Damage

Amrita Kumar has been editor-in-chief, Roli Books, associate editor, Penguin Books India, managing editor, Encyclopaedia Britannica, and freelance editor with Rupa & Co. and HarperCollins. She has also been a copywriter with one of India's leading advertising agencies, research-writer for the Department of Culture, Government of India, editor of a design magazine, and an editor with *The Times of India*. She is currently senior editor and vice-president, Osian's Literary Agency. She lives in New Delhi.

Damage

Amrita Kumar

HarperCollins *Publishers* India

First published in India in 2009 by
HarperCollins *Publishers* India

Building 10, Tower A, 4th Floor, DLF Cyber City, Phase II,
Gurugram Haryana – 122002, India
www.harpercollins.co.in

ISBN: 978-81-7223-674-8

2 4 6 8 10 9 7 5 3 1

This is a work of fiction with some parts based on historical fact. The characters in this novel with the exception of a few well-known historical or political figures are products of the author's imagination and bear no resemblance to people living or dead. They do not depict actual events, they are entirely imaginary and any situations, incidents and dialogue concerning these characters are not intended to change the fictional nature of the work. The places Mugair and Hakra and Bethlehem Square and Chandanpur do not exist.

Typeset in 10.5/13.9 Giovanni Book
Jojy Philip New Delhi - 15

Printed and bound at
MicroPrints India, New Delhi

For Malika and Kaveri,
last of the old warrior clan,
living proof that it existed

I have lived in the desert for years and I have come to believe in such things. It is a place of pockets. The trompe l'oeil of time and water. The jackal with one eye that looks back and one that regards the path you consider taking. In his jaws are pieces of the past he delivers to you, and when all of that time is fully discovered it will prove to have been already known.

—Michael Ondaatje

Contents

Prologue

He flies over the crematorium fence like an antelope, his gentle legs criss-crossing against the wind, making short sharp snapping sounds of weeds and twigs as he descends, his feet picking up the rhythm of the terror that's in his head as he runs towards the converts' hutments. He opens the door to Nanhibai's room, looks at the floor, the bed, the unlit grate, turns around like a trigger drawn into the silence, then walks past the row of hutments, the orphanage, the school, the church, the missionaries' bungalows to the gates of Bethlehem Square to stare across at the highway.

As twilight envelops the small town of Hakra and the highway becomes a steel band running to the end of the world, he remembers the day, six months past, when he and Nanhibai came down that road together. For him who has seen so much it is a day etched in his memory, the sound of a man's Hee-aagh, the crack of his frayed whip against the brittle ribs of a bullock reverberating through his skull as if it were a cavern. He'll spend a lifetime disentangling himself from the web of remembrance, like the narooa doctor who entwines the head of the guinea worm around a needle, forms a sort of windlass with which he proceeds to draw the worm out of its bed, taking care not to throttle it for if that happened the wound would fester, the worm would turn mad with revenge.

The bullocks began frothing at the mouth, he remembers, threads of white foam sweeping the road this way and that as they trudged, one step and then another. It was at that point that Nanhibai had suggested they walk, said she could see the lights of Bethlehem Square in the distance, and he had known she was lying. When they were a hundred yards down the road he'd turned around and seen the knees of the bullocks fold under them gently, their bodies sway to and fro as they fell to the ground. Look Amma look! he'd cried but with a glazed look in her eyes she'd urged him forward.

Six days and nights they'd carried them, and as if they'd known they were sinking, they'd rolled body after body off onto the road to lessen their load, seen the vultures turn eastwards in their trail. It was the rush of wings and the smell of death that remained, not the memory of those they'd abandoned...

The boy is history now, but like the jackal carries pieces of the past in his jaws. His eyes waxing and waning with the moon, his gaze spanning the centuries, days that went before him and those that are yet to come. Both a mirror one to the other, as this day's news recalls an old, old story in his head, of women with nose rings as large as bangles and men on their haunches with their heads in their hands. Behind them the remains of a village once burnt by the sun, today by flames of hatred.

The House by the Nala

I'm Gudda, short for gudiya, or doll, the kind of additional name a parent gives you when you're five or six to cover up for thinking you're a she-devil. I was christened Anandita Chandramukhi Isabella Lawrence but try saying that. Beatrice, my mother was disgusted by the name too which was given to me before I was even born by my father Iqbal, long dead.

How do I begin to tell you who Beatrice and I were? We lived together in a two-storeyed house in South Delhi. It was a nondescript house with a design that was neither here nor there and if you're familiar with South Delhi colonies and the way those assorted houses all jammed together look, lonelier than if they had stood apart, you would know what I mean. It stood at the end of the Lotus Cinema road, the cinema hall itself converted many years before into a dark web of offices with a parking lot that was much smaller than it should have been, making the cars encroach into the residential area so every now and then you would come across a rude notice at someone's gate threatening to take the air out of your tyres if you dared park there. To the east of the colony was Azadpur from where the servants came, an unauthorized maze of jhuggies that the municipal corporation of Delhi razed to the ground periodically but brazenly came up again, and to the west the opulent and mostly empty Trident Hotel that should have been the one to be razed but by virtue of the strength of its impressive sandstone walls probably be the one to be examined by archaeologists and anthropologists a thousand years hence.

The neighbours across the road knew us from Beatrice's clothesline that was strung across our front balcony—her old Maidenform bras, lifeless, large as blouses, stained champagne at the armpits, and her hibiscus nighties with frills. They threw parties often and one day, sent Beatrice a note requesting her to clear the balcony for the evening. Note in hand I turned to her sharply, asked her why she couldn't do the civic thing and hang her clothes on the rear balcony or on the terrace instead of disgracing us. She could, she said, but didn't, and neither of us pursued the matter. That was the pattern of things in that house—neither of us had energy enough to see a thing through.

One of the reasons for this was a state of ill-health caused by the location of the house at the edge of a nala, a dirtwater drain. While the mighty Yamuna at the other end of Delhi was turning into a dribble, this nala, originally no more than six feet wide, expanded with each monsoon until it was the width of a river. Simultaneously the dirt track that ran between the nala and the house shrank, gave way with the force of the water until things came to such a pass that if anyone wanted to go to the rear of the house they had to do it sideways, scrambling at the walls in terror. Ultimately, everyone said, the house would keel over into the nala too but we didn't do anything about it, we didn't know what to do, and I often thought that if such a thing actually came to pass we would probably just shift our belongings to the other end of the house and carry on living at a tilt.

The mosquitoes that emerged from the nala were large and on mid-summer nights of power cuts hummed in our ears like helicopters. The fumes of Flit and kachhua chhap pervaded the house, making us feel protected but causing a sort of emphysema which when it gets hold of women's voices makes them higher in tone. During the monsoons the nala filled up to the brim. Water flowed past at terrific speed, little waves breaking against its shores and on those days I used to call it the Yangtze Kiang for the name had the same lilt that arose in my heart. After the rains, bushes and plants sprouted along its fertile walls. The river didn't dry up unfortunately but settled in stagnant pools from which a stench would begin to emanate. But if you clamped your nose between your fingers and edited your vision by screwing up your eyes just so, the nala became a botanist's delight, a birdwatcher's paradise. Parrots flew from branch to branch and kingfishers raced past in magical flashes of turquoise blue.

The neighbours who threw the parties missed all this, insulated as they were by a high wall hung with bougainvillea. If you stood on our balcony on tiptoe you could see a pretty arrangement of wrought-iron furniture in their garden, all painted a breathless white, and a bar with a blue and white striped canopy. They never saw the colony garbage being dumped in the nala daily, their pulverized mosambi skins and glued condoms being upturned by ragpickers, the row of smooth Azadpur buttocks that lined the nala at dawn, neat brown turds emanating soundlessly.

My bedroom window on the ground floor overlooked the nala directly and all this that I saw offset the unreality within the house. This was partly due to its structure. Beatrice had told the architect she liked havelis so he had given her a courtyard right in the centre of a mere 350 square yard plot that short of creating a vacuum stopped all air dead in its tracks. It was a small courtyard but it gave our two-storeyed house the effect of a skyscraper from within. In winter it was a deep dark well and in the monsoon the rain poured down, making a thunderous racket on the concrete floor, splattering dirt into the rooms around. Caught between two floors it was an acoustical horror for it gave Beatrice's voice from the first floor an echo and turned mine below, for want of privacy, into a whisper. On friendly Sunday afternoons Beatrice would circumambulate the railings above and call out to me: 'Gudda, what are you doing down there?' Sometimes I wouldn't answer and then she would march to the upstairs telephone and dial the downstairs extension and since her phone wasn't too far from the railings, I would hear *two* voices saying, Gudda, *Gudda,* what *what* are *are* you *you* doing *doing* down *down* there *there*?

How do you separate the essence of people from the things they do? It's easy if they don't do anything at all and I couldn't, for it wasn't only Beatrice and I who lived in that house but a host of Christian missionaries who used our house like a railway junction to get to other parts of India. Beatrice was a fanatical born-again Christian. She belonged to a small breakaway evangelical group called the Brides of Christ who'd unleashed a reign of terror in my youth with their rituals of casting out devils, speaking in foreign tongues, dancing and clapping about the house shouting *Halleluiah!* and *Praise the Lord!* We survived on the dollars they gave us. They used to lie between her petticoats in her cupboard and every now and then I would see her counting them in a feverish manner and I would ask her why she never put them in a bank and she would put her finger on her lips and look at me threateningly. Later I pretended those years away, made up stories about the jobs my heroic mother had done to earn a living for us but then at that time I looked forward to those dollars too, an odd sort of fence to be sitting on for my hatred for Christian missionaries was profound. They had always looked upon me as Beatrice's sullen daughter in the grip of the devil and I had seen them as the reincarnation of the devil himself.

There was the Ceylonese missionary called Pila Jayawardene who once tried to masturbate herself on me. I was about fourteen then, lying on Beatrice's bed, reading, when I found her framed against the door, staring at me. Beatrice was out that morning and I thought I was alone in the house.

'It's a good appaurtunitty for us to have fellowship together,' was how she began, in her Tamil–American accent, her teeth standing out large, flat and yellow against the white voile of her sari. Under the sari were no knickers I knew. None of the Brides of Christ missionaries wore them which according to Beatrice was because they were saving every naya paisa given to them by the Americans for God's work. What if they get leucorrhoea? I had asked, then there'll be starchy patches on their petticoats, but Beatrice said *Don't talk about God's people like that!*

'You don't go to school, child?' Pila asked.

I had forgotten that morning and Beatrice never remembered. 'It's a holiday,' I said.

'That's good, that's good,' she said the way Americans do, fill in gaps with an unending stream of upbeat sounds.

'You had breakfast?' I asked equally unnecessarily.

'No child,' said Pila, 'we're fastin' today.'

I hope you die of hunger bloody bitch, I thought, returning to my book while she continued to stare at me. Pila was the one who had first put it into Beatrice's head that I had an evil spirit in me.

She walked up to the bed. It was one of those sultry mornings when people carry their smells around them like an overcoat and every so often you get a whiff of armpit. Hers were stinking. 'Guard promised us rain,' she said abruptly, 'he will fulfil his promise.' Saying this she held up her hands, closed her eyes and began to whisper. I tried to lip-read but her lips were moving too fast. There was a thunderclap in the distance and her eyes flew wide open. 'Praise be to Guard,' she said.

The room grew dark, the curtains began to billow, their rings making guitar sounds against the wires on which they were strung. I turned and looked out the window. Slate black clouds had appeared from nowhere, making it appear like evening.

'I'm going to have a bath now,' I said, sitting up, at a loss how to get rid of her.

'Give me your hand, child,' she said, a glaze coming over her eyes.

I stood upright. 'I have to have a bath now,' I repeated, manoeuvring myself around the edge of the bed to the side where the window was, wanting to concentrate on the nala, on those precious moments just before it turned into a flowing river.

She came towards me. I shrank against the windowsill. Grabbing my hand, she shut her eyes tightly and said, 'I can feel Guard's presence in this room. Don't fight him, child. He's speaking to you.'

Cadaverous breath rose from deep within her fasting bowels, floating in lethal waves towards my nostrils. Her mouth opened and closed over her buckteeth like a constipated rectum. Then she started speaking in a voice that wasn't hers. *'Hum da balla basha, hum da balla basha,'* she moaned, *'Guard have mercy, have mercy....'*

I tried to move but her grip was strong. She was stroking my hair, my face, after which she began to rub her body against mine, in spasms that came in rhythm with the moans that emerged from her throat. My head shook in tandem, banging against the window railings, a wet seat of slime forming under my bottom with the rain that was now pouring in at a furious slant. *'In the name of Guard,'* she screamed, *'I rebuke the evil spirit within this child. Hum da balla basha, hum da balla basha.'*

She was pulling my hair now, her other hand stroking my bottom frenziedly. I'm not sure how it happened then, maybe the spirit she was after flew out of me because I lunged forward and attacked her, hitting her face and her head, pushing her back with each hit until we reached the open passage that encircled the central well of the house where I let go, causing her to slip heavily in the slush, her hand curling around my wrist, her feet scrambling for support.

When Beatrice returned she wouldn't listen to me. '*What did you say to her? What did you do to her?*' she screamed, standing over my head like a wrathful emissary of God, her halo on fire, embers under her feet. She never listened. So I never told her what Pila did, or about Darla, about the shameless hussy that she was, or about Zach and gang not being missionaries at all.

It's true what they say, that the evil that men do is remembered, the good gets interred with their bones because Pila, Darla and Zach apart, most of the missionaries who came and went from our house were probably good people. It was the manner in which Beatrice positioned herself among them that infuriated me—forever awestruck, forever unmindful of me so that Christianity itself began to appear like an international conspiracy against me, one part of that conspiracy being to get me to vacate my room, for that was what she repeatedly demanded of me. For Darla, my room *and* my cupboard *and* the bathroom shelves because she was special, Beatrice said, and we were 'mighty privileged' to have her stay with us.

Darla was a faith healer of international renown and whenever she came posters inviting people to her meetings went up all over town, on lampposts, trees, generator boxes, and sometimes there would be huge cloth banners strung across Ring Road, all with our telephone number on them and in bold letters, CHRIST IS THE ANSWER. For sure Christ was the answer to Beatrice's lousy culinary skills because with the arrival of Darla our table would be full and on those days I ate like a wily camel in preparation for the devastating famine that entailed her departure.

Darla's room smelt of America and whenever she was out I would go in and sniff the air and sometimes I would walk up to her dressing table, open the caps of her numerous pretty bottles and pots and inhale deeply. Unlike Pila, she wore knickers. They were large and diaphanous, with lacy edges and after washing them she would hang them neatly on the line with the clips always dead centre. Her pet project was a slum called Sunlight Colony on the outskirts of Delhi where Beatrice would accompany her as interpreter in Darla's silver-grey Land Rover. In the middle of the slum was a clearing where the meetings were held, Darla and Beatrice wobbling on a little makeshift wooden podium.

'Our heavenly father,' Darla would begin her sessions, head bowed, eyes shut, palms upheld and facing the crowd, fingers twitching.

'Baap Aasmani,' went Beatrice.

'We thank you, Lord, for these precious brothers and sisters.'

'Hum tumhare shukar guzaar hain, khuda baap, in bhai behen ke liye.'

'We ask you to open their eyes to the truth this morning.'

'Aaj inki aankhen khol, khuda baap, taaki woh sach kabool karen.'

'We ask it in your mighty name.'

'Tumhare naam se maangte hain.'

'Amen.'

'Aameen.'

After the prayer Darla would deliver her sermon to the crowd, sitting on their haunches, digging their noses, spitting, but mostly staring at her thick white legs. At the end of the sermon she would make them say 'I love Jesus!'

There would be silence.

'I… LOVE… JESUS!' she would prompt slowly.

'AAYAY LUBB-UH JEEJUDGE!' the crowd would then roar, the cue for Darla to move towards her Land Rover like a Pied Piper, everyone suddenly off their haunches and scampering after her. 'No *juldy juldy,'* she would say.

'Aista, aista,' from Beatrice. *'Sab ko milega. Line se lag jao chup chaap!'*

It was huge, that Land Rover dickey, stacked with bags of atta and rice and strips of vitamins and bottles of Ostocalcium and down the queue these would pass with Beatrice moving alongside, open register in one hand, ink pad in the other. One item in exchange for one angootha chhaap under the heading 'List of Converts'. The longer the list the bigger the funding for Darla's next trip to India. The bigger the funding the wobblier Beatrice's petticoat pile.

One day when Beatrice was out and I thought Darla was out too I entered her room for my daily tour of America and came upon an astonishing sight. There on the bed were Darla's thick white legs intertwined with a pair of thin black ones. Lying curled and abandoned on the floor were her diaphanous knickers. I turned and ran, down the corridor, through the front door, leaping five stairs at a time, down the road to the other end of the colony where the cinema hall stood and then walked all the way back to the house slowly, crept into bed and lay staring at the ceiling, planning on how to tell Beatrice. But when Beatrice came home with a shopping bag bulging with fruits for Darla, her hair in dry wisps around her face, I changed my mind.

That was the day America divided itself into two—dime store America and *Vogue* magazine America and it was suddenly clear to me which one Darla belonged to, with her polyester clothes that never needed ironing and her objets d'art of little Swiss chalets. My secret admiration for her healthy ways, her constant washing and cleaning, her passion for fruits, turned to revulsion, her careful picking of the one serrated knife we had to carve the peel off them, her placing of neat sections of fruit into her mouth, a greedy ingesting cave, a snoring ageing cave into which I dreamed of pouring red hot curry at night. Setting her blonde ringlets alight. The owner of the thin black legs was Pastor Eric Masih, a frequent visitor to our house, and from then on every time he came I left the room as if poison had entered. *'How dare you do that rude girl!'* Beatrice said.

'I'll dare do what I want!' I replied, flashing my eyes at her so that she slunk back, sensing a threat lay for her somewhere although she couldn't fathom quite where it lay.

For many years Darla came and went and then one day she was gone forever. The government was clamping down on foreign missionaries, revoking their visas because they were taking over the entire northeast belt they said, robbing it of its culture, making the hill tribes wear Levis and strum guitars at their meetings. Beatrice said, *'When God closes a door he always opens a window'* so when Zach and gang arrived you would have thought God had no measuring tape on him for the window was larger than the door.

They came flashing tourist visas this time, in a large American bus with picture windows and white frilly curtains and they were young, looking like they had sprung out of a Woodstock album jacket, dropping little squeezed-up nylon bed rolls along their way as they swarmed all over our house, falling on sofas, on beds, on the floor. Some went straight to the refrigerator and downed whole bottles of water, streams running down their moving gullets onto their T shirts. They made American sounds and whoops of joy and relief and Christian sounds, holding their arms up from their armpits, Beatrice hovering over them, her accent changing. 'Man, I'd love a cup of cuawfee,' one said and the rest shouted, *'Halleluiah!'*

'Tere bagal mein chuhiya!' I spat, slamming a saucepan on the gas, glaring at them from the kitchen door.

It was a long while before Beatrice noticed me. 'My youngest daughter,' she said with pride and so started a fresh bout of 'How you doin' sister?' and *'Praise the Lord!'*

'Where are so many going to stay, Mama?' I cornered her in the kitchen amidst water spills and sugar spoons measured out with trembling hands.

'The Lord will provide!' she said and a familiar chill spread through me as I watched her slip away from me once more. The babble of voices receded as I entered the soundproof room I kept ready and furnished inside my head and from that faraway place I watched her arranging and rearranging slices of Britannia cake on a plate, in tiled rows first, and then she dismantled that and placed them round and round in concentric circles so there was a little no-size hole in the middle and I could see it bothering her, I could see her not knowing what to do about it, and it came to me how much I wanted to love her, how important it was that I never let her know.

This was the new breed of missionaries. No meetings. No banners. No polyester. The smell of crotch and sweat. They dispersed from our house in little groups in the mornings, holding tracts in their hands which they shoved into cars at the crowded AIIMS crossing. 'How can they be doing this all day?' I asked. 'What do they do in between?'

'In between when?' replied Beatrice.

A few mornings later I had my answer. It was on page five of *The Times of India*. A small blurred photograph of an American tourist who had been arrested by the police in a seedy hotel in Paharganj the night before. A kilo of smack on him. I knew the face. The caption said that a hunt was on for the rest of the group whom they believed to be involved in the drug trade via Nepal. Beatrice entered the room just then and, swiftly extracting page five, I got up and walked to the kitchen, crumpled it into a ball and buried it deep within the garbage. The next morning before we awoke they were gone. There was a note on the dining table about a sudden change in plans and under the note, a fifty-dollar bill.

That was life with Beatrice, that was it in essence, protecting her from the evil she perpetrated, an evil she was innocent of. Inherent contradictions always make you think. The field was open. Sometimes I put it all down to a fallout of the British Empire, no more no less puzzling than the queen continuing to wear the Kohinoor diamond in her crown but at other times it appeared too pompous, this drawing upon the vast matrix of history to contain a personal dilemma, so I found smaller explanations, and smaller ones yet, until one day there was nothing left and I was ready to move on.

I was twenty-one when I finally left, it was the year 1987, and I wasn't the first person to bid goodbye to that house. Beatrice had three more daughters—Malini Mohini Elizabeth, Sujata Sushila Irene and Aditi Prem Angela—older than me by sixteen, twelve and ten years who had left long before. I hardly knew them; they were so much older than me, my memory of them not going beyond being chased out of rooms so they could discuss their love lives. I for my part wasn't the cute and cuddly baby sister they might have wanted and I don't think they missed me, or I they when they left, their comings and goings not registering on me fully when they returned briefly every few years for Christmas.

That was the pattern I thought I'd follow too, for the rest of my life, but twelve years after I left India changed, Beatrice's world fell apart, my marriage fell apart too, and I came back to live in that house forever.

Shortly after I returned, Malini, Sujata and Aditi returned too, again only briefly, this time to attend a wedding and then some years later, a funeral. It's true about births, weddings and funerals defining your core, marking your passages through life, but it's that wedding in particular that haunts me, for that was the time India, Beatrice, those missionaries, that house all fell into place and I understood their connection. Funny how it all fell apart too just then, for that was also the time images of how I'd imagined it all to be, and how it really was, began to separate themselves like shapes emerging from a mist.

It was fortuitous, my moving on at twenty-one and it happened like this: An American missionary arrived one morning from Lahore without warning. Our fridge was empty that day so I'd gone to the local market for bread and eggs when I saw the neighbours who lived across the road, Mona, Arvind and their twelve-year-old daughter Natasha emerge from the adjoining chemist's shop. They'd moved in a year before when old Mrs Gupta whose children had gone abroad never to return had fallen dead in her storeroom. Natasha yelled out when she saw me, something to the effect of, *'Look Mummy, the one who lives in the house of big knickers!'* and this was so embarrassing, I tried to slink away when I heard that but Mona, equally embarrassed by her daughter's outburst, tried to make amends by catching hold of my arm and inviting me to tea the following day.

Except for the note about the clothesline, Mona had ignored Beatrice and me completely in the year they'd been our neighbours which was why Beatrice was disbelieving when I told her, not so disbelieving as irritated that she wasn't invited as well. She loved the concept of tea with neighbours but no one invited her ever because they couldn't make head or tail of her, so in revenge she started referring to Mona from that day on as a wax doll, moam ki gudiya, and truth be told, I mightn't have gravitated towards Mona to the degree I did in the days that followed had it not been for the pleasure of making Beatrice miserable.

It was the beginning of a brief friendship between Mona and me and it ended horribly. Why, I asked myself, did she befriend me at all? I know she was lonely, but I think she was intrigued by me too because I turned out like no one she had known—I did nothing, said nothing, knew nothing, but looked throughout like I held volumes within, the way vacuous minds sometimes appear. For lack of anything substantial to say to her, I became an attentive listener and of course I balanced all of this out as we went along, started making up things to tell her, learning in the bargain that communication wasn't as mysterious a skill as I had thought, that in everyday life you don't always have to speak the truth or relate absolute fact as if you were in a courtroom and someone had sworn you in.

Over that first tea Mona trashed the neighbours. Over the second she trashed her mother-in-law who was unhealthily in love with her son she said, and at the third, her husband who was not only unhealthily in love with his mother but equally so with all manner of women. But I liked Mona. Six months down the line I found her perpetual whining annoying but initially, accompanied as it was by tea in good china and chip cookies from abroad, our conversations had the dimensions of a world-view. They were a gentle whirring of sultry afternoon air and they lifted my soul out of a dungeon on transparent wings.

In the spirit of communication, when Mona asked me what I did I should have said *I slink, I dodge, I spend my time hiding from Beatrice* instead of which I said I was looking for a job. So she asked What job? and I should have said *Well, I have a degree as a nimboo-pani maker* instead of which I looked at her brightly and said *Media*. It had such an urban sound. Then she said You mean you want to be a journalist? and I should have said *No, I mean I could stand at the AIIMS crossing and distribute tracts about the second coming of Christ to heathens in Marutis* instead of which I nodded enthusiastically and said *Yes,* whereupon she told me she knew the *Indian Post* was recruiting and that a friend of hers, a man called Anand Bharti was arriving shortly from the head office in Bombay to interview people. Did I want her to put in a word? Truth lay somewhere between a scream and a huh? but it came out as an enthusiastic *Yes please!*

Anand Bharti came, Mona put in a word, I met him, and at some point I was asked to fill up a form and among the questions on that form was which branch of the *Indian Post* I wanted to work for and I wrote Bombay, just like that, not quite like that but with the thought that my sister Malini, her husband David and their daughter Neha lived there. I didn't ask Malini, I didn't ask Beatrice, I just did it. Junior as the job was, wholly without experience as I was, the only question Anand Bharti asked me after glancing at my form was 'You're a Christian?' and I could have prolonged the interview by saying 'You're a Hindu?' but of course I couldn't and I came away not knowing if I'd been offered the job at all. A month later, I was.

Beatrice went into a funk. I don't think she meant for me to be making nimboo pani for missionaries all my life as much as she just didn't think, so consumed was she by her own doings. Compounding her discomfiture was the nature of the job because books she understood but newspapers to her were better used to line the kitchen shelves or soak the oil off cutlets.

Two weeks later I was on the Rajdhani Express to Bombay. Mona took me to the station; Beatrice didn't. *Huesht!* was the last thing she said to me as I walked out the door. Every family has its acoustics. In ours it wasn't the sound you make when you swing around on the road to shoo off a dog that's following your crotch but contains within it a world of scorn, hurt, dismissal, the whole shebang, the nine emotions including their thirty-six offshoots, the whole nava rasa.

I dismissed her too. The thought that I was leaving her alone in that house for the first time didn't weigh on me at all.

Uppermost in my mind as I boarded the train was that I was headed for a brand-new life now; Malini would help me define that life.

What I didn't think at all was that Malini might have her own life, one in which I might be an intrusion.

The Life and Death of Douglas Bharti

I'm standing outside Malini's door, Darla's old suitcase beside me, my hair turning to noodles in the humid Bombay air. Malini's smile is so wide, her voice so loud as she opens the door that I know something is wrong. I'm here, I say, and she holds out her arms to enfold me but something is wrong.

She picks up my suitcase and I follow her into the house. It isn't like I thought it would be: curtains matching the sofa covers, glass bookshelves with curios between the books, a mahogany dining table, ashtrays so clean you could eat off them. Beatrice and I weren't like that at all, we would cover up mounds of things with pieces of cloth and every now and then we would pick up the cloths and shake them on the side like bullfighters and then place them back again so the dust would fly around looking for new places in which to dwell, gnomes with young faces and baggy eyes that stared at you from the joints of chairs, from under the bed, from behind the refrigerator, the underbelly of the bathroom sink.

Malini takes me to her daughter Neha's room which I'll be sharing she says. I hope Neha won't mind, I say, but Malini doesn't answer because the doorbell rings. It's Neha, bronze and sweaty and glowing with health, home to grab a teatime snack and Malini says Look who's here, look who's here and Neha rushes up and puts her face against my leg and says Aunty Gudda, Aunty Gudda. Five minutes later she's gone.

The bell rings again. It's David this time, briefcase in hand, and I say Hello I'm here and he puts down his briefcase and gives me a hug and says Welcome and congratulations on your new job. Malini goes to the kitchen to fetch a tea tray and the three of us collect around the mahogany table that's shining like a mirror and I am about to place my cup down when her hand slides like quicksilver across the table with a coaster, my tea spills a little in shock and Malini rushes to the kitchen and emerges with a napkin to wipe it and I feel awful, I keep apologizing, keep apologizing.

An hour later Malini and David are gone.

A week passes. I'm walking from kitchen to bedroom when I hear Malini on the phone, in a whisper. My house just isn't the same any more, I hear her say, she's always there you know what I mean, following me around, and I stop and listen and she says No no no, yes, of course I know, I know…but why did they have to give her a job here of all places when they've got branches all over the country…

In Bombay, unlike Delhi, you learn fast. While the searing Loo from the flat unseeing Thar empties your mind of all direction, the Malabar sea breeze quickens it with its unpredictability, waxing and waning like the tides that can be heard far inland and on the topmost floors of skyscrapers around which it whirls and swirls its way into air-conditioned rooms before turning back to the great brown Arabian, sometimes leaving behind a message of disaster.

One of the first things I learnt at the *Indian Post* was that most of a big newspaper isn't a newspaper at all and that the most important people working there aren't journalists. Anand Bharti placed me in the Outreach Department that produced supplements that had nothing to do with news and everything to do with ads and money. The real journalists sat one floor above and they referred to the one below as the whorehouse.

Two weeks after I joined the market crashed, the ads didn't come in, so I was shifted from supplement to supplement, very few of which saw the light of day. During this period Anand Bharti developed a liking for me and the way he expressed it was by taking a deep interest in supplements and in all of this false interaction a base of sorts began to develop and I learnt that you can hide in the folds of a thousand-strong organization forever without being discovered, that a base can exist without anything rising on it. I began breaking out into hives. Coin-sized dark red patches on my neck and arms as well as my elbows, the latter traumatizing my thinking position. So I thought less and less, using my energy to wander towards the canteen instead for bread pakodas that the *Post* canteen was famous for.

Six months went by.

Anand Bharti began poking his nose deeper and deeper into my non-affairs. I couldn't fathom what it was about my dour persona that interested him. Every time he did that I simply leaned back on my chair, blanked out and waited for him to go away. But his nose came nearer and nearer and sometimes I could positively feel his breath on my shoulder. Then one day his hand brushed against mine and something told me it wasn't an accident. Raised like I was, my immediate thought was to look for another job but I knew no one outside the *Indian Post* and within Outreach everyone seemed to be looking to get the hell out of there too so the job market was a big secret that everyone hugged to themselves in case you swiped something meant for them. But that's how it happens with all jobs. You have to leave one to look for another but if you leave one before you get the other you won't get the other.

So in between the bread pakodas I took up smoking, simply because in a filthy, dingy, paan-splattered staircase running behind the *Post* building it was allowed. That was where all the fellows from the upper floor congregated with steaming paper cups of coffee and I would hear snatches of their conversation and I began to envy them, began to wonder what it would be like to be a real journalist. I asked Anand whether he would consider transferring me to the upper floor but he was evasive. Having hired me he thought he owned my soul. I raged against him internally but turned meek and malleable in his presence, a combination that should have translated itself into a stomach ulcer but turned into something much more unfamiliar. I found myself straining for the sound of his footsteps.

Every woman at the *Post* was in love with him. Anand was a good-looking man in his mid-thirties. History holds many examples of well-placed men running after plain women but why he ran after *me* was an enigma although it might have been precisely because I didn't fall over him like every woman at the *Post* seemed to be doing, never mind what I felt inside, I just wasn't brought up that way, I continued addressing him as 'Sir' which nobody else did. It's the same wily principle that women use to trap men in a higher league than them except that that wasn't what I set out to do at all, I was genuinely frozen in the face of his behaviour and I think, just like Mona, he might have grown intrigued by the do-nothing, say-nothing, know-nothing air about me.

I also suspect that underlying Anand's interest was the usual misconception about Christian girls being available, especially bare-legged ones in skirts. Maybe he thought that under the gloomy persona lay an item girl waiting to be liberated, not that the dresses lasted too long, Malini made sure they didn't, she kept buying me new clothes, either on account of sisterly love or not wanting to be ashamed of me, I never could tell what Malini was all about, what *I* was about, suddenly in different clothes, and it might have been this confusion of sartorial identity that made me eventually succumb to a man I might never have succumbed to had I remained the way Beatrice had fashioned me.

A sinister element existed in me too. My initial alarm at being wooed by the boss transmogrified into fascination at the thought that a Hindu might be interested in me, a majority-community, regular kind of guy, one who couldn't say *Halleluiah* if you held a knife to him. I don't think I thought all this through when the affair began, it's in retrospect that we understand the things we do, subconsciously Anand began to emerge in my mind as my passport out of Beatrice's world and into the real India, a country I wanted to belong to and somehow didn't, always living with the feeling that some big security fellow was about to come up and take my arm.

I was in the canteen one day munching a bread pakoda when I received a message that there was an urgent call holding for me. I couldn't understand who it was at first. I heard sobbing. Then the person disconnected. Then the phone rang again and this time I heard Mona clearly. She was launching into a tirade against someone. I thought she meant her husband. 'Mona, can I call you back?' is what I said. She had begun to irritate me with her calls, making me listen to an endless saga about her husband's love affairs. So I didn't return her call for two days. On the third day Beatrice called, hysterical. She said there was a police jeep and an ambulance standing outside our house. Mona had hung herself.

I ran to tell Anand Bharti. He looked stunned for about two seconds. 'Oh god,' he said, and then seeing how distraught I was, put his arms around me, whispered into my ear that he had a meeting with the chairman so could we talk later? We did talk later, over wine and more wine at his place, without any mention of Mona because Mona went into a CLOSED FILE after that hazy night but she must have been watching the two of us from wherever she was because many years later, when I had almost forgotten she existed, she came back for revenge.

It was the morning after that Anand proposed to me and I turned him down. The concept was good, the reality unnerving, nor did I fully believe him at the time. There was also the question of Beatrice. How on earth would I introduce the two of them? Malini's, Sujata's and Aditi's husbands were all Christian, so I pretended that night and that morning hadn't happened, laughed in Anand's face, he turned cold, and this had a terrible effect on my job. He began excluding me from department meetings, ignoring me in front of my colleagues, at the same time calling me up at odd hours to heap all sorts of work on me that I wasn't hired to do.

I thought of quitting once again but the myth of sisterhood had completely crumbled by then so I'd also thought of moving out of Malini's house into paying guest accommodation and so I couldn't risk a break in salary and so I didn't quit. I simply despaired.

In the stillness of my despair I didn't know that life was about to change once again. But this is what always happens. Change creeps in through the back door just as you're beginning to accept the view from the front.

Malini and David were out for dinner; Neha was fast asleep. I was rummaging through Malini's cupboard for a pair of pyjamas she had borrowed from me when I came across a letter hidden deep between her clothes. It was addressed to Beatrice. I had no business opening it but of course I did. *Dearest Mama,* it went:

I hope you are well and happy. I am not. I am writing this letter to ask you to please ask Gudda to return home. She treats this house like a hotel, comes and goes at all odd hours, sometimes in the middle of the night. I have to get up early morning to send Neha to school so this is extremely inconvenient. Moreover she leaves lights on all the time—you have no idea how high our electricity bills have been since she came. Above all she's an extremely rude person and I don't see why I should have to put up with this in my own house. She never had any manners, this we all knew, but she's become worse since the job.

I'm also worried about another matter. At first I thought of not telling you anything but she's getting too friendly with a Hindu fellow in her office. He is equally rude and keeps calling her up at odd hours and you know how particular David is about these things. I also think she's started smoking on the sly. I didn't want to upset you but David and I both came to the conclusion that she needs a mother to supervise her at this stage in her life, not a sister.

Please don't mention this letter. I would prefer that you ask her to return for reasons of your own.

Your loving daughter, Malini

I looked at the date on top. It had been written a week before. Perhaps Malini never intended posting it, perhaps she was only hyperventilating, but I couldn't take the chance. So I got rid of her, Beatrice and that pathetic job in one fell swoop. I picked up the phone and dialled Anand.

I married him.

Why Anand wanted to marry me in the first place was a mystery to me. It could have been because although I'd spent a night with him I hadn't technically surrendered my virginity yet, or maybe he was tired of living alone, maybe it was because I spoke English better than he did, knew the difference between Beethoven and Schubert, maybe he wanted children, there had to be *something* that made him want to marry me because it wasn't love.

The harsh sunlight at Alang ship-breaking yard touches the region behind your eyes so that one moment you're a tiny speck on the shore looking up into the mangled guts of ships and sometimes a giant Alice peeping into a perfect little doll house. Not that there's anything fragile about them; no pretty porcelain teacups within to push around with your finger but heavy metal as it falls with a resounding clang even as a tilted Eiffel tower-like crane plucks out a four-poster bed from deep within the heart of a ship with the delicacy of a violinist, the kind of medley Salvador Dali would have created were he a sound recordist. Such a profusion of images and men at various heights, depending on which discarded part of a ship they're standing on, their faces grease-black as if they'd dragged the dregs of the ocean up after them. At night soldering sparks fill the heavens like a strange death rite, a spectacle, if you put aside the sound of your heart as it breaks against the great unmoving ship walls and then ebbs into the sea in search of a memory...

No New York or London or Switzerland, not even Ooty or Manali leave alone Khandala for a honeymoon but the Rann of Kutch where no one but the wild ass roams. And Mahatma Gandhi, a long time ago.

Anand's grandfather, now dead, was a Gandhian. He had accompanied Gandhi on the Salt March to Dandi and I don't know what that had to do with Anand but he wanted to go there and pick up a clod of salt in his fist. That's how our marriage began, driving through the vast, eerie salt pans of Gujarat and Kutch, the occasional salt hills breaking the monotony of the landscape the way those brown dung heaps in the midst of green fields do up north, but the salt you could mistake for snow even in summer if you had dark glasses on which both of us did because there's nothing as blinding as an endless sheet of white, not even a cloudless sky at noon. It was a reflection of what our marriage was to be, the silent expanse of the Rann where not a bird twitters, salt workers from a distance looking like they're dancing in the shimmering pans.

From Dandi on to Bhavnagar where we stayed at the palace hotel of the local maharaja and from there on to Alang, the world's largest ship-breaking yard where, seated on plastic chairs on the discarded deck of the *SS Iona*, I understood what Mona's last and agitated phone call to me was about. It wasn't about her husband's numerous affairs at all but Anand's. Anand's and mine. Almost in a manner like he were discussing the weather he said what a coincidence it was that the last two women in his life not only hailed from South Delhi but lived on the same street, facing each other. My mouth fell open.

'You're joking,' I said.

'No, I'm not,' he answered, looking surprised. 'I thought you knew.'

My tongue clove to the roof of my mouth even as the sound of screeching pulleys rent the air and the giant hull of a ship went nose down into the sand. The iron gates of the port flew open just then for a tempo to pass through, with a sudden voice-over of trucks plying on the road beyond the high walls that enclosed the port. A scrap-iron trader leaned his head out of the window, screaming instructions in Gujarati. In the distance an inventory was going on—cupboards, mirrors, washing machines, a piano with one leg broken.

'This tea tastes of iron filings,' I said then, putting my cup down.

'I'm sorry,' he repeated, continuing to look surprised. 'I thought Mona and you were good friends, I really thought you knew.'

Sorry? It was like several doors being slammed at once and then opening and swinging so you couldn't tell which one to go through. Not only had I not taken Mona's call, I had stolen her boyfriend. For all I knew, I was responsible for her death.

In the car returning from the port back to the palace I put my arm casually through Anand's and a few minutes later, my head against his shoulder, either to convey it didn't matter now, or to jumble his radar but my arm felt like it were hanging on to the edge of a cliff, a yawning abyss below.

It *did* matter. Our honeymoon nights, every night but one thereafter, were spent in cold silence.

Back in Bombay, not two months into the marriage, Anand's promiscuity came to the fore. But I didn't leave him, I simply continued not sleeping with him although we shared the same room. When you marry in a hurry it's assumed by the world that you're either pregnant or otherwise contain tremendous passion within you and it was the latter image that slipped on to me like a satin negligée through the part-shocked, part-envious looks I received from everyone. After an arid life I liked that look. Second, there was Beatrice and Malini, a matter I couldn't undo without hurtling into space like a misguided comet. Third, there was Anand's house on Malabar Hill, one wall in Jodhpur blue, Michael Aram chairs, that sort of thing. Fourth, there was Anand himself. You could pee in the same pot as him without having to wipe the seat first.

It was no kind of relationship, and I had no job either because I'd had to quit on account of office policy not allowing married couples to work together. I handed Anand his cup of tea in the mornings, asked a few civil questions about work when he returned in the evening and on the whole, wasn't particularly devastated to be rid of either the job or the prospect of sex, the half-sex I'd had with Anand before marrying him reminding me more of Darla and Pila. The pleasure I *did* get out of that marriage was hurting Malini who was almost as rigid as Beatrice about Hindus although I suspect she was grudgingly impressed by Anand's status and wealth.

As the days went by I began to realize how important it was for Anand to be married to someone like me because that way, when he embarked on an affair, the girl in question always knew that the relationship couldn't go too far, he could profess the deepest love without having to make a commitment, he had to go home after all to the unquestioning one, his see-nothing, do-nothing, know-nothing woman.

Those affairs were brief but they always ended badly. There was a *Post* journalist who stood outside our house one day, threatening to set it, and me, on fire. She tore into Anand's new Mitsubishi in the middle of Marine Drive. Another time that might have appeared like a ménage à trois was when a gentle Sufi woman entered our lives, creative head of one of Bombay's largest advertising agencies. Anand began to meditate at her behest and listen to tapes she gave him and went round trance-like and all positive, thanking people, thanking me for the smallest things I did, thanking God in the morning for the sunshine, in the evening for the moonshine. The Sufi told him to be aware of everything around him. I mean are you aware of your shoes, for instance, she'd told him. Do you ever think of thanking them for the many miles they've taken you? Have you ever said *Thank you shoes for protecting my feet*? The next morning Anand got out of bed and slipped his feet into his slippers half-asleep. Then he remembered and quickly withdrew them as if they had caught fire. 'Thank you slippers,' I lip-read from the corner of my eye. Then she convinced me to try it too. So in the kitchen one dawn I noticed a lizard, dashing from the sink to the Aquaguard, its carbon tube casting a blue reflection on its body. *Do not concentrate, just be aware,* is what she had told me so I tried to look at the lizard while not quite looking at it. The water was boiling. I looked at the bubbles. Bubbling, bubbling, like a hot spring, like blisters. I picked up my cup and wandered into the living room, put on a Beethoven album and looked out into the dark. The streetlights were on and that's when I saw it—the patio lit up like an oil painting in which the artist had painstakingly outlined each leaf, the fluorescent colours of green, not dead, not sad, not silent as they were in natural light but every molecule in the air moving back and forth and in and out of my head as if the garden and I were one. Then I looked up at a tree and I could swear I saw the leaves on its topmost branches dancing to Beethoven's Ninth.

I couldn't say with any certainty whether I grew to understand, accept or even hate Anand. Indeed I waited for the sound of his footsteps but I'm uncertain what I felt for him because after a while he wasn't entirely there. He began trailing a kind of shadow after him, not letting me see more than the shadow, me, who had always lived in the perpetual fear of vanishing herself. Sometimes when we were together I would examine his hands and think of touching them but he belonged to the sea alone and I watched him from the shore, ebb and melt. There were times when I spotted the occasional froth on the water's surface and I wondered whether I'd imagined it all and I would watch till evening shadows lengthened and I could see no more. Then I would turn back with a leaden heart, and just then I would hear a rustle behind me and I would turn and see that the sea had changed.

One night that is dark in my memory now, I took a turn in bed and found Anand not there. He was in the living room, crying, a piece of paper in his hand. I took it from him. It was the Sufi. She had written him the most cruelly worded Dear John letter I had seen in my life. I had no choice but to do what I did then, and it was only with morning's first light when I felt the sensation of my head against his arm, the dribble from my mouth on his skin, that I knew what I'd done. Damage doesn't make for good bedfellows. It only rises in the morning to brush the debris from its hem and sometimes it straightens its back and stares at itself in the mirror just like I stared at Anand and saw that if I knew him now it was no more than an echo knows a hollow well.

After a period of sulking Malini came around. That's another perk that comes with losing your singlehood—sisters begin to look at you with respect. After she got in touch, Sujata from London and Aditi from Columbia got in touch too. There was another angle to the whole thing. Anand was vice-president of the *Indian Post* now and the *Post* ruled India. It had been launched pre-independence and then in the eighties, around the time the *Sunday Mail* and the *Observer* came up, it had turned into a rag but INR figures were now placing it above even the *Hindustan Times.*

Sometimes there can be all sorts of thoughts in your head about things, about ways in which you should be behaving but you end up behaving differently for the sake of convenience. Just like a parallel economy, there are parallel lives—one upholding the other, one at war with the other but only on the surface, a moral code under a survival code, a palimpsest that smothers your screams in the middle of the night. That's how Malini and I became friends again, the first tentative coffee at the Blue Moon progressing to sizzling steaks at Touche, moving from there to art and kathi rolls at the Jehangir Art Gallery until finally the two big men, David and Anand met and got along famously, turning the whole business into a fait accompli. What was bona fide in the end, and what wasn't, didn't matter. Men have that power, that quality of giving sanction to things. Women watch.

If something was wrong in that state of Denmark, it was Beatrice. Three years had passed but she wouldn't relent. I tried, Malini tried, but the message was loud and clear: Over her dead body would she accept a Hindu son-in-law. *'The Lord said, do not be unequally yoked!'* she once thundered at Malini on the phone as I listened in on the extension. I shudder to think what either of them would have said had they known that Anand and I didn't even live as man and wife but that part was reasonably secure. Anand was a toucher and due to the manner in which he held my hand in public and every so often slung an arm around my shoulders, no one could tell. Besides, because of that night I was pregnant now, so even if I chose to tell, which I felt like once or twice, who'd have believed me?

Then she came around. Literally. She had to.

Anand had to attend a meeting in Madras. I decided to accompany him. We were at Meenambakkam airport on our way back to Bombay when I detected a stain on my behind. My first thought was to pretend I hadn't seen it. Then I became anxious about forming a blood map on the aircraft seat. 'Anand, I think we're losing the baby,' I said. 'Look.'

'You must have sat on something,' he said coolly, sizing up the stain with the detachment of a cartographer.

My palms around the steel rails of the trolley began to sweat and the smell of fear was beginning inside my head. What can you do at an airport in the middle of a queue? You haven't left and you haven't arrived. It takes as long to turn back and locate a doctor in a strange city as it does to go home. So we boarded the flight and by the time we reached Bombay there were huge uncontrollable sounds coming out of me, full of vowels and spit.

Anand took me straight to a hospital where I was asked to down five glasses of water before an ultra sound. It was all a blur. I remember him shouting at the Malayalee nurse at the reception. 'Is this really necessary?'

'Bladdarr fulll honay ka,' she replied.

A full hour later the doctor came. My bladdar was bursting by then. 'There it is,' he said, tapping the screen next to my bed.

Swooshing lines moving up and down like a radar sighting. No heartbeat.

'Can I use the bathroom now?' I said.

'Look at this,' he said, tapping the screen again, and then to me, 'Afraid not,' and then to the nurse, 'Get her a bed pan, sister,' and then to Anand, 'Would you wait outside please, we have an emergency here,' and then back to the nurse, 'Get the OT ready. Page Dr Desai. Patient turning toxic. Fluid in Pouch of Douglas.'

I was a kangaroo with a pouch and there was a half-dead baby sitting in it called Douglas.

'I'm so sorry,' was the last thing I said to Anand, holding out my hand, but before I could feel his in mine I felt my eyeballs rolling backwards. 'Out, please everybody *out*,' is the last thing I heard. I saw Anand move like lightning towards the door, turning around to take a look at me, hitting his shoulder against the door in the process. I felt myself dripping—Number One, blood, Douglas, I wasn't sure.

'What the hell is a Pouch of Douglas?' is the first thing I heard when I regained consciousness, hours or days later, I couldn't tell. It was Anand whispering to Malini.

And there was something else in that room. Something I hadn't seen in a long, long time. It was sitting on a sofa and it was shaped like Beatrice.

By the time I came to my senses completely she was gone. And then everyone pretended she hadn't come at all. Anand didn't talk about her nor did Malini and that was odd but I didn't pursue the matter for two reasons. One, I came to the conclusion that there must have been some unpleasantness between her and Anand. Two, after that miscarriage the world changed colour. Anand was solicitous for about three or four days. After that he withdrew his attention from me as swiftly and coldly as money from a bank account.

Spring Quintet in G Minor

Damage occurs at many points in our lives and we normally source it to a happening outside ourselves. An evil deed, an ill wind, a natural disaster. Also, we are surrounded by people of motley intent and we enter their ambit for a while, suffer a degree of damage and then move on. This is presuming we were victims and not self-flagellators who imagine that mostly damage stems from within.

For a year I hung around the house in a vapour of disbelief, everything smelling of chlorine—food, doorknobs, bathroom sinks. My hair grew tangled with grief. Around me were the bleating sounds of the slaughterhouse, the smell of blackened blood. I could feel the jagged ends of lacerated pink flesh on my body, the crusted tips and the flapping ends and I could do nothing but wipe the perspiration off my upper lip repeatedly with the back of my hand. Huge curtains of air, thick and gelatinous, pulsated into one another and the world itself rose and fell like the breath of an asthmatic.

Anand's silence didn't precede any kind of reincarnation. It was a dead, stupid thing that persisted in existing like an appendix so I dealt with it as best as I could but when nothing would come to mind I would grow silent too and silence waits for more silence to multiply within itself until it's larger than you and I would try and rectify what I'd done by saying the occasional something and that would be a mistake because there would be no answer and by then I would be enveloped in this great white senseless sheet.

From silence he drifted into the opposite, being mean to me, little smoke fires that sprang up from nowhere. Beatrice had described hell to me once. She said it was a place where there were hot coals under your feet so you kept jumping up but every time you jumped someone hit you on the head with a stick so you spent eternity wondering whether it was better to stand there and burn or jump and let your brain pour out of your skull.

I could have picked up my things and left but I hung around from sheer fatigue, looking at my pieces dumbly like a passer-by does an accident. It was only when the hormonal fog around me began to clear that I began to look for solutions. I thought of travelling, keeping out of Anand's way but I felt uncomfortable asking him for the money so I began toying with the idea of becoming a travel writer. I asked him if I could contribute to the *Post*'s travel supplement and whether they would pay me but he made it sound like incest, as if he had grown scruples suddenly.

That's when I bumped into Behroze Modi. I had met her initially at the *Post*. From writing she had moved to being written about, hugely fêted for her spirit of adventure that had taken her to remote parts of the world. I saw her walking along Warden Road. I stopped my car and ran after her, convinced that she it was who would be my saviour. If she recognized me and was nice to me initially it was probably because of who Anand was but I let that go as a petty detail in the face of my larger plan which was to get away from him and simultaneously get him to want me back. But Behroze said travel writing paid nothing. She suggested I try travel photography instead. So I bought a second-hand camera and began learning.

Four years later, she and I produced a book together on the fishing villages along the Malabar Coast. After that she introduced me to *National Geographic* for whom we did a feature together on Malana, the little village in Himachal inhabited by the descendants of Alexander the Great. From one camera I now had three and an impressive array of lenses. Anand could go to hell is what I thought and so could Beatrice. But not Malini. She had hung around those years. She was the one who had loaned me the money to travel, the money for my first camera.

Can sisters exist outside the womb that brought them together? By then I thought someone would have to do a DNA to find a connection between Beatrice and I. She was ancient history, an occasional wrenching of the heart but mostly something I could do nothing about, a memory like a beehive in my brain, safe if ignored but with the knowledge that you couldn't ignore it forever.

Then perhaps you could, because Beatrice gave in to her pique one day, she did something awful.

Malini called one afternoon. It took a while for what she said to register and when it did it was as if the floor, the walls, the molecules in the air around me had grown silent. She had just received a copy of Beatrice's last will and testament by courier in which it was stated that she was leaving her house jointly to Malini, Sujata and Aditi. My name was mentioned briefly in the last paragraph to the effect that since I had already enjoyed the comfort of her home for several years previously I should not consider that anything more was owed to me.

Sometimes when we are stunned we do this funny thing—we skirt the issue at hand, deny its import to us and move at a tangent to some other issue entirely. In retrospect the two would be related, howsoever unclear it may seem then. Mozart when he was told the family home had been left to his sister told her he didn't give a damn but proceeded to compose the *Spring Quintet in G Minor*, the saddest piece of his career, nothing to do with houses. Just like that, after I placed the receiver back on its cradle I began to think about damage—whether it had more sources yet that I was unaware of and it came to me that damage could be a part of one's inheritance. It could have begun a thousand years before in some deed committed by a forefather. It could explain a phone call a thousand years later.

It isn't an unfamiliar phenomenon. When the topmost branches of your tree of life begin to turn yellow you turn to their roots for answers. How could Beatrice have done this to me merely because I married a Hindu? It wasn't the house that bothered me as much as the fact that she had turned me into a nobody, and if I was nobody, who was *she*? Who the hell was a Christian? Who the hell was a Christian in a land of a billion Hindus? How could Beatrice forget that her own forefathers were Hindu? As far as I knew *everyone* in India was originally Hindu. Which forefather of mine decided he wasn't?

But we *had* no forefathers, Beatrice had always said.

All I knew was that we hailed from the Thar desert in Rajasthan, from an old Hindu warrior clan called the Dahiryas but everyone was dead, she'd always said, their houses had fallen, the graveyards were gone, and thank god we had 350 square yards in South Delhi to our name. Thank god we had nothing else because relatives and histories and photo albums and letters can complicate your life. Those 350 square yards was where history entered a blind alley, tyres screeching.

It's a phenomenon peculiar to the Christian convert in India, a blanket amnesia that keeps the heart of the onion safe. An as-is-where-is policy that lets you walk about unfazed in a land of a billion Hindus. It's also a bit like that pillar of salt in Greek mythology. You never look back, not even if someone takes away your view from the front, not without everything falling about you like a house of cards. Our colonial masters had done that to us. It was there in their Book of Knowledge and Truth, in the small print, after you were done with the adjudication, the promises and the blessings, what would become of you if you looked back, for the same god who led you through the terrible wilderness, who could bring forth water out of a rock, would smite you with all manner of things, *with the botch of Egypt, and with the emerods, and with the scab, and with the itch...with madness and blindness and astonishment of heart*...so Beatrice never looked back, to the right or to the left, turned cross-eyed from following the tip of her nose, her nose and her forming an unwavering queue to heaven. She was the flying leap in Darwin's chain, between her and the year dot, monkeys. On a micro level I also imagined that perhaps some relative might have hurt her feelings once which was why she said what she did and so for all these reasons I had never questioned the absurdity of what slowly became my truth—we had no forefathers.

Thus I had no inheritance.

Who then was Beatrice to disinherit me *now*?

Inheritance is a complicated thing, made devious by a misunderstanding of what the word really means. No doubt it's in material things, in property or fixed deposits or jewellery lying hidden in lockers but it's also in the repository of collective memory, in the great epics, in stories your grandfather or an old toothless servant might have told you while cracking a betel nut.

In the material sense I now had nothing, in the real sense I never did have anything, and from that comprehensive nothingness into which Beatrice had placed me, bits of my own memory began to return. Meagre, unsubstantiated, blowing in the wind.

Way in the recesses of my mind was a dead aunt, Flora, for instance—things I'd been told about her by Malini, Sujata and

Aditi that didn't amount to a halfway reasonable description of a person. She was like the Bhootni in *Bees Saal Baad,* a witch with ringlets who draped herself in jewels from head to toe, dragging herself down corridor after misty corridor of a desert mansion making tinkling sounds.

There was a granduncle called Andrew, also dead. If I thought hard enough I could remember something about his jaws, something about them being like the jaws of a Basset Hound. Another dead granduncle, Billy, who everyone referred to as a Tidda, locust, I never knew why. As locations went I knew only that Beatrice had grown up in a house called Grace Place somewhere in the Thar, the Great Indian Desert, the name of the house and the desert not matching at all.

Oddly, I knew hardly anything about my father Iqbal, not even why he had a Muslim name. Beatrice I knew had been named after Queen Victoria's youngest child but his name was a mystery, including the peculiar combination of names he'd inflicted on us. No one explained, nor did I ask. Having died before I was born he hadn't meant much to me at all. The little I'd heard about him hadn't endeared me to him, especially the tales about his temper. If he didn't like what was cooked he would pick up the hem of the dining table cloth and send the food cascading to the floor, Beatrice mopping it up afterwards, weeping. Once, Sujata told me, he threw a tiffin-carrier out of a train window but it had opened up mid-throw and the food had pasted itself along the window bars and they had to look at it the whole journey through because he was too proud, and they were too scared, to remove it. There was also a bunch of letters lying somewhere that he'd written to Beatrice once. Beyond this I knew nothing. No one ever spoke of him, nor did I ask, but with Beatrice having abandoned me now, I suddenly began to think of him and he grew larger and larger in my mind.

Some of us manage without a personal history. There are those who go to their graves not knowing where they came from. Property or bank accounts have the power to fill that void besides which one might say there are other histories far bigger and more significant than one's own. It's a trade-off, the dynamics of which don't dawn on you until you're deprived of both and that's how I made up my mind that day to look for my forefathers, look for the Dahiryas, look for Iqbal wherever they lay buried for I saw that unless I did I would never find my way back to the present, the last signpost to which Beatrice had just obliterated.

I didn't tell Malini my thoughts because she wouldn't have understood, she would have thought I wanted the house, she would have asked me how a bunch of dead people equalled a house. *Oh dear!* was all she'd said after reading the will out to me, like she hadn't the power to pick up the phone and scream at Beatrice, put her right, like her will had been carved by the finger of God into a tablet of stone that Moses had thrown on the Israelites.

Looking back, I see that it was my inability to accept the fact that Beatrice had abandoned me that made me look for those men and women long gone, look for links between past and present, sometimes where none existed, but then at that time I was convinced that nothing less than a huge historical revelation could return to me a sense of time and place.

History wasn't a matter of linear progression that day but a collision of comets racing across the sky, both past and present in combat, eyeball to eyeball, the abdication of one to the other, the one unwrapping itself from around pillars to slink under stairwells weeping, the other pretending it had no way of knowing quite what it had done.

I'm walking down a dark street lit by puddles that in the moonlight appear like sheets of glass. History's a stranger in a greatcoat and hat, leaning against a defunct colonial lamp, watching me approach. As I cross him, he takes the cigarette from his lips, grinds it under a patent leather shoe, tips his hat over his forehead and starts following me. I walk faster, looking over my shoulder briefly like a coquette, increasing my speed in tandem with the decreasing distance between him and me but the two together are immeasurable because of the physics involved, the light years, that business of looking at an old moon, thinking it was new…

Not having been a student of history, my search began with a map of Rajasthan, a couple of brochures picked up from the Rajasthan tourist office and a coffee table book from the Strand bookshop. The book contained chapters like 'Fifteen Ways to Tie a Turban'. Royalty like petrified glass. It's what has happened to Rajasthan since it became part of the Golden Triangle. There's so much to unlearn. Of course there were libraries, reference sections, little drawers labelled A to Z where I could scramble and unscramble dates like a Rubik's Cube freak, or an alchemist, except that the libraries revealed nothing either. Almost. *One* paragraph in Tod's ancient three-volume tome in which he admits to knowing nothing about the Dahiryas beyond one Dahir who he refers to as 'the despot of Sinde' and who met with a tragic end at the hands of Cassim, lieutenant of the Caliph of Baghdad. In conclusion, Tod writes, 'Whether this prince used Dahir as his proper name, or as that of his tribe, must be left to conjecture.'

One more nugget of information emerged in the form of the *Chatees Rajcula,* the catalogue of the thirty-two royal races of Rajasthan in which the Dahiryas are enlisted. Placed against Tod's information, it raised a question in my mind as to whether the Dahiryas were the prince's soldiers or sons. What could Tod have meant when he referred to them as his 'tribe'? He himself pointed to the former, that the Dahiryas were in all likelihood a martial race, not royal, and that Prithviraj Chauhan, Raja of

Chitor had bestowed some sort of title on them in gratitude for their defence of him. That he also granted them several acres of land so they never returned to their home in Sind.

Soldiers, aristocrats, or kings? Finding that beginning was like lying in bed trying to catch a blade of the ceiling fan in your vision, eyeballs going round and round, muscles screaming. Accuracy lay *somewhere* but I didn't know where to look for it. Untutored in research techniques and hopeless with dates I fumbled along in a fog. Three things confused me further. One, an English translation of an ancient song of the Manganiyars, folk singers of the desert who referred to Dahirya as a place where the legendary churails of the Thar dwelt. Then one day, Malini, who'd discovered by and by what I was looking for, dropped a bombshell: 'You're wasting your time, Gudda,' she said, 'there isn't a drop of blue blood in us, or even black. We're peasants.' Sujata all the way from London disagreed. 'Don't tell anyone, Gudda,' she said on the phone in a whisper, 'I think we're bandits.'

So I began all over again, poring over old gazetteers, maps, historical tomes, at times regressing into an old nightmare of lessons at school, things I never understood then or now, the ryotwari system, the zamindari system, this reform, that bill, some tenancy act or the other, after which I began flipping through files of the Thuggee and Dakaiti Department of British India. So wounded was I that I went back to the year dot, collected pictures of gnarled tree stumps dating back 180 million years to the Lower Jurassic Age in the Mesozoic era, to bizarre hybrids of ferns and palms belonging to an age when dinosaurs roamed the region; an excerpt from Kautilya's *Arthasastra,* written around the third century BC; a seventh-century description of the Thar by Huien Tsang trying to get to Sind from Gurjardesh, now Barmer, and something I'd always hated: dates, dates, dates.

A year later a picture emerged. This was the story of the Dahiryas as I understood it: Rajasthan had through the centuries been ravaged by war, by dynasty overthrowing dynasty and in the process sometimes entire communities were swept away or family documents lost, or branches of families severed from parent stock. Things came to such a pass that few could remember who their ancestors were any more, and given the Rajput's legendary vanity on this score, his insistence on distinguishing his ancestors from the herd of mankind, imagine the void. Only he could have done what he did then, for when he couldn't find his ancestors on earth he looked towards the firmament, began to lay claim to primeval parents of celestial origin—the sun and the moon—and failing that, of demoniac.

Legend goes that when the cards were being dealt it was the latter that fell to the lot of the Dahiryas. It came to be believed that this ancient warrior race was descended from a churail, that breed of vampire with uncombed hair who roams the desert by night on feet cranked backwards. Embittered by the reputation imposed on them, the Dahiryas migrated from the dunes in the west to the Aravali mountains in the east where they laid down their arms and became peasants.

Not far from those mountains was a commercial beehive where trade with Europe, Africa, Persia, and Arabia was conducted through the old Silk Route and it was this, along with the once fertile fields of Rajasthan that brought the British here. With the British came taxes. As the economy of the Thar transformed into the classic colonial pattern, the old rural system began to disintegrate and with it the finest cornfields of India began turning into barren, hard stretches. The Dahiryas began cultivating poppy for its commercial value. An agrarian law then limited its cultivation but the law was forgotten by all, including the rulers who were its chief beneficiaries.

How much opium can you sell before you begin to lose track of what you're consuming yourself? Already the Dahiryas' abilities as warriors had diminished and now as peasants they grew increasingly inert. Staggering through their fields in an opium haze one day to the diamond-studded plait of a rich begum en route to Palli, they chopped off her plait whole and made off with it, sold the diamonds in Palli for a killing after which good luck some of them abandoned their fields and began plundering caravans along the Silk Route.

1868. Into the uncertain lacunae between two sets of morality, two nations not of one blood, the forces of nature stepped in to change their lives forever. Dreams of the harvest were stillborn. Water wasn't to be found even at depths of two hundred feet. The earth sizzled and cracked. After the drought the rain came in torrents but just before the harvest, calamity struck again. The heavy rains after the drought had set off a population explosion of the hungry locust, tidda, the most dreaded of the species called the farkha. Their meagre crop of makki was destroyed that year, huge colonies of locusts moving in concert from the makki to the sugarcane until all was laid waste in minutes. It's said that no Rajput worth his salt abandons his land but hunger couldn't be postponed. After yoking the few bullocks left standing in their fields they joined the caravan of peasants crossing the desert. It was the beginning of the greatest exodus mankind has ever known, an enquiry commission estimating the death toll from that famine and many others that followed in the latter half of the nineteenth century at approximately 1.5 million people.

From churails to warriors to peasants to opium-eaters to bandits to the Lawrences of Hakra. After wandering interminably through the scorching plains of Rajasthan in search of succour, they arrived at a small town at the periphery of the Thar, at the gates of a Scottish Presbyterian Mission. Only thirty-two had survived that journey. Among them were two families, one consisting of my maternal grandfather, a man called Hubair Singh, his wife Rosan, his brothers Bilawal and Rundoo, and his sister Haria. They became Hubert, Rose, Billy, Andrew and

Harriet Lawrence. The other family consisted of my paternal grandmother, a widow called Nanhibai, and her son Iqbal. Nanhibai became Nancy, and Iqbal, for reasons unknown, remained Iqbal. Seven others were individuals who had lost their families along the way. The rest of the Dahiryas, eighteen of them, died within months of their arrival and lie buried in the Mission cemetery, three rows of headstones with no names, overgrown by the dhooba grass of the desert.

What became of Dahirya? The present generation of Lawrences deny it existed at all. It's only old British War and Foreign Office maps that could confirm its exact location but they're lost, either in England or in the fly ash of India's colonial past. Only the Thar remains and it's speechless, now the dust bowl of India, dotted with gnarled stumps of trees from fires that once raged through its bone-dry forests.

Hai Ram!

I have a dream of home, another world, other smells. They've got to be there somewhere. A house with fruit trees all around and some without fruit that are much taller, casting a shade over a picture-book dwelling. An old-fashioned larder with pickle enough for a generation, in huge brown and white ceramic jars in various stages of readiness, and fruit in baskets, asleep in the straw for ripening. Kaju kishmish badam in old colonial apothecary bottles. My window overlooking a mango tree and an untidy little path running through the back garden to nowhere. The kind of sisters that wake you up at midnight on your birthday with a steaming chocolate cake. Mother, whose eyes reflect the wonders of her lawn as she sits on a chair on the patio, and Father, whom no one speaks to out of reverence but things change in the house whenever he returns. Sudden movement and sounds, cups gently placed on saucers, that sort of thing …

September 1997. I was still wading through Tod, Lawrence James, old gazetteers, antique maps, government reports to see if I could spot Bhootni and Basset Hound and Tidda somewhere when the wheels of history suddenly began to turn. Like the churails of the Thar, in the wrong direction. It began with a small news item at the bottom of the first page of *The Times of*

India. A Father Christudas of Dumka, Bihar, had been stripped naked and paraded through the town while being beaten throughout. Among the spectators were the district collector and the superintendent of police. A few days later it happened again. Slightly higher up on the page. A Christian priest was dragged out of his vehicle in Chennai by five men and beaten mercilessly with iron rods. Shortly after, the Bajrang Dal called upon Christian converts to leave India. 'We will compel them to leave India by virtually launching a Quit India movement against them,' they said, 'they do not have a moral right to stay here.'

It was a year before, soon after the BJP had come to power, that a hate campaign had been launched against Christians. Dozens of fanatical Hindu organizations under the umbrella of the RSS had begun to make their presence known. I hadn't taken their babblings seriously.

Christian missionaries were CIA agents in disguise.

They had links with the drug mafia.

Their educational institutions and social work were a cover-up for conversion.

They were utilizing welfare funds from abroad to bribe the poor Hindu.

They were destabilizing India by funding terrorism in the North-east and Jharkhand.

Dates and figures were splashed all over the media:

The Seventh Day Adventist Church was pumping in Rs 700 crore to fund conversions in India.

Out of the 2.25 crore Christians in India over 2 lakh were active missionaries. Their aim: to set up 9 lakh more churches by 2001.

> *The Christianization of India was part of a global strategy decided in the US in November 1995 when Christian leaders of 77 countries held a conference in which they decided to evangelize the whole world before the twenty-first century.*

Nowhere was it mentioned that Christians constituted only 2.34 per cent of India's population.

It was similar to the build-up preceding the demolition of the Babri Masjid in 1992. Six years had passed since the event and thousands of RSS shakhas and balopasana kendras propagating Hindutva had sprung up across India, armies of gymnastically oriented young men in starched khaki knickers who thronged the parks morning and evening to practise judo and karate, their uniform a symbol of Hindu revivalism. It was xenophobia taken to an extreme.

> *Muslims weren't Indian because they were loyal to Pakistan and Saudi Arabia.*

> *Christians weren't Indian because they were loyal to the West.*

The VHP was proposing a 'holocaust museum' to show the oppression of Hindus by Islamic conquerors and later, the British. Appropriating the heart and soul of history was another project to resurrect the Sarasvati river. The RSS wanted Hindus to be able to bathe in its sacred waters once again. Through state power a mythical past was being created in exaggerated colours of Hindu glory. Researchers were being commissioned through government agencies to put together anecdotal, scientific and Vedic evidence to prove that the Sarasvati was much more than an exotic tale. Remote-sensing specialists, hydro-geologists, archaeologists and historians were sent off to drill up the one witness to India's glorious past, the river, never mind that it vanished around 1500 BC.

Next came the announcement that the VHP was preparing a Schindler's List of Christian missionaries. They were going to teach them a lesson for making fun of Hindu gods, going around calling Lord Ganesh a pot-bellied baby elephant and Lord Hanuman a monkey. In an angry newspaper article Amartya Sen reminded Hindus that if Christians made fun of Hindu gods, Hindus did it now and again too, that popular theatre in rural Bengal had always depicted Hanuman as a comic character and the epic poem *Meghnadbadhkabya* portrayed Ram as a coward, his enemy Indrajit as a hero—not that the Hindu heartland read elite professors from Oxford.

After the knickers had warmed up to the cause, they were given saffron bandannas and tridents, told by their leaders how Hindus were being persecuted in their own land and that the onus of saving the nation was on them. After that they were let loose like cannon.

Churches were vandalized, Bibles burnt, bodies of converts exhumed from graves and dumped by the roadside, villages torched. Little-known places became newspaper headlines: Jhabua, where four nuns were raped; Dangs, a poor but peaceful tribal area in Gujarat, known until then for its near-zero crime rate, where soldiers of the saffron brigade went on the rampage, shouting *Hindu jago, Christi bhago*, leaving in their wake poverty-stricken tribals clinging to broken crosses and the burning remains of small sad village churches; Manoharpur, Keonjhar, where the Australian missionary Graham Staines was burnt alive along with his two sons by a mob led by one Dara Singh.

The prime minister on his part didn't even order an enquiry. Instead, in the manner of a peacemaker at the family dining table, he called for a national debate on conversion. To salvage his image in the aftermath of the Staines murder, he announced a fast for communal harmony, symbolically scheduling it on 30 January, as if no one remembered it was the same day Mahatma

Gandhi had been assassinated fifty-one years before by a member of the RSS.

It was the morning after the Staines murder, staring at the headlines in *The Times of India,* the photograph of Staines's blackened jeep below, that I broke down—like I knew him. He was *nothing* to do with me, I told myself, *nothing at all,* but the tears wouldn't stop, and we all know this about human nature, it could have been the cumulative effect of my miscarriage, Malini, Anand, Beatrice's will, I can't really say it was *all* about Staines, it was the first time I'd even heard of him, the very first time anyone outside Mayurbhanj had heard of his existence but there he was now, his life exposed to the world, his charred bones on the same page as his gentle face, the impossibility of merging the two images.

It's possible others wept too, who knows, those pictures were heart-rending; it's also possible they wept and went on with their lives, but I couldn't. Of course I'd already been angry at news reports through the previous year but that was it, I'd been angry, but Staines was different, that photo of his, those eyes, I looked at them, they were the eyes of Beatrice.

A radical change began coming over me in which my embarrassment at Beatrice's world, my old world, began to transform itself into fierce pride. I knew I would never come to terms with Christian missionaries and their ways but they suddenly didn't seem so alien to me any more, not as much as the world outside Beatrice's door.

Someone was taking my country away from me but returning my religion to me, neither with my permission. The RSS had achieved what my Bible-thumping mother hadn't in forty years. I was suddenly the thing I'd been trying so hard not to be—I was a Christian.

Shortly after the Staines incident India went to the polls. Anand, to my astonishment, expressed his intention of voting

BJP and I walked out on him the morning the elections were held.

Those were My People; Anand was not.

This is what happens when a small community is threatened by a larger one. You don't stop to think; you simply reach for your sword.

Anand wasn't a fanatical Hindu, if he was he wouldn't have married a Christian but he was something worse, an *unthinking* one, to me the bigger crime, one that was taking place all over India, spreading from the heartland to the cities.

I didn't speak my mind to him, partly because I hadn't understood the change in me fully and partly because Anand had changed radically too. He was given to rages in which he would pick up things and start smashing them around. And had I even spoken what would Anand have replied?

You don't expect me to vote for the bloody Congress do you?

Or,

Have you forgotten the Sikh riots?

Or,

This is not a personal issue, Anandita!

Or worse,

Is this a mother–daughter issue?

And then in a kind voice,

Nandu Nandu Nandu ... she doesn't even think of you as her daughter any more.

Or, the prize,

But you yourself told me you suspected your mother was a CIA agent and had links with the drug mafia!

And what would I have said in reply? No, Anand, it's a historical issue? Women leave their husbands over *history*? So what I said to him instead was that if it were Staines today it could be Beatrice tomorrow and that I needed to return to Delhi briefly to warn her, to get her to mend her ways.

'Get the old bird to mend her will,' was what Anand said to me in return.

I wasn't sure if I meant to get Beatrice to mend her ways. I wasn't sure I knew how to. I wasn't even sure I wanted to go back home, not after what she had done to me, but what was also true was that what she had done to me turned small in the face of the insults that were being heaped on her and her religion and while a part of me wanted to say to her *serves you bloody well right,* the greater part of me was furious on her behalf.

I left Bombay in a rage. If Beatrice hadn't dropped me off at the station, Anand didn't either, so I waved goodbye to a couple of urchins who watched me load my suitcase into a taxi, smiled at the pot-holed road in front of our building to which I would never, God help me, return. At the end of the road the tears came and the pain, on wings that made a fearful sound.

What kind of person allows a government to govern their personal life? I wasn't an illiterate from the Hindu heartland who would believe he was who the government told him he was, or wasn't, but at the same time a government has the power to topple your internal bona fides. God knows how other Christians took it all but I was suddenly driftwood in the ocean of a new India in which Beatrice's house began to appear to me the only discernible shore.

Such is the tenacity of the idea of one's childhood home that I put aside for a while the fact that she had made it clear that even that wasn't mine.

Return of the Prodigal

I returned to the house by the nala without fanfare, twelve years after I'd left, a week before Easter, both Beatrice and I pretending away her will along with Beatrice pretending I hadn't been away at all. And I almost believed it because apart from the fact that she was older and the house a little shabbier her world was still turning on its own axis like an independent planet, sending its UFOs racing across my sky. Her clothesline on the front balcony was flying full mast, those Maidenform bras announcing the size of her breasts to the world and as I stood on the balcony on my first day home I found myself wondering why I had returned at all. I was confused. If Pila, Darla and Zach were who I had always believed they were, why was I now enraged on their behalf? It was one of those questions that remain in the air like so much fluff.

Malini, meanwhile, had gone and reported to Beatrice that I'd been showing interest in our history.

Beatrice was furious. 'Why are you behaving like an FBI agent, Gudda?' she said. 'Let the dead rest!' While I'd begun my search for the Dahiryas for one reason, the RSS had given me another so that was the one I presented her with. I tried to reason with her, tried to explain how important our history was in the face of the accusations that were being hurled at us, that we needed to open up the past and show them they'd skipped an entire chapter of Indian history, that she wasn't to take it personally, that I wasn't threatening *her* in the least but all of this was beyond her, she behaved like the past was a rare diamond cursed by the gods to lose its lustre if you so much as looked upon it, and it was so sad because if only she'd had the capacity to remove herself from the centre of the universe my task would have been so much easier, but no, she stood there like a Dobermann guarding the gates of history like she owned it all.

There were two Dobermanns, snarling at you from opposite directions, the VHP now announcing that all Muslims and Christians must accept that their ancestors were Hindu. True they were Hindu, but it was as bad as asking Christians to accept that Jesus' grandfather was Krishna or Ram because Christianity's like that, it leaves no room for hospitality of such kind, Jesus is the one and only, the Alpha and the Omega, you can knock the socks off a Christian by telling him something like that, and it was so ironic because I'd been trying to knock the socks off Beatrice already, that logic was *mine,* but with the RSS entering my playing field I was forced to abandon it, and since Christianity's a black-and-white religion unlike Hinduism, it doesn't allow you to sit on a fence, and since the RSS wasn't about to wait till I'd worked my way out of the conundrum I had to walk over to the other side and declare that *everything* they were saying was wrong. The irony was that they could have found in me their greatest champion but this is what fanatics do to you. Force an argument on your plate when you have none. Set a cycle of contrary opinion in motion.

The manifesto of the Hindu Jagran Manch was suddenly in circulation that year, its principal objective to make converts realize the folly of their ways and return to the Hindu fold. The

VHP declared that it didn't want to punish the Christian, just generously welcome him back, give him a royal homecoming, a ghar vapasi through a shuddhikaran ceremony. So, in a leaf out of the Christian missionary's book, shuddhikarans began to take place all over India. With a sprinkling of holy water, the chanting of *Om*, the presentation of a saffron cloth and a flower, the reconversion of thousands of frightened Christians to Hinduism began to take place.

Nothing consolidates a micro sense of community as much as the slipping away of it in the macro sense which was why, when Beatrice asked me, I agreed to go to church with her on Easter morning.

So she made a huge concession for me. She snubbed off her own bunch of loonies to attend St Paul's Cathedral on Hastings Road where people behaved with a dignity she despised. For me, who hadn't entered a church in twenty years, it was a surreal experience, the old familiar Easter whiff of morning breath laced with mothballs from silks packed and hastily unpacked for the occasion. The opening hymn was getting over when we arrived and Reverend Joel Das, resplendent in his robes, was emerging from the vestry to climb the tiny wooden spiral stairway to a freshly waxed mahogany pulpit. 'Please be seated,' he said and then into the hushed silence boomed, *'The Lord is risen!'*

'Halleluiah!' Beatrice shouted back, all on her own, loudly, making a thousand heads turn.

Two minutes into the listening I realized that something was wrong with the Reverend's syntax and diction. He was emphasizing all the wrong words. 'And then Mary *went* to the grave,' he was saying. I cast an angry sidelong glance at Beatrice but her head, after that initial burst of enthusiasm was curled into her chest like a bat in stasis. The huge helicopter blades on either side of the church were whirring slowly, no breeze coming my way. My eyelids grew heavy and Pastor Joel Das's voice began to recede. 'And so my *brethren*, the lesson *of* Easter...' he was saying. I saw the pallu of Beatrice's sari flutter like a wing gathering momentum and she rose into the air like a bird. Then she flipped over horizontally with her feet behind her, her bunions forming two little rear engines. She flew out of the pew and onto the pulpit and with one nylon wing distended, she raised her arms from the armpits and said, *'Halleluiah, halleluiah, halleluiah!'*

'Tere bagal mein chuhiya!' responded the congregation, raising one cheek and farting in unison, the cue for Beatrice to take over the sermon.

But it didn't sound like one. She was banging a spoon and plate together and whistling through the whistle of a pressure cooker, jumping up and down the pulpit, singing a crazy Brides of Christ ditty after which she moved on to serious theological issues beyond her ken and from there to the big one, the question of questions that no Christian on earth can answer intelligibly. 'What had I done to deserve this terrible life? I asked Him, Lord,' she was saying, 'but he said that I hadn't and *this*, my brethren, is the lesson of Easter because someone hung and died on a wooden cross for this mysterious non-reason. He bled and he bled, from his palms and his feet, the centres of them...*he bled and he bled and he bled* and at this point in the story I get terribly confused because I looked up the meaning of Redemption in the dictionary but what it says is different from what I feel. *Why did that man die?'*

My eyes flashed open. 'Why did *Christ* die?' boomed Pastor Joel Das. 'Ask yourselves this *my* brethren, on this precious Easter *morning*, and why did he rise *from* the dead?'

There was no answer. The congregation was dead. Incinerated by Beatrice's breath. Not a shard of a bone on a pew. She had forgotten to brush her gums that morning. I would have to have a word with X-files. They were running out of ideas, bringing snakes out of people's goiters now. Mulder and Scully would march up to Beatrice and hold out their cards and say 'FBI, would you answer some questions please?' and Beatrice would get up trembling, clutching her Bible to her on which would be written Placed by the Gideons so they would see that she was a hotel thief too and they would bark at her and say, *'And put on your brassiere when we talk to you!'*

'Hey hey *just a minute,* you don't talk to my mother like that!' I interrupted.

'Will you tell her Mulder or shall I?' said Scully.

'Tell me what!' I said, but the service was over and that firstquestion lastquestion about who Christ was went *whatwhatwhatwhatwhat* as it flew up the rafters to settle on the pigeons' backs, making them flutter their wings and make guttural sounds.

I elbowed Beatrice sharply.

'What?' she said, clutching her beat-up purse and Bible in the flurried manner of someone hiding the fact that they had slept through the sermon. 'So how did you like the service, Gudda?' she said, looking up at me eagerly.

'Utter nonsense!' I replied rudely.

On the way home she was silent. Her lips were dry and she looked straight ahead at the wind rushing against the speeding car. As if there was nothing to her but flakes and those too would blow away if I said anything to her. *But the way she sat!* Her hand around the handle that nobody holds, the one above the door. Like she was the wife of somebody big. As if she had rings on her fingers and a retinue of servants to whip awaiting her.

The roads were like boulevards that Sunday morning, so empty that we didn't even stop at the traffic lights. *'Hurry up!'* she'd said when we were leaving the house that morning, *'or we'll be caught in the traffic jam!'* but as the magnificent procession of her went by it was only the grey asbestos shutters of the new India that saluted her.

Hardly anyone came home that Easter to wish us. Most of the foreign missionaries had fled India in fright and some of the darpoks she knew had reconverted to Hinduism. I went off to Wengers for hot cross buns and marzipan eggs for tea but they lay like so much still life on the dining table, and if it hadn't been for the occasional fly cruising over them you would have believed they were sculpted. So at the end of the tea I gave them to Beatrice's cook Ram Bhajan to give to his children, turning the whole thing into an act of Christian benevolence, as if I'd bought extra deliberately.

Viewed from the house by the nala Christ definitely didn't rise that Easter, if he rose at all, and as Beatrice and I drifted from the dining table to the sofas to sip our tea into the evening light I found myself chattering about this and that interminably to drown out the sound of her heart, a sound like a chain around my ankle, *my* heart. *Don't talk nonsense!* she said once, I remember, looking as proud as ever, and since I was like I was, that was the cue for me to speak even greater nonsense, to hurt her with my remarks and some of those remarks were about Christians and about her last anchor in life, Jesus Christ, and they were cruel remarks and I saw her wilting like those Easter lilies that appear only for the day and that was how that evening went, without comfort—that odd, comfortless connection between Beatrice and me. Me lashing out at her to hide my fear, watching her life walk away from her as if it had been stuck to her all that while with cheap glue. Her heart like a surreal nightmare leaning against a door with no hinges.

'You're causing a social schism in the community, Ma,' I said, flipping through a copy of *India Today*, an interview with the BJP General Secretary.

'Social *what?*' said Beatrice.

'Pay attention,' I said. 'In a village hamlet of 300 people, if 120 get converted to Christianity, it makes life difficult for the other 180. It is not merely the addition of one more god in the row of pictures. Its effects penetrate deep down, affecting societal amity and disrupting material well-being and harmony. Where earlier all 300 accompanied a funeral procession to the crematorium, now 120 go to the burial grounds. And where does the graveyard come from? Often the land owned by the 180. This is a complex social phenomenon, it rattles those who are not converted.'

'Bund karo bakwas!' said Beatrice.

Funny how we transfer our own fears on others, because Beatrice herself was shameless. Through the entire furore about the Christians she redoubled her efforts to convert everyone around, not with a war-cry like the Muslim, but like a sweet little woodpecker gnawing at a tree until he's made a hole in it.

A few days after Easter a thousand copies of a pamphlet entitled *Operation Tell Everybody* were delivered at our door. It delineated the remotest areas of India, with a paragraph on each, on what the Mission was doing to convert them. Remember the Latur earthquake of 1993? Flipping through the pages of that pamphlet I came across a paragraph which if touted efficiently could have successfully brought the entire Hindu heartland to the feet of Jesus:

> *Pastor John Osteen of Houston, Texas helped me some years back with $40,000 to conduct 40 evangelistic campaigns, and we planted over 80 churches in Latur area as a result of this. Remember the earthquake which hit this area three years back killing 45,000 people in a few seconds? It was in this region. The earthquake hit 117 villages, killing people*

> *and cattle, even destroying hundreds of buildings. But in these 80 villages, wherever there was a Christian, no person or animal died and no building was destroyed. The earthquake just zig-zagged these villages but destroyed other ones where there were no Christians. Praise GOD.*

I turned the packet around to look at the name of the sender. It was that bloody bitch Pila Jayawardene.

A month later I saw her on Doordarshan. She had been hacked to death in the backwaters of Orissa where she had gone preaching. An NGO was demanding an inquiry to confirm whether she had been raped as well, a suspicion brought on by the fact that her corpse had no panties on.

Leave aside that I hated Pila, did she deserve to be taught a lesson? Probably, going around converting people the way she did, but she wasn't breaking the law. Article 25 of the Constitution clearly states that 'Subject to public order, morality and health and to the other provisions in this part, all persons are equally entitled to freedom of conscience and the right freely to profess, practise and propagate religion.' The very soul of Christianity is missionary. It would cease to exist if it disregarded the parting words of its founder: *'Go ye therefore and teach all nations...'* Besides, Christians weren't the only ones conducting conversions in India. Billions of dollars were being sent every year to India by VHP organizations abroad for converting Muslims to Hinduism. In tribal areas Hindu missionary organizations like the Ramakrishna Mission, the Gayatri Parivar and the Brahmakumaris were active *with* the assistance of the State. The RSS was raising a bogey about conversion as if India were a stranger to the phenomenon, as if it hadn't known conversions since time immemorial, since 500 BC when conversions were carried out by Buddhists. Then, due to preaching by Hindu religious leaders like Adi Shankaracharya the Buddhists converted right back to Hinduism. There are accounts in the Puranas too, historical allegories if not verified history, of forest dwellers and animist tribes being made to accept Vedic ways of worship. During the Muslim period many who converted to Islam continued to be governed by Hindu laws of succession...a complex phenomenon indeed, rendered simplistic by that overtly innocent but inflammatory question *Where does the graveyard come from?*

Pila's murder stunned me deeply. It was too close to home. Suddenly fear wasn't just a state of mind; it could mean the pounding of Beatrice's door in the middle of the night. It was that rape business, never confirmed, that led a thousand Christians, along with a band of writers, artists, newspaper editors and intellectuals to march to Parliament House in protest.

I joined the march.

Beatrice didn't. She was nearly eighty by then and I'm not sure she was fully aware of what was going on. She never read the papers, besides. It was the Book of Revelations that gave her all the information she needed, she said, reading bits aloud to me, making ancient prophecies sound like the nine o'clock news. A sad thing had happened to her while I was away. The Brides of Christ group had expelled her. It had objected to the meetings she was holding in her drawing room independent of the pastorate. Initially they'd appeared harmless, consisting of a sermon by the foreign missionary in residence followed by an invocation to the holy spirit to descend, the latter accompanied by Beatrice's three-piece orchestra—a pair of bongos, a tambourine and a pair of cymbals, further accompanied by an outpouring of hysterical gibberish. Naturally Beatrice was MC, it was *her* house, but gradually she began showing tendencies of megalomania. She began directing missionaries to villages of *her* choice, at a time chosen by *her*, making them report to *her* on their progress and then one day she did the unforgivable, she held a meeting on a Sunday morning and the church looked up sharply.

She said the pastor was jealous of her, that he was playing power games with her but the fact was that he was the one invested with power, not her, and though she carried on with the meetings, consolidated her own little ragtag group under the aegis of a dubious Texan Mission, upgraded the Britannia cakes to pastries, partly in defiance, partly to lure people to attend, she was gradually cut off from the mainstream, from news and views and plans of action.

Fired by the march I hired a security guard for her and this was ironical in a way because even while the storm outside was raging, the missionaries who had comprised her world had reduced to the solitary diehard or two. They were no more than clones of what had gone before, shabby little imitations of the original devils, sans dollars, often sans even knowledge of the religion they came in the name of. Texas had money but it wasn't enamoured of the East. Invitations from Beatrice to them to hold conventions in India were met with polite silence. It was the state of Christianity all over India by then with only twenty-three million left in a country of one billion to keep the flag flying. The religion had lost its roots, its original mentors had gone and whatever new money was being pumped in through Missions or individuals was serving only to embellish a dying community's last rites. Beatrice's three-piece orchestra had fallen apart to be replaced by a katori and chammach, our old brass dinner gong and the dhakkans of two dekchis for cymbals that when banged together produced what you might call a dreadful cacophony but to my ears the sound of a breaking heart. There she sat, on sofas that had lost their sponge, banging away and singing her sing-song, her maid Lajo to the left of her, Ram Bhajan to her right, a magnificent congregation of three accused by the Government of

India of threatening to upturn 5000 years of Hindu civilization. It was so odd, because at the same time as the community was dwindling, because it was suddenly being made to stand up and be counted, it began to appear as if it consisted of hordes, threatening the soul of every Hindu in sight. It was what happened to the Jews. They seemed to be in hordes always too, spilling out of train compartments, huddled one on top of the other at concentration camps on three-tier beds.

Staines was still in the news and the hunt for Dara was on. Because he was Australian the incident had drawn worldwide attention and protest. Newspaper editorials were declaring that India was hanging its head in shame but the election results belied that. Anand's vote had been only a drop in that ocean of hate because the BJP returned to power. Former RSS chief and premier ideologue M.S. Golwalkar's *Bunch of Thoughts* was being circulated along with the party's manifesto. That litany of hate closed with the statement: 'So long as Christians here indulge in such activities and consider themselves as agents of the international movement for the spread of Christianity, and refuse to offer their first loyalty to the land of their birth and behave as true children of the heritage and culture of their ancestors, they will remain here as hostiles and will have to be treated as such.'

But Beatrice wasn't the kind of woman to be *treated* as anything. Hostility she viewed with joy, prove as it did all the prophecies in the Bible about Christians being persecuted in the Last Days. To the faint-hearted Christian who was contemplating returning to the Hindu fold through those shuddhi ceremonies being held all over, a counter threat of God's revenge was laid on them, in one word—the promise of HELL.

Beatrice stood at the gates of St. Paul's one morning, handing out a tract entitled 'The gates of hell opened?', an astonishingly inept translation of an article that had appeared in a Finnish newspaper. *Do you believe man's vanity appears to increase with knowledge, and the tail of evolution grows proportionately therewith, does it?* was the opening sentence of another translated Finnish pamphlet I found lying on her mantelpiece one day, it being anyone's guess whether such a sentence was the product of printer's devil or dislocation of the convert's brain, and in such an ethos, journalist Arun Shourie's vicious attacks on Christians began to appear like someone were taking a corpse out of its grave and flogging its remains. As if no one had noticed since the Bible was written, he declared there were grave contradictions between the four gospels.

For all their scholarly tone his articles in the *Asian Age* were as senseless as the pamphlets on Beatrice's mantelpiece but people read those articles and people wrote letters to the editor that were sometimes boxed in with rules around them, making them stand out on the page and suddenly after all those years of no one in India knowing quite where Christians had sprung from, everyone was discussing them in drawing rooms, suddenly everyone had opinions on them but none of those opinions even remotely touched upon how it felt to be one.

Murder in the Fourth Degree

How would you feel if someone who doesn't know you suddenly starts telling you who you are? What your religion is about? What your religious texts are about? It was a horrendous invasion of privacy, a taking away from Christians a sense of self, of belonging.

Who was I?

Who was Beatrice?

In what way were we responsible for what a man called Hubair Singh had done a hundred years before? In what way was *he* responsible?

As if in answer to a cry of anguish, an angel of God in the form of Pope John Paul II descended on India to tick a few people off. Holy men have a strange effect on the public conscience. A nervous Archbishop of Delhi greeted him with '*Shanti, shanti, shanti*', leaving the 'Om' out. An equally nervous prime minister went, 'You know, Holy Father, India is a land of religious freedom, but we have some intolerant fringes.' Not to be left out, the President dug into his bag of good deeds and told the Pope he had attended Catholic primary school. To show the Pope how secular India really was, an interfaith meeting was organized between Hindus, Muslims, Jains, Sikhs, Bahais,

Buddhists, Zoroastrians and Jews, in which however the Pope boldly declared that 'it was the moral duty of Christians to spread the gospel throughout Asia'. This got the RSS into a frenzy; it was *already* in a frenzy before the Pope came, at the very thought that he should come, organizing rath yatras with flying banners declaring *Ram chahiye, Rome nahin*! In the midst of it all came terrible wisdom from a French journalist who suggested through an article in the *Indian Express* that everyone stop, they were already brothers, the word 'Amen' was derived from 'Om', the structure of the church resembled that of the Buddhist chaitya, and Sri Sri Ravi Shankar had found out something that had escaped even Christians, that Christ himself sometimes sported that Hindu symbol of renunciation, the saffron robe.

India was so alive that year. India was dead.

From Beatrice's balcony I looked across at Mona's garden and saw that it had died too. It was overgrown with weeds. The blue and white canopy had faded in the twelve years I'd been away and was now trailing at one end, as if Mona had tried dragging it along with her when she went and then suddenly let go. The wrought-iron chairs were no longer white either. They looked like they had taken root, like they were fossils from another era which was why, when I peeped over Mona's gate one evening on my return from the market, the last thing I expected to see was someone sitting on one of them. It was a replica of Mona, as if Mona had been sitting there all these years waiting for me.

'Oh my god,' I said, jumping in fright.

Mona's ghost stared back at me. I was about to turn and run when it got up from the chair and said, 'Guddamaasi, is that you?'

'Natasha!' I exclaimed. The gawky fat kid I had known was

now a svelte woman. And she had the strange good looks of one who had weathered a terrible storm successfully. 'My god,' I repeated, as I went forward to hug her.

We sat on the fossils. Her story emerged. After Mona died, Arvind went off abroad with another woman, left Natasha with an aunt with whom she'd lived for five years after which the aunt died too, of cancer, so Natasha, now twenty-four, had returned to the old house and had been living alone since the age of eighteen.

So I adopted Natasha in my mind, partly to assuage my own guilt about Mona and partly with the thought that Natasha could be the daughter I would now never have. She was a busy girl with a full-time job with Action Aid but whenever I saw her I smothered her with attention and surprisingly, instead of being jealous, Beatrice liked her. Natasha wasn't like other kids her age who bypass old women as if they were already dead. She wasn't like other kids her age in other ways too. One of those ways I mistakenly put down at the time to the residual trauma of having had a rotten father because although Natasha was attractive and had a host of girlfriends she didn't appear to have a single boyfriend. Kitchen psychology is a dangerous thing and it can be so off the mark.

One more neighbour—an invisible one—welcomed me in his own fashion. I was standing at the garden gate one day when I felt something descend on me. I looked around. I looked at my clothes. There was nothing. Then I felt my hair. It was wet and slimy. There was no tree above me so it wasn't crow shit. It was clearly a gob of spit. Above me was our balcony and there was no one there but connected to our balcony and alongside it was the neighbour's balcony. It was a narrower one than ours and unlike ours you could see their curtains as soon as you looked up and I saw them billowing just then as if someone had gone behind them quickly. Not possible, is what I thought, mentally measuring the angle between that balcony and me, but it was certainly odd. There was absolutely no one around, the sky was a clear blue, not a bird or a plane in sight. I went in and scrubbed my hair. What was it? Flying snot? Flying piss from a soundless aircraft?

The following morning when I awoke and went to the front door for the newspaper I got a strong whiff of something. I saw a huge mound in the centre of the garden. There were about a million flies dancing above it. It was a mound of garbage, neatly emptied, poised atop it a used sanitary napkin. I banged the door shut, my heart pounding. This was inconceivable. It was six a.m. None of the neighbours emptied their garbage that early. Someone had obviously done it in the middle of the night. I asked the guard outside whether he had seen anybody coming. He hadn't, he said, and that was inconceivable too.

By eight I had it cleared, by ten I'd called the security agency and asked for a change of guard after which I told Beatrice what had happened but Beatrice gave the matter no importance. The nala was only six feet away, she reasoned, and some sleepy head must have misjudged the distance. Are you an idiot? I wanted to say, but she was already an idiot in about a hundred other ways that had called for me to expend greater energy than I was motivated to do over a mound of garbage.

It was after that incident that a depression came over me. And paranoia. For years there had been a sticker on Beatrice's car that read JESUS SAVES and I decided to remove it but car stickers don't peel off just like that so I had to use a blade and after that we had to look at this rectangular gummy patch on the rear windshield with scratches on it which wouldn't go away no matter how much I scrubbed and spat at it and then the gum collected lint which turned the patch opaque and the whole sequence got me into a purple rage.

Beatrice was furious too—that I had removed the sticker. Nothing I did or felt those days gained me any credibility with her. The old mark of treason was engraved too deeply on my forehead, and as I watched her watch me from the balcony struggling with that sticker I saw that her eyes held absolutely no gratitude for my concern for her. *Father forgive her for she knows not what she does!* is what her eyes spoke, as if *I* were the one tearing her life from her, lynching her skin away inch by inch with that blade.

I misread those eyes. I didn't misread those eyes as much as I didn't read the duality in their myopic depths.

'Gudda, what are you doing down there?' she called, as if she didn't know what I was doing.

'Nothing, Mama,' I replied, scrubbing away, as if I didn't know either.

'Can you come up?' she said.

I stood absolutely still for a minute. It was a new trick I'd developed, something that grew me an armour before I faced her. 'Coming,' I replied, which if I could reverse the clock, I would never have done. *What would I have done*?

I climbed the stairs, thinking wearily on my way up that she was going to make a big issue out of that stupid sticker, make it out like before the cock crowed I had betrayed Christ thrice.

'What is it, Mama?' I asked, settling down on a sofa, lighting a cigarette.

'Close that cigarette!' she shouted. She had some papers in her hand. 'I want you to read this,' she said then, a crazy sort of look of pride on her face.

'What?' I snapped.

She was always giving me stuff to read, about the end of the world, about the Second Coming of Christ. But this looked different. A passport-sized photograph of her was pasted on the upper right-hand corner of the first page. I put on my glasses. I read the heading. It was the Last Will and Testament of Beatrice Lawrence.

'What is *this?*' I shoved the papers back at her, fear turning my heart ice-cold. Was she dying? Was she dying without informing me? Seeing a will feels different from hearing about it on the phone. It spells instant death.

'But I want you to read it, it's important that you read it,' she said, looking snubbed.

Did she imagine Malini hadn't already told me?

'Why me?' I said. 'How dare you show this to me?'

'Why not?' she replied. 'Parents make wills. Children must read them.'

'Right,' I said. '*Children*. I'm only *one* of your children. What about the other three?'

'But they're not here,' she said.

'Then leave it with a lawyer,' I said. 'That's the way it's done in movies.'

'But the lawyer gave it back to me. He said I should give it to you, that you should keep it in safe custody.'

'Why *me?*' I began all over again, sounding hysterical.

'Read it,' she said firmly. 'You'll understand.'

So I read it. Not once but twice. It wasn't the will that Malini had read out to me.

This one said she was leaving everything she owned to me. Her house, her car, her television set, her bloody pamphlets. At the end of the will was a clause that passed a paltry Rs 300 per month from my earnings to the Mission. I looked at the date on top. It had been written just two weeks before. It invalidated her earlier will. Numbly, I looked at the term 'household and personal effects'. Why was she thrusting her underwear on me? Her bottles of Cod Liver Oil and Waterbury's Compound?

My mind ran over her things like a thief in the night, past furniture, past crockery, past the tacky Christian calendars that hung all over the house, the picture of The Last Supper over the dining table and I saw that there was nothing in that house, nothing that you could call an inheritance in material terms and since my mind had reached an impasse it began to wander along a path long shrouded in memory, when things were different and we had a Villeroy & Boch dinner set, and Irish linen, a Rud Jbach Sohn piano, a silver tea set, a little meat safe in the shape of an English cottage. Where had they gone? Why was our house so empty? The piano had gone to the Mission, I knew, but the rest had simply vanished along with Malini, Sujata and Aditi who had taken themselves away, turn by turn, leaving me with Beatrice, and now, here I was, the little ragpicker, mentally rummaging through their leavings. Their leavings and the shell of an ugly house. Who enraged me more? They or Beatrice? It was just some more fluff to try and pin in the air.

'Why are you doing this?' I asked quietly. 'What about the Mission?'

'The Mission has enough money,' she said.

'What about Malini, Sujata and Aditi?'

'Who are they?' she said bitterly. 'And even if they are somebody, they have enough money too.'

I stared at her. Why had she done such a turnabout?

It couldn't have been in gratitude for my return, for my desire to shield her from a changing world because according to her those changes were *written*, that dreadful things would happen in the Last Days, that Christians would be persecuted all over the world and so, rather than any help I might render to her, I was more likely in the way of God's plan! I examined the clause at the end of the will, the bit about the 300, tying me to the Mission for life, a nasty bit of revenge she'd concocted for all the years that I had troubled her. Was this her way of humbling me? Machiavelli, Queen Lear, all sorts of names Malini–Sujata–Aditi used to call her behind her back and the memory of this came back to me now, exacerbating my unease. What was she up to? What if I broke a leg and ceased to earn? Would it mean surrendering my soul to the Mission? Alternately, little pieces of the house, room by room? What if she had already paid someone off to break my leg, say, six months after she died? It was ludicrous, the path my mind was taking.

'Okay, I'll keep this for a while,' I said awkwardly, rolling up the papers into a funnel. 'Let me think about it.'

'There's nothing to think,' she said, 'what are you going to think?'

What was I going to think? Among the things I thought on my way down the stairs was that I now owned a piece of the earth. A piece of earth in a country I no longer felt I belonged to. What I didn't think at all, because I didn't know it then, was that Beatrice's little Christian ghetto by virtue of its location in South Delhi was prime property, and that the land on which it stood was worth seven crore. But before this came to my notice, something else did, making my new status as landed gentry pale into insignificance.

Two days later I decided to spring-clean the house. It wasn't a clear-cut decision, about the cleaning up. It began with merely shifting her pamphlets from the drawing room to the bedroom because in the atmosphere pervading the country I saw no reason for her to announce to every stranger who entered the house who we were. One thing led to another. I found that her bedroom shelves were chock-a-block with pamphlets too so I created a sort of study room for her in another room and therefore some of the things in that room had to be moved out and in all of this shifting and settling she kept hovering over me, interfering and passing unnecessary comments and so I turned aggressive, delving into more and more of her junk just to irritate her and through the process I noticed an old black trunk under her bed, under lock and key. Was it full of dollars?

Was the trunk worth more than the house? Was *that* what she intended to give to the Mission, fooling me into thinking I was getting it all?

It wasn't greed that made me focus on that trunk, just curiosity but in retrospect perhaps it was more than that, perhaps it was the hand of God that moves when the time is ripe, when the time has come for you to finally open your eyes, to see. I say this with a sense of drama because what emerged from that trunk made her will appear as worthless as the paper it was written on, the creatures that flew out of Pandora's box look like butterflies, the proverbial skeleton in the cupboard look like a mannequin in a shop window.

I hid her keys. I waited for her to go out and then, locking myself in, headed straight for the trunk. Identifying the key wasn't hard, it was the oldest one in the bunch, but I had to hit the lock with the ball of my palm several times to get it to move. The first thing that came to me as I lifted the lid, along with the smell of old mothballs, was disappointment. It was no Fort Knox that trunk, just a collection of household and personal items. There was the white lace tablecloth she used to lay out at Christmas once upon a time, some crocheted cushion covers, a set of three English Yardley Lavender soaps that Sujata had given her on her birthday two decades ago and other such old-woman odds and ends. Shuffling between and under her things I felt a small compact bundle with my hand. Lifting up into the air the pile of things above it I saw that it was the same bunch of foreign aerograms she had shown me a long time ago, letters from my father Iqbal to her, written many years back from London.

Placing the pile on the ground I picked up the bundle and debated whether to go through the letters again. No, I wouldn't, I decided and just at that moment the old sticky rubber band around them came apart and the letters slipped from my hand.

Placing them together I saw that the one at the bottom of the pile was different. It was a local aerogram, not foreign, and the handwriting wasn't my father's. Unfolding the flap I looked at the signature below. It was from Basset Hound.

My dear Beatrice,

You will be surprised to hear from me. Not unpleasantly I hope, although you turned your back on us three years ago in anger. It was a harsh step you took and not entirely in balance with what had occurred between Iqbal and you but perhaps at that time you were disturbed due to your delicate condition. Wrong timing has been the cause of much heartbreak in the world as it has no doubt been with you.

There was much I wanted to say to you then but you weren't prepared to listen and now it's too late perhaps. I hear you are well settled in New Delhi and have utilized the money your father gave you to build a beautiful home for yourself and your children including the little one who I never had the joy of seeing. I couldn't help but feel sorry for Iqbal that you took his children away from him although both Mercy and I were angry with him too, which unfortunately you chose not to believe. We spent many an evening with him trying to understand his behaviour and we came to the conclusion that if he was unfaithful to you it was not because he loved or cherished you less than he ought but out of his own insecurity and lack of emotional stability.

The fact of the matter is that Iqbal stopped visiting us after you left. We heard rumours that he had taken to drink and then a year later I met him at the Hakra bus stop and could scarcely recognize him. He said that he had finally come to terms with the fact that you had left him but that without you and the children there wasn't much point in his staying on here. I asked him where he was planning to go and he replied that he was returning to Dahirya, the only place left on earth that he could call home. That's when I realized that something was gravely wrong, that he had grown delusionary due to drink so I stood there with him for a while, trying to convince him to return home with me but he was adamant and I had no choice but to leave him there waiting for a phantom bus.

I have not heard of him since.

Now to the real reason for this letter. Your father Hubert left Grace Place to me and your aunt Mercy. Mercy departed from the world two years ago. I myself have been suffering from tuberculosis and do not have long to live. I have drafted a will through my lawyer, leaving Grace Place to your unborn child. I did not name the elder three whom you would probably have convinced by now to take the same stand as you, nor did I name you for you had sworn to me when you left that you would never return. I am hoping your youngest one might some day and thereby connect with a small corner of the world where we were happy once. I have thought long about this. I have thought about the mistakes I have made in life, some of which it's too late to rectify now. One of them is that I wasn't supportive enough of you when Iqbal let you down. Forgive me, my dearest Batto, and allow me to make it up to you through your child. My will and the house registration papers are in the custody of my lawyer who will be in touch with you on the occasion of my death.

Yours affectionately,
Uncle Andrew
Grace Place
Hakra

The letter was dated 29.7.69. If Andrew had seen Iqbal a year before, like he said, it would have been in 1968. Give or take half a year to accommodate human error there was still something wrong for Iqbal had died in 1966. His grave with the date of his death writ large on his marble tombstone was there for all to see. If Iqbal was dead, who then was the man at the bus stop? If that was Iqbal, who was in his grave?

I tried to recall the circumstances of my father's death, what I had been told about it. The story went that *both* he and Beatrice had migrated from Rajasthan to Delhi in 1966. Malini, Sujata and Aditi had been left behind briefly with Beatrice's sister Flora because Beatrice couldn't look after them along with the double load of shifting and being pregnant with me. Shortly after arriving in Delhi, Iqbal had died of a heart attack. He was buried at the cemetery on Prithviraj Road. Beatrice had erected his tombstone before Malini, Sujata and Aditi could join her. In other words no one had witnessed his death and only two people, Beatrice and I in her womb, had attended his funeral, and it came to me in the manner of a thief divining a code in the dead of night that there had never been one.

I thought about Iqbal's grave, about the flying angels on top of the snow-white marble. I had put up with looking at their cherubic faces for years whenever we'd gone to place flowers on his grave, the cheapest the flower-seller on the road outside had, the ones wasps cling to in delight. That's all he deserved, Beatrice had muttered once, and as we'd stood around his grave I had imagined she was angry with him for dying; I mistook the emptiness in her eyes for profound grief, her faraway gaze for a philosophical denouement of unspeakable loss.

As the puzzle began to take shape I began to understand why she had strewn our lives with corpses. It was because relatives excel at asking awkward questions, so after telling us Iqbal was dead, they had to be dead too.

Such a Long Summer

Stories should have some sort of linear progression; life doesn't. It would have been in the order of things that I confront Beatrice, wring the truth out of her, then board the very next train for Hakra, wherever that was, from Hakra find out where Dahirya lay. But shortly after I found the letter the longest summer of my life began and I was rendered speechless.

Beatrice fell ill and illness in the hands of a megalomaniac is a fearsome thing. She directed its course, used it as a tool to harness attention and when that worked, directed the illness to remain. It was secondary that in the bargain her own suffering was prolonged because that's the essence of megalomania. You're willing to die just to get a crowd to collect.

Perhaps she'd sensed something, perhaps she hadn't, I don't know. I kept telling myself I'd confront her as soon as she stopped looking vulnerable but the moment never came and then it was too late. I began to fear I might kill her, reviving the past like that, crushing her pride, bringing her life down like a house of cards, so those questions like so many others before remained in the air: Had she done what she'd done because a widow got more respect than a woman deserted? Where was Iqbal when Malini, Sujata and Aditi had been left behind in

Hakra? How was it possible those three knew nothing? Had nobody dropped Beatrice off at the station when she left for Delhi, watched her boarding the train out of Hakra alone? Does TB affect the mind—was Andrew delusionary? Was the date on the letter a simple mistake?

Is it a lie propagated by children that parents fall ill just to harass them? Of course it is, but with Beatrice and me there was always a sinister, convoluted truth beneath the more rational lie which was why it took time for me to understand the extent of her anger towards me that summer, that it was greater than mine towards her. What had *I* done? It was more a case of what I had stopped doing. I had stopped seeing her as synonymous with Christianity. The circle of which she had once been the centre had turned inside out. I had begun seeing her as a single member of a community, a helpless community that I was suddenly taking up cudgels for. Not because of my association with her but because I was a bona fide member of that community. Strangely, she and I were on the same side now but this robbed her of the importance I had earlier allotted to her and the only way for her at her age to tower over my life once again was to fall ill with a vengeance.

It began with her looking windblown even when there was no wind. Wisps of hair forming a tired halo around her head. Her lips looked dry and they were white at the corners every time she came home and her breath smelled. Her skin looked as if epidermis was all she had left and under that, bones with no marrow. The white nylon saris she had taken to didn't suit her but cotton she said was too much trouble. I would watch her from the balcony as she emerged from her car, her shrinking figure encased in billowing nylon. She would enter the house and go straight to the sideboard and pick up a tin of foul-tasting biscuits called Threptin as if new life lay there. She would open the tin with the back end of a spoon, dig one out and put it whole into her mouth. Then she would sit at the dining table and stare at the wall in front of her as if there were miles and miles of ocean there.

I suggested she see a doctor but she refused, not out of a sense of martyrdom but fear that the doctor might find nothing wrong with her. Then one day she agreed. But she insisted on going alone and later I discovered why. It was the doctor who told me. He said she'd walked into his clinic saying she wasn't there to consult him but that she'd had a vision the previous night that his soul needed saving. After that she proceeded to deliver an endless sermon to him while his patients practically expired in the waiting room, thrust all sorts of pamphlets about the Rapture on him to scare the living daylights out of him. Now, the doctor who was not only a staunch Hindu but had surrounded himself with innumerable little statuettes of Lord Ganesh in that clinic, was also a good-natured man. He laughed in an affectionate way telling me all this, about how important it was to indulge the old and then he went on to compare West with East and how in the West nobody would have listened to her, they would simply have dumped her into an old-age home and between that overly kind and secular doctor and Beatrice I felt diddled and I grew angry which isn't saying much because I had been angry for a while. But *this* was *it*. I decided to ignore her, turn on my heel whenever I saw her. She on her part was bewildered. She had given me her house, so what more did I want? Why was I breathing fire and brimstone?

Simply to indulge her one day, the doctor ordered a blood test. The result she insisted on collecting alone too, looking strangely triumphant when she returned from the lab. I watched her from the balcony as she shuffled past the gate, through the garden, then from the top of the stairwell, her calcified nails whitening against the banisters, a small dinosaur heaving itself up step after step on the dead meat of its thighs. At the landing she half-straightened, eyelids falling over her eyes like two shy turtles. I waited for her to tell me the blood test was clear. She didn't. She told me nothing. She sank onto a dining chair instead, legs dangling like a foldable table whose joints had swollen so they couldn't go back into their niches.

'Do you want a cup of tea?' I said finally.

'Huh,' she said, her eyes opening slightly. What did Huh mean? Yes or What?

'Do you want a cup of tea?' I repeated a little louder.

'Half a glass of Rooh Afza,' she said, rubbing her hand up and down her chest. 'Don't shout.'

She had taken to Rooh Afza of late. So much had changed. The colour of her irises, that switch to nylon, and that breath.

After a few sips of the Rooh Afza she told me she had tuberculosis.

I turned ice-cold. I could hardly breathe. I couldn't look at her face.

Tuberculosis be damned, a lie of such magnitude stood between her and me now so that all I could bring myself to look at was her photograph that night when she was fast asleep.

I took it out of an album and I looked at it and I wept.

As the months went by I began to wonder why I should look for Hakra or Grace Place or Dahirya at all, look for a man who had abandoned me because even though Beatrice was the one who'd abandoned him who asked him not to look for me?

Anger to absurdity: What did I care about a dead man's house? What if Andrew's lawyer was dead too? What if he wasn't dead but when I found him he said *Who the hell are you?* I would need to bring Beatrice forward to prove my bona fides but to make Beatrice come forward I would have to get her arrested first but if I dialled the cops they'd ask *What did she do?*

and what would I say? I'd say that *She's a thief* and so they'd ask *What has she stolen?* and I'd say *She's stolen the past from me* but that would sound odd so I would strengthen the accusation with *And now she's beginning to steal the present too, God knows about the future when there's such a thief around* and there would be silence after which the cop would say *Look lady we've got work to do* or more likely, since this was Delhi and he a Haryanvi Jat, *behenchod,* and I would be left holding a dead receiver.

Worse, what if I found the house?

Because if I did I would have to walk up to it, ring the bell and a man would open the door and say 'Yes?' and I would stare at him, not knowing what Yes meant. Who on earth turned Yes into a question? Yes was the opposite of No. Yes meant you were agreed to something.

So he would rephrase the question. 'May I help you?' he would ask.

'Yes,' I would reply, but nothing would come to mind after that so again he would say 'Yes?' which in the second instance of its utterance would have magically turned into an 'Is that so?'

'Actually this is my house,' I would venture then, but my voice would emerge like a spent wind, sighing as it lays down its head, dispersing time across miles and miles of desert sand with its last sad breath.

'What nonsense!' the man would say.

'This is my house,' I would repeat. 'See, there's been a terrible mistake. When Beatrice ran away and Andrew died...'

'Who?'

'When Beatrice ran away and...'

'Listen dear,' he would be kindly now. 'This house has belonged to my family for a hundred years...'

'But that's impossible,' I would say.

The man would look helpless then and yell for his wife who would come running to the door to block my view so I would have to prop myself high on my toes to look past the two of them at Andrew's things which I wouldn't recognize.

'Sweetheart,' he would say to his wife, 'this young lady says this is her house, I mean this young lady says this *was* her house a hundred years ago...' and as if suddenly understanding would have dawned upon him, he would without moving his head swivel his eyeballs downwards in their sockets to look at my feet and he would see that they were cranked backwards.

That's when he would bang the door shut on my face.

And that's when the sequel to my life would begin, the return-walk through the desert, back to Beatrice, for if you were exiled before you were born it isn't destinations, rolling miles and vistas that are given to you but the twisted story or two, everything outside your own head a mirage, one that recedes as you near until it breaks up with a shiver into a thousand unrecognizable pieces.

With new medication Beatrice's health began to improve and even though the pills continued for a while we almost forgot she had TB and started going about our normal ways but only briefly because after the tuberculosis it was her kidneys, after the kidneys her osteoporosis, as if the one up there was watching her pain and knew no other way to distract her from it but by sending her another. The kidney problem began with an ordinary urine infection. The doctor prescribed Furadantin. She demanded I get her Pearl's Barley that had gone with the wind along with the Brits so I wrote to Sujata to hunt for it in London but that particular letter she said she never got. So Beatrice had Rooh Afza instead, gallons of it, the whole house, her clothes, her dribbling chin, everything smelling of a Mughal harem. But Furadantin, not Rooh Afza, she said, was what was making her reel, and she didn't complete the course so the infection returned and this time she was given a stronger drug and it made her worse until the day came when she was immune to them all. No longer were they urine tests she required but urine cultures that took forty-eight hours to develop during which period she was in despair, sitting on the potty and burning, pouring mugs of water between her shrivelled thighs.

You don't abandon somebody when they get like that, you don't abandon the living for one who might be dead so I put my plans for Hakra and Dahirya aside and I told myself there was always tomorrow. And some day, I told myself, Malini, Sujata and Aditi would come, but they took their time. *'Thank goodness Mama has you,'* they wrote.

But I wasn't enough, not when Beatrice began to lose her hearing. It was Gentamycin injections that caused this to happen and I had been warned they might have that effect but erratic medication had brought her to a point where if I hadn't agreed to them she might not have lived. 'Why are you whispering?' she would say if you spoke to her in a normal voice and 'Why are you shouting at me?' if you raised it. And then in between the Gentamycin injections, in collaboration with Ram Bhajan, she began a course of homeopathy behind my back which brought out the infection from its roots and there were little drops of urine on the floor as she walked and then she reneged on the homeopathy as well because it deprived her of her cups of tea and this went on until we learned to live with it, learned to think of sickness as a way of life.

It had a smell of its own, that life. Of phenyl and urine laced with fermenting garbage from the nala and to compound matters there were frequent power breakdowns that summer so the smells from the nala didn't waft in and out but hung there in a cloud and if you ran around shutting the windows along the side of the house that faced the nala you'd be locking yourself in with those other smells, the phenyl and urine and the Rooh Afza, and worse, the new smell that happened that summer, the smell of a stomach jiggered by antibiotics. She chewed Digene after Digene. The pressure of wind on her rectal muscles led to haemmorhoids and then to bleeding haemmorhoids so she was afraid to sit on the potty and so she developed constipation. So she farted some more, to the extent that she started lifting one cheek to make the passage of wind easier. Initially, if anyone was around, she'd jump in pretended shock and say *'Who did that?'* and then gradually she ceased to bother to do even that.

Her deterioration was rapid. The doctor suggested panty liners so I bought a packet. Drawing one out I tried to explain to her what they were about but she looked at me with contempt and I saw that the time had come for me to exercise authority. 'Show me your knickers, Mama,' I ordered, heart thumping, telling myself this was no more than a plumbing job, a little stuffing up those old washers.

She scuttled off, returned with a shapeless garment which she spread on the dining table. 'India Gate,' she said, introducing her knickers to me.

'Not tight enough,' I said in a tone like I'd been in the business of fitting panty liners into crotches all my life.

She looked bewildered.

'Show me the one you're wearing, Mama. Lift up your nightie and show me up to where they hang.'

She lifted up her nightie slowly, like it were a velvet curtain going up at a grand concert. Then she looked down at herself and said, 'There!'

To my horror I saw that she wasn't wearing anything at all. 'Hush, Mama, I'm thinking,' I said. Then I saw it. A little trickle escape from her crotch and move down her thigh. 'It's no good, Mama, put it down,' I said, turning my face away swiftly, fear zooming through me like a spacecraft in a Spielberg film. You can't go much further than your thoughts and I had none at that moment. It was as if all my thoughts had got together to stage a strike against me, shutting down the equipment that manufactured my very life.

Fear amplifies everything and it's infectious.

I began to fear everything, from the state of the nation to the house which I imagined was about to fall down. I also began to fear how I'd manage if Beatrice died. Would Malini, Sujata and Aditi be in time for the funeral or would I have to buy out Perfect Ice? In those few hours between the refrigeration of Beatrice and the defrosting of her, when there would be little streams running all over the house turning it into a skating rink, would I cleverly, just a few minutes before they arrived, bury her? Tell them I waited and I waited and the whole city ran out of ice and the streams had begun to dance with her pus cells and so here's the mound of earth under which she lies and you can kiss that now and that's my revenge on you for living all over the globe about which the chief idiocy is that you can never hope to be on time for your mother's funeral.

I was also afraid that Iqbal, if he wasn't dead already, would die before Beatrice.

What became of my profession? The photography assignments I'd taken on to remain afloat after my return began to dwindle. I began dropping invitations to photography exhibitions into the waste paper basket as soon as they came because I knew I couldn't go. My To Do List began with Give Mama tablet and ended with Give Mama tablet. If I so much as glanced in the direction of the door she would sit upright and say *Where are you going?* Ultimately I lost most of my assignments and worse, I lost my credibility. A *National Geographic* project I had been promised went to somebody else. They didn't even bother to inform me. It was the photographer they'd chosen who rang up to tell me he didn't have a reputation of pinching other people's work so what was he to do? Do what you have to, I said, and I'll do what I have to too, but I didn't know what that was and so I told myself it was time to take stock of the situation but that is a phrase that has always baffled me, what it is people take stock of when everything's gone.

Time comes when you begin to lose your elasticity, your capacity to spring surprises on people, to invent a brand-new way of being. You rely on people younger and less tired and grieved than you. It was too late for me to invent an alternative to photography, too late too to regress to being a nimboo-pani maker. Besides, there was hardly anyone to make it for now and moreover the price of nimboos had gone up ten times since.

Two years had passed since I'd left Bombay and as far as I could see I had no marriage left either. Anand didn't call once nor did he write me a single letter.

'Is something wrong with your marriage, Gudda?' Beatrice asked me finally one day. Now that she knew she was safe, she was enquiring about Anand as if she had long back accepted him as family.

'Not at all,' I replied.

'Then when are you going to have children?' she asked.

'Never. Can't have children doctor said.'

'Rubbish!' she replied. 'I also had two abortions.'

'It was not an abortion, it was a miscarriage.'

'So what? I hope you know what you have to do after a certain age.'

'No. What is that?'

'After he has made love to you, you have to lie down quietly, pillow under your buttocks to raise them a bit, thighs squeezed tightly together. Don't wash for at least half an hour,' is what she said.

It was clearly the turn of the new generation.

Right on cue, Malini called, shrieking. Neha had returned from Harvard with a black Jew ornithologist fiancé in tow.

'She wants to marry a hupshee?' Beatrice exclaimed.

'Hush, Mama, nobody uses that word any more!'

Neha was only twenty-three. I was deeply shocked. It was proof that *my* life was over.

Malini demanded that Beatrice and I attend Neha's wedding in Bombay. I told Malini it was quite impossible, that Beatrice wasn't strong enough to travel but she wouldn't believe me. Then she called again to say she was shifting the venue from Bombay to Delhi and that I should *stand by*.

I thought that was cheeky, making me sound like auxiliary forces in a war but that's what it turned out to be eventually, a war camouflaged as a wedding.

It was I who was responsible, I or my Christian upbringing that had caused me to do something foolish. I had sent photocopies of Beatrice's new will to Malini, Sujata and Aditi, thinking they would appreciate my openness but they were livid.

If expressed at the outset rage isn't that difficult to resolve but they replied to me in loving terms. The fact that all three letters were in the same vein should have been a warning to me but I turned my face from that warning, so overwhelming was the discovery that Iqbal might still be alive. Overriding all else was the conviction that I had to find him and that Malini, Sujata and Aditi, the only people apart from Beatrice who had known him, would help me.

Faced with the prospect of meeting them I began to imagine the expression on their faces when I told them about him and then sprung the next surprise on them, about Grace Place now belonging to me, which of course I would share with them to make it belong to the four of us. That there had never been a 'four of us', and therefore might never be such an entity, didn't dawn on me once.

But before Malini came Anand's call.

He wanted to know why I wasn't replying to his letters. Initially I thought he was playing a game, confusing me with some fictitious letters because apart from everything else that Anand was he was also a liar.

But the letters turned out to be true. I found them under Beatrice's mattress. Through all that burning and piddling she'd taken the trouble to go to the letterbox three times a day to intercept them. She was mid-breakfast when I found them. I went to the table and threw them at her violently. *'Then what is this!'* I screamed. I had asked her *just* that morning, right after Anand's call because I had suspected her but she'd looked so hurt by my questioning that I had felt guilty. So now I lost control. *'You sick bloody bitch!'* I yelled.

Dumping her fork on her plate, making one piece of papita fly, she picked up a stained, unironed napkin and dabbed her lips with it. Then she rose from her chair upright and, slamming the napkin on the table said, *'Forgive her Father for she knows not what she speaks!'*

The letters themselves were nothing much. Mostly news about the *Post*. Anand was no sort of writer I discovered and one of the letters even read like the minutes of a meeting. But on the phone he was different. He said he was coming to Delhi soon, that he wanted to talk to me about things.

What were those things? I imagined it was about our marriage, about the possibility of repairing it, and truth be told I would have accepted an apology, even an insincere one, not because I was unintelligent or even an accepting kind of creature but because I was so tired by then you could have lain me down on the ground and stamped upon me and I would have looked at you with eyes of hope.

Dead Woman Walking

It was a week after Anand called, a month before Neha's wedding, that the doorbell rang. A very tall, very old schoolmarmish woman with short hair was standing there in a sari blouse with a Chinese collar, Magyar flips at her elbows, pallu neatly pleated at the shoulder and held together with a glittering brooch. There was a steel trunk by her side and she was staring at the doorbell nervously. 'Is this the house of Mrs Beatrice Lawrence?' she enquired in a convent accent. She was holding out a small piece of paper with our address on it.

'Yes,' I said hesitantly, not in the mood to welcome one of Beatrice's crazies and this looked like the mother of them all, with her bob cut and the wrong shade of powder on her face.

'Then you must be Aditi,' she said.

'No, I'm Aditi's younger sister,' I replied.

'My goodness me!' she said in a high-pitched nervous tone, 'then you wouldn't know me at all. I'm Flora, your aunt, your mother's sister.'

'That's not possible,' I said coldly, 'my aunt died a long time ago.'

'Fiddlesticks!' she exclaimed, walking right into the house and into the drawing room where she settled down comfortably on a chair, suddenly not looking lost at all.

'But they told me you had ringlets,' I said stupidly.

She giggled like a schoolgirl, patting her bob with her fingertips. 'I certainly did, my dear, I certainly did.'

I felt the blood rush to my face from embarrassment. 'But this looks good too,' I said, as if I had known her in her ringlet days, but the way she'd positioned her head made me feel she expected me to compliment her and so absurd was the scene that I yelled for Beatrice right into Flora's face. Of course Beatrice didn't hear me.

'Where's that little minx?' Flora said. 'Where's my little sister?'

I charged towards Beatrice's bedroom where she lay fast asleep and shook her roughly. 'Mama there's a horrible woman sitting in the drawing room who says she's Flora.'

'What?' said Beatrice.

'Why did you tell me your sister Flora was dead?'

'What?' she said again, sitting up.

'Your sister Flora's sitting in the drawing room. Why did you tell me she's dead?'

'When did I say she's dead?'

'*Go* and check if that's Flora, *get up*,' I said roughly.

Beatrice hustled out of bed and started walking down the corridor, I behind her. Suddenly she stopped, did an about turn, and jabbed me. 'My teeth,' she said, 'get me my teeth.'

I bounded back into the bedroom and picking her dentures out of their bowl, bounded back with them dripping. This was the first time I had touched them. Slamming them into her mouth she turned around, chin quivering and dribbling and then for the second time I did something for the first time, I wiped her chin with my hand.

'Flora!' she exclaimed the moment she saw her and my heart pounded. I watched them fall upon each other, Flora's face screwing up, Beatrice's shoulders heaving, and with things being the way they had been that summer, I accepted Flora's return from the dead not just with equanimity but as an exciting precursor of things to come, the prospect of dead relatives walking out of closets from around the world.

There were two good things about Flora's emergence, or so I thought. One, I could grill her about the past, about who we were, about Iqbal and Basset Hound and Tidda and Dahirya and Hakra and Grace Place; and two, when I learnt she was here to stay, that I would be in a position to travel. I would dump Beatrice on her.

But Flora turned out to be a dimwit who could scarcely take care of herself. And she was bone lazy. She never seemed to bathe, kept dabbing that awful powder on her face with a giant puff, the likes of which nobody had seen that century and she kept that puff open on the dressing table instead of keeping it in a box or tin or something so for about ten minutes after having got dressed she appeared to be walking about in a dust haze. She was a small-town miser too. I took her and Beatrice to Moti Mahal, for a tandoori meal, and she picked up the cut nimboo off the salad plate and squeezed it into her glass of water after which she said she was having a bout of low blood sugar and could she have some sugar please but when it arrived she stirred three spoons into the water and then chuckled that she'd got nimboo pani for free. To my disappointment she hadn't emerged from either Dahirya or Hakra but Mugair, and she seemed to have lost touch with everybody too, if they were alive at all, besides which Beatrice guarded her with her life, hovering over her constantly, sometimes brazenly positioning herself between Flora and me like a human wall.

I tried to be equally brazen. I also tried to take advantage of the fact that Beatrice was losing her hearing but I discovered it was a highly selective losing. So then I tried a third tactic. I tried speaking to Flora loudly, right into *Beatrice's* ear in order to flummox her but it flummoxed Flora instead who sat speechless in the face of such unheard-of tactics, looking nervously at Beatrice.

'Okay,' Beatrice relented one day, 'you can tell her about Mr and Mrs Darling.'

So I swung my feet up on the sofa, propping a cushion behind me, readying myself for Flora's first story. For history from the horse's mouth.

'Mrs Darling didn't like to cook for Mr Darling,' Flora said, 'so she took him to every wedding in town, invited or not, made him have his dinner there and then stuffed her handbag with food for his next day's lunch.'

'*Oh my,* she never got caught?' I asked.

'Simple,' replied Flora. 'She told the bride's side they were from the groom's side and the groom's side that they were from the bride's side!'

'Good *heavens!*' I said, and then egging her on, 'And then?'

'What and then?'

'Where are they now, this Mr and Mrs Darling? Who are they?'

'Arre baba sab mar gaye!' said Beatrice, lifting one cheek and farting loudly.

What I *did* understand from Flora eventually, late at night while Beatrice was fast asleep, was the layout of our part of Rajasthan as well as the tail-end of the migratory pattern of the Dahiryas. I'd already located Mugair and Hakra on the map but I was as bad with maps and directions as I was with dates. You could tell me the colour or shape of a house and I could find it but if you gave me the number, the address, the name of the street, specially a map with the street delineated on it, I could chase my tail forever. One side of my brain isn't developed; I require descriptions, stories, and it was a chance remark by Flora that caught me, something about the Rajpootana Rifles regiment that I wouldn't normally have paid any attention to because she was like that. She could talk about kofta curry, Hindus, Timbucktoo all within minutes. Both Beatrice and I had stopped listening to her with any attention, we just nodded in her direction, let her prattle on. So she prattled something about the Rajpootana Rifles but then it emerged that she was actually talking about Hakra where the Rajpootana Rifles were based. One thing led to another and Flora began prattling about some English lieutenant in Hakra who used to give her the glad eye and from all this it began to dawn on me that Hakra was a cantonment town.

A pattern began to emerge. Mugair–Hakra–Dahirya, in that order, was the route I needed to take.

Mugair, apart from being the old Residency, was the old railway capital of British India, and as far as trains went in that direction, so I would have to go to Mugair to get to Hakra or Dahirya. Mugair was where Flora and other relatives had migrated to from Hakra in the late forties, including the parents, now dead, of someone called Maddy, a relative of sorts and the only one Flora was in touch with.

Hakra cantonment, where Grace Place was, lay at the periphery of the Thar amidst the Aravali foothills and was two hours west of Mugair by road. A few relatives, Flora said, might have stayed on there because not everyone had migrated to Mugair.

Dahirya, the most important on my agenda, was a blank. I knew it was up in the high Aravali but Flora said she hadn't even heard the name.

And when it came to Iqbal she turned deaf like Beatrice. I didn't pursue her, that's the way it had *always* been about Iqbal.

How do you begin a journey into the unknown, one that refuses to begin? There are only three ways given to man: The first is through desk research, the second is to initiate a dialogue with someone who's been there, and the third is to get up and physically move in the direction of that unknown, so at 6.30 one morning in June I boarded the Flying Ranee for Mugair. Two days, I calculated, was the time I could trust Flora to keep an eye on Beatrice, enough for a quick recce around Mugair in preparation for a longer trip into Hakra and Dahirya as soon as Beatrice's health improved.

I was armed with just three things: Maddy's phone number, the keys to Flora's house and a diary to keep my notes.

Uncertainty often begets a peculiar regressive leap in the mind, as if the mind in its anxiety were returning to foetal position. As the wheels of the train cranked and clanked into motion and we began passing the dreary slums on the outskirts of Delhi, memories of long forgotten journeys in the opposite direction with Beatrice and Malini–Sujata–Aditi returned. Those chocolate and emerald fields up north, and huts like doll's houses whizzing past and Kathgodam station where we would descend in the middle of the night and then rush to another platform with our trunks and hold-alls, bleary-eyed in the halogen light, to catch some other smaller hissing smoking train that took us further uphill. But those days were truly gone, and I was alone, and of course there's a huge difference between those old trains and the Flying Ranee that's full of hippies doing the Golden Triangle, their fluorescent nylon rolls stuffed into overhead racks, and posters of Hawa Mahal and the City Palace along compartment walls, all of which made my heart sink for I had had this absurd expectation from the moment I committed myself to the brave act of purchasing a train ticket that the past would respond and begin unfolding before me but it was all happening the other way round, an aeon had passed since I'd been on a train, the aloo purie had turned into cheese sandwiches, the kulhads into plastic teacups, the emerald and chocolate fields to jade and soufflé and as the wheels of the train picked up speed I thought I could hear the Dahiryas, smothered by air-conditioning, going *we waited for you, we waited for you....*

The First Journey

'Who are YOU?' said the Caterpillar.
Alice drew herself up and said, very gravely, 'I think you ought to tell me who YOU are, first.'
'Why?' said the Caterpillar.

—Lewis Caroll, *Alice in Wonderland*

June is the worst time to go to Rajasthan. The first thing that hits me is the heat, and vertigo, the feeling you get after a train ride, of walking along a platform that's moving like a treadmill. Sweat pours down my neck in rivulets like I've broken a vein. Loudspeakers blast my blocked ears open with high-pitched repeated announcements of the arrival of the Flying Ranee on Platform number 6.

Mugair junction is the familiar synthesis of Gothic and Saracenic you see in all small towns where the British settled, thick walls and pillars now laced with paan stains. Outside the station auto drivers, taxi drivers, seedy hotel touts are making a din, mostly around the hippies. I learn from the touts that the best place to be is the four-star Prithvi Palace at the other end of town. I take a three-wheeler with rubber flaps flying on either side like a mad elephant's ears.

Mugair is a dusty little town, a faded old painting in which the lines of demarcation have merged. It's surrounded by a ring of low, bare dun-coloured hills, the occasional acacia and zizyphus accentuating their emptiness. There's an astounding assortment of vehicles on the roads—cycle rickshaws, phatphats, obsolete cars, rickety buses spewing carbon monoxide, and snaking between them girls in salwar kameez and helmets riding Lunas. Railway crossings too, tracks seemingly thrown across crowded roads by a maniac when actually it's the town that's arbitrary, a confusion of building styles, mildewed old structures squeezed between newer uglier ones.

The Prithvi Palace stands on the banks of the Vidyasagar like an incubator for artificial respiration in the midst of chaos. The air is cold and crisp within with a whiff of magnolia—a huge bouquet on the reception counter, probably imported from somewhere because nothing grows in these parts besides cacti and bougainvillea.

I pick up my keys, take the lift to the second floor, walk down a corridor past an abandoned housekeeping cart to a room at the far end. Dropping my bag on the bed I walk up to large bay windows leading to a faux Rajput balcony from where I get a panoramic view of the Vidyasagar, silvery, dancing in the sunlight, speaking to me from its depths, promising to return to me the stories I own, about the years and the people I never knew, the key to incomprehensible mysteries about the people I do, the changing face of my country. I pluck up the courage to pick up the phone and dial Maddy, heart thumping as I hear a click. 'Mandira Wilson,' says a voice, impatient, out of breath. 'Miss Maddy?' I say awkwardly.

She has a hard time understanding who I am, thought Beatrice had only three daughters. Speaks English with a liberal sprinkling of Hindi, merging the two so well you would think they were one. Not unfriendly, but with many pauses in the conversation in which I don't know what to say and in between she asks me about some relative in Delhi I haven't even heard of, and then suddenly as if she's nevertheless made up her mind about my bona fides, asks what I'm doing in a hotel. Says hotel like it were a four-letter word. *Wasting money*, she says, as if she knows me or knows how much money I have or haven't. Does this convey acceptance of me as a relative or could she be poor or stingy or simply hospitable and inviting me to stay?

I'm going to see her now, not with my suitcase but with an onion in my armpit as per her instructions, because people do that here, she says, or die of heatstroke. I forgot to ask if I'm to peel the onion first. And how on earth do I ask room service for one onion?

Babu, the taxi driver has bloodshot eyes and rubber chappals on his feet, the heels of which appear to have melted away in the heat. His taxi's a white Ambassador with the back seat higher than the front one so my head keeps hitting the roof and there's no leg room either because he's adjusted the front seat further back than it normally is. I can't breathe. Why in this weather does he have a rug on the seat? It's fluffy and ugly and ochre coloured and it keeps shifting around and gathering folds under my bum.

I read Maddy's address out to him. I tell him I don't know the roads so he should keep telling me where we are which he interprets as my wanting to know everything about him, like his life were so inextricably intertwined with every street and gali of Mugair that he has no choice. It's a small-town thing I think, the impossibility of perceiving a place as outside oneself and in a strange way and despite my annoyance, the distance between Mugair and me begins to reduce as we go along and I begin to be grateful.

We're headed towards Nicholas Bridge, a gaping hole under it that emerges on to the opposite bank of the Vidyasagar. From here the lake is large and comforting, stretching beyond what the eye can fully see to a haze of hills in the distance. It was on one of those hills that the legendary ruler Prithviraj Chauhan once waged a battle. Strange how history returns to you a sense of the present. Perched on a crag is the whitewashed British Governor's House, high and lost and lonely, a touchstone to the fear inside that I might never find what I've come here for. The town had been sold to the British by the Marathas in 1818 for a mere Rs 50,000, not sufficient today to buy one room in Beatrice's house! Growing along the hills to my right are the lofty battlements of an ancient fort. On coming into the hands of the Raj, I'd read somewhere, it was dismantled by order of Lord William Bentinck and converted into a sanatorium for the troops stationed at Hakra.

Maddy lives in Indra Nagar. We drive up to Number 4, a faux colonial structure painted white. She has a garden, flowerbeds carved out of cement, rockeries with cacti growing through pretty arrangements of pebbles like miniature desertscapes, bursts of blood-red bougainvillea along garden walls, little marble statuettes all over, women with hourglass figures balancing pots against their hips. There are over a hundred pots here, some terracotta, some ceramic, some on the ground, some hanging on rope baskets, a few large urns in a corner that belong in a Greek garden.

At the sound of the taxi a woman rises from among the plants, hands covered in dirt, wisps of hair around her face. The voice on the phone doesn't match her appearance. She looks my age, has blunter features than mine but the hair, the skin, are the same, like I'd been carrying her under my skin all these years and now there she was outside of me. She isn't overly effusive; I see that Maddy's not given to drama and I like her instantly.

Why did I imagine she lived alone? She lives with a grandaunt, a brother, a sister and an uncle, the uncle turning out to be Tidda, my *dead* granduncle Billy.

Her house is a bit like Mugair, not so big but so full of things that they turn two steps into the longest journey. To get from the dining to the drawing room you have to skirt a Chinese screen, to get to the sofa, turn left at the coffee table, right at the teepoy, circumambulate the lamp, hit your thigh on a chair placed at an angle to the sofa. Things behind things, things among things, enough to fill a mansion. A rug with a Chinese dragon, embroidered birds on the walls amidst ceramic plaques engraved with verses from the Bible, money plant, a brass bell, a plaster-of-paris duck, paper roses, a basket of ceramic fruit at the centre of the dining table, old issues of *Women's Era* and *Reader's Digest*, a French brass boot next to a marble Victorian lady next to three Chinese wise men. Among the curios a plaster-of-paris lizard. Another one on the windowsill that turns out to be real. Rajasthan is heavily populated with a variety of lizards. This one is pale, with a jaw and chin to be taken seriously and a thin whiplash tail at least eight inches long.

Each of the people in this house has something wrong with them. Maddy's grandaunt is blind, her brother Daniel has Parkinson's, *dead* Granduncle Billy has twelve broken bones, keeps asking if the tiddas have been fed when there're no tiddas around, farts loudly, shouting *Honky Tonk Woman* after each blast, and Maddy's sister Milly has the worst disease of all—she's not married.

Maddy, a widow, appears to be the only normal one around. The one thing that's wrong with her is that she's a compulsive locker of doors and turner-offer of lights. In the vast historic canvas unfolding before me, thieves and big electricity bills are Maddy's chief concerns. But Maddy appears to be a large-hearted woman so I'm not sure the reason is bills. Maybe she doesn't want to see the world wholly, who knows, creates microworlds full of curios in the shadow of dim lamps.

Maddy's grandaunt is not my grandaunt; Maddy says I should call her dadi. I'm not sure why but it's fine by me. Her name is Imarti, like that convoluted strain of jalebi and she looks it, her thin plait deadened by repeated applications of oil, six stanzas instead of the usual three coiled tightly to match her name, the sixth an olive-green nylon ribbon snaking through the other five to culminate in a flouncy big bow. Dadi's plait follows the contours of the enormous hump in her cervical. She's 102, her dentures are loose and over lunch they drop into her curry with a plop, she doesn't see the curry fly, she picks up her dentures and starts sucking at them, and then she says: '*Bones bones bones, there's nothing but bones in the meat today.*'

I ask dadi where she lived before this house, shout actually, because she can't hear very well. 'Christianganj,' she says. 'And before that?' 'Before what?' she says, looking like I were asking her about a previous incarnation. In return she doesn't ask me a thing about myself, accepts me as if I were always around, either that, or new things don't register with her. Her stance with me is almost as if I've come to Mugair to enquire if all is well with her; apropos nothing she tells me I needn't worry, she's being looked after well, Maddy bathes her regularly, washes her chhichhi-pippi. Then she asks me if I know of a boy for Milly, a Delhi boy. A second later she's fast asleep, just like that, hand still dipped in her curry bowl, head tucked against her shoulder like a bird. I think Maddy will move but she doesn't. 'Shouldn't we get her to bed?' I ask but she says, 'She'll wake up in a minute and start eating again, she hasn't finished.'

Maddy doesn't ask me much either, beyond whether I know why Aunt Flora upped and went to Delhi and I want to say I'd like to know how Flora upped from the grave to begin with, but of course I don't, after which she enquires about Beatrice's health, out of courtesy, because she wouldn't have known Beatrice at all, couldn't have been born when Beatrice left these parts, would only have heard of her. It's difficult to unravel such mysteries without sounding rude. I'm the one on the far side of the time barrier, I can hardly ask what the fuck she's doing believing me, believing who I am, *what's the use locking your doors all the time woman when you let someone like me walk in just like that*? I don't tell her I'm here looking for Iqbal or for Dahirya but that I'm interested in Rajasthan generally and in catching up with my relatives.

She says she'll introduce me to someone called Philomen. I ask her who that is and she says he's someone who knows everything about Rajasthan, takes notes just like me. When I persist she says he's my uncle, in an accusing way like I should have known. But Beatrice had no brother, I'm about to say but I don't, because that's the way it seems to work here, it's rude to pinpoint connections. He works in a mandi in Hatundi. I don't dare ask what she means, just nod as if it's the most normal thing in the world to have an uncle who's a sabziwala and takes notes on Rajasthan in between.

She also offers to introduce me to someone called Wilma who she says is a cousin and again I'm about to say I have no cousins, and again I don't, because by now I'm liking the idea of free cousins and uncles; it's the opposite of what Beatrice did to me. 'Don't faint when you see her girls,' Maddy says, so I ask her what's wrong with Wilma's girls and it turns out she's referring to Wilma's breasts!

Then I ask her about Granduncle Billy, why he's in the condition he's in. 'Because your grandfather Hubert beat him to death,' she says. 'But he's alive,' I say and she says, 'You call this alive?' What happened many years ago, I learn, is that dadi found Granduncle Billy in the backyard of Grace Place, the day he was allegedly beaten by Hubert, snuck him away and brought him here, letting Hubert think he was dead. After that dadi's late husband insisted there was no need for a doctor, that Billy's early morning spit rubbed on his wounds was enough and so there he lay and there he continued to lay decades later like pieces of a jigsaw puzzle that no one knew how to put together, the twelve broken bones healing on their own in any which direction.

I take the opportunity to ask Maddy about Grace Place. It's in the cantonment in Hakra, she says, and a 'very rude man' lives in it now but why would I care, it had been sold aeons ago. *Who sold my house!* I want to say but I'm uncertain whether to tell her about Andrew's letter. Then she tells me my grandfather Hubert owned a hunting lodge too, beyond Hakra in a village called Ranigaon, but that it fell down a long time ago, and is now a heap of rubble smelling of dog piss. I shouldn't even think of venturing into those parts, the area's full of drunks. And go-s. 'What's a go?' I ask. 'A thousand-legged Rajasthani monitor lizard that flies at you, wraps itself round your neck and squeezes you to death. A hundred men can't pull it off,' she says.

I change the subject swiftly and ask Maddy if she ever goes out. 'Yes there are restaurants and cinema halls but I never go, I have to give dadi her tablets.' A chill runs through me. Then she asks me if I know of a boy for Milly, a Delhi boy.

'D'you think dadi knew my father?' I come out with it then. 'We know nothing,' she says firmly, her face closing up.

We run out of conversation waiting for dadi to finish eating/sleeping. Maddy draws the curtains against the afternoon glare, plunges the room into darkness and then switches on one 40-watt lamp by whose glow we sit, side by side on the sofa, thinking—I about the similarities between us, she the differences.

In Mugair afternoon siesta is mandatory. A hush falls over the residential parts of town. The roads continue to be jammed and chaotic and honking but none of this is apparent in places like Indra Nagar.

Maddy wakes me up at five with a cup of tea in her hand. She'd accepted dinner with relatives at Christianganj, she says, they're celebrating a child's christening, would I accompany her? 'They're very simple,' she says, 'they're Bhils.' I look up in surprise and she explains that fifty years ago her father's cousin had fallen in love with a Bhil over which there was much furore in the family which was all forgotten later. 'Of course I'll come,' I say, delighted at the unexpected opportunity to meet the ancient warlords of Rajasthan who I thought would have vanished off the face of the earth by now or languishing in the Andamans where the British had dumped them.

Two hours later we leave for Christianganj. On the way I ask Maddy whether the Bhils still follow any of their ancient customs. 'What are those?' she asks and I tell her about something I'd read in Tod, about divorce among them being so simple, the husband simply tearing a shred from his turban and handing it to his wife who then places two jars of water on her head and walks off, the first man easing her of her load becoming her future husband. Maddy looks zapped. Then, *'Tu pata nee kaunsi duniya mein rehti hai, kya kya bakti rehti hai,* what nonsense!' she says.

Christianganj isn't Christianganj now, but Krishnaganj, renamed a few years ago, although the Christians, including Maddy, continue to refer to it by its old name. It's a small slum-like colony of about fifty houses growing out of each other in the manner of a beehive. Nobody appears to have employed an architect here and they couldn't have because some of the houses are so small an architect couldn't have drawn more than four straight lines on a blueprint. I see a small church hard by a garish temple made of multicoloured bathroom tiles, the smell of incense pervading the atmosphere, the sound of bhajans and bells raucous, like some sort of exorcism were on to banish the white man's heathen god who persists in lingering in these parts long after the white man has gone. Nobody attends the Sunday service any more, Maddy says, they can't hear a word the pastor's saying on account of a loudspeaker fixed on a lamppost facing the church, belting out Hindu bhajans at precisely the time the service begins. It's been fixed by some RSS workers, she says, so who has the courage to remove it?

We arrive at the Bhils' den. 'Satya Paul' is the name at the gate. The thought that I'm about to meet what Tod describes as 'the most ancient tribe on earth' quickly dissipates at the sight of that gate, bronze with blue and pink wrought-iron lotuses forming a kitsch pattern worthy of the Smithsonian. *'Praise the Lord!'* is how Parveen Paul our hostess greets us, a tall dark woman in a pastel-blue nylon sari. What follows is so far from Tod that I spend the evening in a daze. There are about twenty people present, all family Maddy says, and yes, there's physical evidence of a distinct anthropology here, camouflaged by cheap tubelights turning their dark skins not white but a pale mint green. Good teeth, good corneas, wiry black hair on their heads, eyebrows glowing like beetles against calcium-deficient patches on their mahogany faces.

Maddy introduces me around after which she joins a group of women around the baby that's been christened and who's in a stiff white nylon frock several sizes too large, a broad white nylon ribbon on its head. One of the women leaves the group and walks up to me. 'I love Jesus,' she tells me, apropos nothing. I take a step backwards. A surge of anger runs through me *and this isn't the end of her sentence mind you,* '...and *after* that I love my husband and children.' Trapped against a wall I nod at her as if I approve of her profound prioritization thoroughly. She should have been standing on a fearsome crag with a bandanna around her forehead, flying arrows at me instead of behaving like one of Beatrice's loonies. The enormity of what the British did to the Bhil hits me; they completely rewired their brains.

We're in a large courtyard that leads to a kitchen on one side, another small room on the other where I catch a glimpse of a young girl on a bed vomiting into a bucket. I turn away swiftly. There's nothing more to this house and I try and calculate how so many people could be living here, I imagine a row of charpais laid across the courtyard at night like a dormitory, all of them sleeping under a starlit sky and a pang of loneliness overwhelms me, I recall our courtyard back home, that terrible empty hole, that peculiar buffer zone between Beatrice and me.

The courtyard is being cleared now, two men bringing in sunmica tables, laying them in a long line, wobbling, none quite aligned with the other in height or width. Pulao-curry follows, huge steaming dishes exuding an aroma that finally subdues that smell of incense. Our hostess appears to have a very 'Hindu' respect for her elders. Invites them to the table first, doesn't speak to them head-on but takes a small step backwards when addressing them. A combination of two cultures, quite opposed, quite baffling. Maybe three, because the prayer at the table is in chaste Urdu. Another enigma. Why do some of the Christians here have Islamic names and why do they speak chaste Urdu? Why do some of the Rajputs have Islamic names too, like Iqbal? Did Muslim conquerors get to the Aravali even before the British? I know that fanatical hordes of Pathans and Mughals spread terror across north India once but my knowledge of history's so poor, I'm confused. Could I be mistaken in thinking I had Hindu origins? But along with names like Iqbal and Parveen there's also my grandfather Hubair Singh alias Hubert Lawrence...a complete confusion of caste and identity that I cannot even begin to unravel.

There's a special word for me in the Pauls' prayer in which Satya refers to me as his 'sister', come all the way from Delhi to see them. How does everyone here accept strangers so readily? Tears prick my eyes. Simultaneously I baulk at the presumption. Another question: Forget the converted, why have the Rajputs with their obsession with caste and rank always looked upon themselves as the superior race, the Bhil as the inferior? It's the Bhil who was the original inhabitant of the Aravali, the Rajputs mere interlopers who arrived much later from the banks of the Oxus in Central Asia, moving through the valleys of Afghanistan from where they forced their way into India, driving the Bhil into the recesses of the mountains. It's like the Americans, turning Red Indians into an object of curiosity while coolly usurping their land. Is that what I've done tonight figuratively? My ignorance of India's history, my voyeurism even while basking in the Bhils' legendary hospitality embarrass me acutely.

Dahirya, Iqbal...none of that figures even remotely in the unsuspecting canvas before me.

Morning: I'm headed towards Flora's house at Tarapur Gate and I'm thinking of that silly woman, of what she means to me and what she doesn't, and I'm wondering why I'm going to see her house as if it were the embodiment of history.

As we pass the lake once more I see a group of people with all sorts of instruments in their hands. I lean my head out of the car to see what they're staring at and I see that indeed the water has something in it, a blue-green algae like deposit. I'd read somewhere that the Vidyasagar was dying, being choked by sewage and agricultural effluents and that environmentalists were objecting to its obnoxious odour. Cyanobacterial bloom it's called, I think. Had the Brits stayed on might Mugair have been a picturesque lake resort? Look what we've done to that lake and what do those environmentalists think they can do now? What has anyone done about the Ganga? Can anyone bring a dead lake back to life? Dredge its stories out of its depths and return them to those who own them? But those stories had fled long before, taken refuge in the myopic recesses of old women's eyes, women like Beatrice who transplanted them in the big city where they changed shape and colour so no one can find them now.

We near a colony of houses, a mish-mash of building styles to give me a headache. We snake through its lanes looking for Flora's. Unlike Maddy's it's genuine colonial and it's named 'Rose Villa', presumably after my grandmother Rose Lawrence. Flora's nameplate 'F. Lawrence' sends shivers up my spine for until this moment I think I hadn't fully believed the woman existed and suddenly I begin to understand why I'm here, what it is precisely that my aunt means to me.

There's a rusted lock on the gate and I'm dismayed because she'd given me the keys only to her front door but the gate collapses as soon as I touch it, dry weeds intertwining through its bars along with it. The garden is overgrown. I look around for snakes. A single bright red anar hangs from a tree, half eaten by a parrot. A rusted red-orange iron jaafri encloses the porch, concave, bending inwards like it had been rammed by a truck. At one corner of the porch lie some old utensils, practically cemented to the ground. I am bewildered. Flora hasn't been away that long.

The first thing I see as I enter the house is a dead pigeon on the floor. Not smelling surprisingly. Its feathers still grey. Probably dashed its head on a windowpane trying to escape or suffocated for lack of air and I think, how like Flora, she would have sailed out of the house without a backward glance. I calculate the greyness of the pigeon against the vintage of the utensils, the weeds, the gate, the jaafri and come to the conclusion there's no mystery here, Flora simply didn't clean up ever. The house is dark, with a quality of antique coolness, and it's full of old colonial furniture worth a fortune. Everything's covered in dust and there are a million mosquitos in here, large ones that strangely don't bite, don't fasten themselves to your ankles but fly around wistfully like ghosts.

The city girl in me does a quick inventory. Not everything here is valuable. There's also a cheap poster of Christ over a mantelpiece in the living room, ballooning out of its frame, probably on account of the extreme temperatures here. On a table in the bedroom stands a Murphy radio where I imagine Flora hunchbacked, turning its knobs, searching for *Binaca Hit Parade* on Radio Ceylon, lowering her head to the right until her ears met with a crackle. On the dressing table is a box of Coty Powder, Rachel shade, a bottle of blood-red Cutex, a half-used Feather Touch glove, all frozen in time just like those pots. A ripple of fear runs through me. I see Beatrice back home at Flora's mercy, I see Flora powdering her face, her neck, her ears, Beatrice behind her cemented to the ground, weeds growing out of her ears.

This house fills me with an unfamiliar shame. Sitting gingerly at the edge of Flora's dusty bed I see that the counterpane is part of a set, the other half of the one she brought to Delhi, as if this one had been left behind as collateral against the possibility of rejection. I try and quell the shame, I do not understand it, I summon up scorn, humour, academic doubt to be reflected upon from a distance, but it all turns tail, grows into rage at myself, a recognition that Flora had come to Delhi looking for nothing more than love, a love I never even gave her. A thought that history *is* love, sometimes just the journey in search of it, the mud on those wheels that *turn turn turn*…

Evening: Maddy and I take a phatphat to Wilma's house that's built like a train including two round beacon lights on either side of the front door, a huge brass ding-dong bell. It's on the Mugair–Hakra highway. This highway begins in the heart of town and leads on to the Hakra cantonment. It's as straight as a ruler, no detours anywhere. Highways are normally located at the periphery of a town as this one probably was except that the burgeoning population of Mugair turned it from a thoroughfare into a muddled extension of the town so that on the left of Wilma's house is a three-storeyed eye hospital, on the right a row of mobile phone shops, smaller makeshift shops in between selling imitation Levi jeans and school bags, a petrol pump next to a row of vegetable shops, trucks queuing up outside, spewing carbon monoxide onto the vegetables, a government office in a combination of Rajput and Mughal architecture, newly built in pink sandstone and hard by an excessively tube-lit chemist's shop right next to an open-air barber's shop under a neem tree, its clients unaffected by the din and the passers-by as if there were an invisible wall around them. In short, a hundred years after that magnificent highway was built by the British it's only a bird that could tell you it's a road. And despite it being straight as a ruler you could get terribly lost on it.

Against that montage, and if you needed guidance, Wilma's girls could serve as a landmark. If you were looking for the Levi's shop, for instance, rather than say it was near the eye hospital, I would tell you to skirt Wilma's girls, take a right at the end of them, then a left. And if you were looking for the hospital, three-storeyed though it may be, I would still tell you to first look for Wilma's girls, that's how big Wilma's girls are, physically not as big as the hospital but notionally enough to place that entire highway in oblivion.

'Don't faint huh?' Maddy whispers again as we get off the phatphat and so I am somewhat prepared but rather than make fun of Wilma, now that I've actually seen her girls, I'd say she needs medical help. They're probably full of cysts and tumours. And she treats them with scant respect. She's waiting for us outside, girls draped over the gate and then inside the house she

picks them up like a pair of watermelons and dumps them on the dining table around which we sit. I'm thinking, when she's old, when those girls turn to laukis, will she pick them up and fling them over her shoulders to get them out of her way, hang little Rajasthani bobbles on her nipples to make you think she were wearing a chunni? Everything I say to Wilma at that table smacks of insincerity thereafter—you just can't get past those girls.

One of the first things Wilma asks me is if I knew her father. How the hell would I know her father? Later Maddy tells me she has a thing about that father, a station master, goes around asking any and everyone if they knew him. So Wilma and I have something in common! She ignores me thereafter, addresses only Maddy, picking up threads of her last meeting with her, discussing things I couldn't possibly understand, people I haven't a clue about, the kind of conversation in which there's no point your even looking interested. So I pretend I need to use the loo and in the process look around her house. It's like a train from within too. We were in the first bogey and there are four more, five compartments in a line, the loo at the far end. The second compartment has three antique wooden beds in it (including a beautiful four-poster) with three cheap, unmatching bedcovers on them. A large Chinese Checker board from the British era hangs on a wall along with verses from the Bible in ceramic. In the third compartment, amidst ordinary furniture is an exquisitely carved armoire and a set of beautiful planter's chairs, quite out of place. Maddy tells me later that Wilma stole the armoire and chairs from Grace Place, apart from several other things, that just before Grace Place was sold she ripped it apart, that even her ceiling fans are from there. But that was later. I didn't know this then, only wondered how the scale of objects in Wilma's house didn't match its size and character. I'm a bit mystified at

Maddy's tone though. She sounds like she's accusing Wilma of having stolen something from *her*.

On my way back from the loo I see a heavily carved sideboard outside the kitchen, overstuffed with plates and cups and glasses. There are all sorts of other odds and ends in there besides, including a whole pile of sugar and coffee sachets filched from trains. Hundreds of them, which means Wilma's a serious magpie because if she were a casual one she would have used the sugar and coffee, not hoarded it like that. On one of the shelves is a framed certificate in Grandfather Hubert's name, some sort of appreciation from the British for services rendered during the world war. Nobody told me he had anything to do with the war and, what's his certificate doing in Wilma's house, and *who is Wilma*? On another shelf is a Wedgewood dinner set. I freeze. It has the same looping rosaries of pink and blue flowers as a single plate lying with Beatrice and which Beatrice told me she brought with her to Delhi to remember her father by. I count Wilma's plates. *There are exactly eleven*!

Wilma is cool about my having taken a tour through her house, doesn't look guilty or nervous at all which she should have because legally those would be *my* plates, *my* dinner set worth a fortune. There are three additions around the table when I return. Friends of Wilma's. Between them a plate of pastries, plump and staggering with green and pink icing topped with blobs of red jam, just like those pastries that come out of tin trunks at hill stations, excellent, far better than the elegant ones you find in Delhi's patisseries but I don't know who those women were, I think they were nurses from the hospital next door, because Wilma doesn't bother with introductions, it seems to me she lined them up simply to make me feel excluded. Maddy tries, but Maddy's explanatory powers are limited I discover. She's lived in that world forever; she can't conceive of it as something that needs to be explained to another. She's also confused about my note-taking. She doesn't know what's worthy to enter my diary and what's not. She must have done a course in botany some time because apropos nothing she suddenly takes me outside the house to show me a tree, tells me its botanical name and insists I write it down.

Back at the table one of the women pulls an old black and white photograph out of her wallet and shows it to me. Naturally I don't recognize the fellow. That's her father and she looks disappointed that I never knew him. As Alice would say, the tea party gets curiouser and curiouser. I wonder whether it's my turn now, whether this is the cue for me to say something about Iqbal but I hadn't bargained for this club of middle-aged children all looking for their fathers and a strange fact dawns on me, my mind goes back to Beatrice's loonies, to church congregations, births, christenings, funerals and so on, and I realize that the Christian community in India does indeed consist predominantly of women, fatherless children, stunned widows standing in queues at post offices battling the red tape of modern India to get to their husband's pensions. Where have the husbands and fathers all gone?

And who indeed is Wilma? She's Beatrice's aunt's daughter's niece, too convoluted a relationship for me to unravel. And, among the women at the table was anyone a Dahirya? Wilma hadn't even heard the name. Thought on account of my extended visit to the loo that I was telling her I had diarrhoea. Then, that I was asking her about a river, a dariya.

At the gate as we leave I say it, casually. 'And my father Iqbal...did you hear of him at all?'

Wilma opens her mouth to reply when Maddy pokes her in the breast with her elbow. 'She doesn't know anything,' she says firmly, waving to a phatphat.

'How do you know she doesn't know?' I say to Maddy in the phatphat but a truck blows its horn violently just then, farts carbon monoxide right in our faces and she covers her ears and then shakes her hands about to indicate she can't hear me. But she does hear me. I can tell from her eyes.

At night I board the train back to Delhi feeling stupid. Between that ignorant thieving broad with big breasts and Tod, between that born-again Bhil and that poor pigeon alone and dead on the floor, between the hoary past and the mindless present, and just like that highway that's both straight as a ruler and deceptive as a maze, I'm completely lost.

Where Have All the Cushions Gone?

A week after I returned they arrived one by one, Malini, Sujata and Aditi, the three witches of Macbeth boiling a terrible brew, Beatrice's defence of them through the years having petered into a whimper and finally into a *Who are they?* on the day she had shown me her will when I had asked her why she had forgotten them. So had I, but waiting night after night for delayed flights, sipping airport-coffee after coffee that I didn't really want gave me ample time to remember. What I remembered the most was the manner in which they'd disappeared. Because of the *Post,* Malini I'd got to know since, but Sujata and Aditi had gone off the radar completely, writing rarely, arriving every four or five years for Christmas in a flurry, unpacking and packing in a flurry, speaking to Beatrice and me in a flurry.

For reasons of emotional brevity we chisel our perspective of a family member down to a symbol and this symbol gets further abstracted through the years so that even while casting rude or loving glances at them as the case may be, we do not let them leap about our cells like a debilitating cancer but having set the parameters around them go about our daily business with felicity.

Thus Malini was a uterus on account of her never-ending period problems, erratic bleeding, erratic behaviour that Beatrice referred to as meena-pause; Sujata was a misguided comet, the kind of woman who rushes to a gymnasium to tighten her buttocks when everything else in her life is falling apart; and Aditi was a clock that had lost its cuckoo. But 'Who the fuck is Arun Shourie?' was what they all wanted to know and ironically, he was the man who had rendered the question of our individual identities redundant through his newspaper articles, herded us into his intellectual gas chamber where no symbol, no description could take us beyond the hard fact that we were a blot on the face of India.

Their anger was justified. Why was the man leading such an angry crusade against a dying community? That Beatrice and her ilk were converting the poor through unethical means was a drop in the ocean of spiritual corruption that was India. Besides, if that was the bone he had to pick with Christians, why was he flaying the gospels in his articles, gospels that amounted to a mere paragraph among the reams of spiritual literature in the land of a thousand gods? Why didn't he read the fucking Vedas, Malini said, or the Koran, which he wouldn't, because the Muslims would do a fatwa on him.

Aditi, who taught a paper on Salman Rushdie at Columbia, responded only to the word fatwa, looked up sharply, eyes widening, but for the rest of her stay in India remained in a state of jet lag. In a time warp too. It was the third time I was seeing her since she had left and each time she appeared to me to have no sense of time or location. At the same time she did this funny thing, made everyone shift their clocks backwards for her. Go back twenty-five years to the time she had first left. Adjust themselves to her dated perception of them. The years in between she just wouldn't believe. The strange part, mind you, was that though she still called Janpath by its old colonial name 'Queen's Way' she kept *herself* twenty years ahead.

Kept saying 'Why does everyone in India make so much *noise*?' 'Why is no one worried about cholesterol?' Casting an imperious glance over the Azadpur jhuggies one day, she pronounced, 'It is now *known and proven* that asbestos roofs cause cancer.' *'So crude!'* she called Beatrice's servants.

Sujata's anger towards India stemmed from another source entirely. Was everyone in town thinking she was the descendant of some poor tribal? was what worried her. She was deeply class conscious and the stress that was being laid in news reports on conversions among the lower castes infuriated her beyond measure. It left every other kind of Christian out.

'What about us?' she said, as if we were Christian for love of Christ alone.

'What about us?' I replied. 'We know nothing about us.'

So it went, this pointless questioning of our identity. It was the new India that had done this to us, turned us into insecure victims of a past and a history we were not responsible for and it was this that took away from us the ability we might have had to survive in a group so that we turned on each other like scorpions trapped in a bottle.

But first everyone turned on Beatrice. She it was who was responsible for it all, a woman who could have been swooshing along quartz-crested mountains in a nine-yard ghagra but ended up in a nightie in a house in South Delhi instead, banging plates and spoons together. But, 'If Gladys Staines can forgive India,' Beatrice announced, 'so can we.' No relation between the two but that was Beatrice and it was only because I'd read the letter from Andrew that I understood that her capacity for relating diverse elements and turning them into a whole was something to be feared. Pick this, pick that, put it all in one plate.

Tell your children their father's dead because he had a roving eye.

Forgive India!

What is it that defines the word Family? How does the furniture fall into place? The spontaneous combustion that's supposed to occur when one member of a family walks into a room and collapses on a chair with one jean-clad leg over an armrest and then another member floats in seamlessly and so on until many members congregate and one of them tells the rest what happened to them on their way to somewhere and another sings along with the TV commercial....no, no such thing happened with us ever. Not even at the Christmases we'd spent together in the past, when instead of dealing with the event at hand everyone opened up their baggage, let the years tumble out in the form of boulders to throw at one another. That was how the week before those Christmases always went, being mean to each other and then a few days later, on Christmas day, making joyous sounds, falling upon each other's necks when the gifts were opened, all that dazzling coloured paper and ribbon flying around like sad neon lights over the deserted city.

It was clear soon enough that Malini had relocated Neha's wedding to Delhi for reasons other than Beatrice's health. Beatrice had nothing to do with it. *'Nani's nuts nuts nuts'* was the sum total of Neha's acknowledgement of the location, skipping past Beatrice's room in the pre-nuptial girlishness that afflicts women in love.

'I don't know about India,' went Bob the hupshee, 'but back home we normally institutionalize them at this age. It's far kinder.'

'Institutionalize her?' I repeated coldly, 'You mean make an institution out of her?'

'After my wedding! After my wedding!' shrieked Neha, wanting all focus on her.

'But suppose she misbehaves at your wedding?' added Malini, perhaps not really thinking, perhaps simply prolonging a conversation brainlessly as one tends to do when surrounded by family and I could have stood on high moral ground but I didn't because Beatrice and I were incidental to that wedding in a sense, as if *Malini* owned the house and Beatrice and I had only dropped by on our way to somewhere.

Perhaps Beatrice knew and perhaps she didn't. *'No respect!'* was the strongest she came out with when Neha called six friends for dinner one evening without her by-your-leave. And she didn't even introduce Beatrice to them. Maybe I imagined her pain, maybe it was *me* throughout, transposing images of my own fearful destiny on her, but every so often I would hear the sound of chatter, of many people talking at once about things way beyond her ken and I would swing around and look at her and each time I thought I could hear the walls pick up the beat of her heart like a giant stethoscope.

At least technically speaking it was *her* house, *her* walls, *her* floor, *her* furniture but Flora poor thing was nobody. Kept examining her clothes on her own and expressing grave doubt, doubts that nobody was willing to clear, as if it didn't even matter what she wore, or came to the wedding nanga. Malini, Sujata and Aditi could hardly remember who she was, wouldn't even let me finish telling them about her being dead in between. Aditi had looked at me cross-eyed. 'Common consensus is that you're a liar, Gudda!' she said.

Bob who knew nothing about nobody went, *'Matilda told such dreadful lies, it made you stop and blink your eyes…!'*

But I wasn't a liar, Aditi was only preparing to accost me on Beatrice's will later, fertilizing the ground by laying seeds of doubt in Malini's and Sujata's mind about my integrity. Funnily, the fact of Flora's existence registered fully on me only then. Lies have that effect on truth.

About Iqbal, about Grace Place, about my trip to Mugair… between the varieties of racket they all made, I didn't even get a chance to begin.

'Thirteen glasses of milk!' I heard Flora hiss to Beatrice as I was passing her room one day. The two of them were in a huddle over Bob. By the looks on their faces they were concocting a scandal.

'What?' I said, unable to pass such a thing by.

'Shhhhhhhh,' went both of them, Beatrice patting the place next to her on her bed.

'What?' I said, sitting down, lowering my ear towards Flora's mouth.

'It's not right, Gudda, it's very bad of Malini to allow this,' she whispered.

'What?'

'Woh Neha *ka* boyfriend,' she said. 'Why should they sleep in the same room like that, they're not married yet.'

'How d'you know they sleep in the same room?'

'Arre bhaiyya, are we stupid? First he sleeps in the other room, then he slips into Neha's room and then he goes to the fridge for milk. It's shameful! Last night he went *thirteen* times!'

'Are you worried that he's in Neha's room or that he drank so much milk? Americans are like that, Aunty, they keep drinking milk. They keep drinking juice, they keep drinking cuawfee, they're like that only.'

'Why are you saying cuawfee for coffee?'

'Arre chup ho jao Flora, get to the point!' hissed Beatrice.

'Bhaiyya, what shall I tell you? *Why would someone have THIRTEEN glasses of milk in the middle of the night?* Because they need E-N-E-R-G-Y!'

Even I was shocked. *'Haaw!'* I said with my hand on my mouth. *'Thirteen* times?'

'Badtameez!' said Beatrice. *'Hupshee hai*—Africans are like that. *Kala kaloota, baingan loota,'* and then in a surprising show of modernity, 'I hope she's having birth control *nahi toh army kardegi kale kalooton ki.'*

'Hai hai!' went Flora.

I felt so depressed. Not at the vision of thirteen black children but that everyone in the world but I was having sex.

Then Bob went away for two days to Bharatpur and I was heaving a sigh of relief at the respite when Anand showed up. Since he was about the hundredth person coming and going from the house that season I greeted him, maybe not like he was the hundredth but at best the fiftieth or sixtieth. Just like Malini and David had been, Sujata and Aditi were impressed by his corporate good looks and in the middle of that crowd no one could tell and even I almost forgot that there were unresolved issues between us.

Beatrice was so confused by then and, moreover, was already trying to come to terms with the fact that she was about to be related to a hupshee who was a sex maniac to boot that she said to Anand *'Welcome to the family!'* as if she hadn't met him that time in Bombay when I was in a dead faint and had probably said *'Get out of the family!'* for all I knew, and it was such an awful anachronism her saying that *now* that I had no choice but to go around looking flushed and soft and warm the morning after Anand's first night in that house as if I'd just had great reunion sex with him.

Sex with Anand was an impossible thought but families are like that when they get together, their brains get addled, they keep on chattering and forgetting, chattering and forgetting.

Leave alone Anand, who the hell would have sex with me? If I relaxed my muscles and looked into the mirror sideways I looked three months pregnant. My hips too were broadening. Unattractive little lumps here and there that followed me around like the children I would never have. I became two people in one. One who did the eating; the other the watching. In the silence of our bedroom when I was brushing my teeth and changing into my nightie I saw Anand look at me with disgust.

The one part of me recoiled in fear; the other didn't seem to care at all.

Anand himself had deteriorated. He had stopped exercising; he was eating too much too, lying around like a beached whale in the sun. You had to kick him to get a rise out of him. I tried. I pranced into our room now and again pretending I was afflicted by the jollies but effort after effort came apart like the petals of an old rose.

Poor Anand. He was surrounded by Christians. In all our years together he hadn't even learnt to pronounce the word properly. Like the rest of India he would go Crisshan, Chrisshian, Crisshun soldier, black Christchun alternately, sometimes Christchen tart or *fucking convert* when he hated me. And like the rest of India he didn't know the difference between Catholics and Protestants. For a long while he had thought that if Amarnath was the Hindu's ultimate destination and Mecca–Medina the Muslim's, ours was the Vatican City.

What were the *things* he had mentioned on the phone that he wanted to talk to me about? It was nothing about him and me but about his own future. Anand had been sacked. He didn't tell me he'd been sacked but that he was thinking of leaving the *Post* and starting a furniture business in Gurgaon. He was sick of Bombay. How I deduced he'd been sacked is that I'd read in the news about a scandal at the *Post*, about the management being shuffled around, axed ruthlessly. I didn't feel glad or sad, just uncertain as to what I was to think. Anand never said a word about us, as if it were incidental to the issue and I began to suspect he was simply using me now to create a base in Delhi, glossing over the fact that we had ceased to be married.

In all fairness to him I'd never told him I was leaving him forever and so he talked vaguely about us getting a plot in Gurgaon and since he referred to a plot and not a flat, it meant he had plans of building, which meant he was here to stay, but the implications of that were lost on me temporarily because of the wedding. There was simply too much to do and that marriage of ours came back on the tracks out of sheer necessity just then, a derailed train whose mangled bogeys stood up on their own, shuddered and clanked and queued up behind each other as if nothing had happened to them and they were still going somewhere. It began with me giving Anand five wedding chores to do. Progressed with him actually setting about to do them. Then those chores grew tentacles. People say have children if you want to hang on to a man but I say, make him attend a family wedding. Except that I hadn't really wanted to hang on to Anand at all so those bogeys went in whichever direction they pleased, one to Amritsar, the other to Kanyakumari.

And Bob as I said, went to Bharatpur. There was a furore that year about the Siberian crane having suddenly changed its migratory pattern, not having arrived in Bharatpur at all. It was feared that the birds had been shot down in Afghanistan or Pakistan or Uzbekistan en route to Bharatpur and I don't know what business Bob had with that but he'd made himself part of a project to bring back the bird. It involved training the birds to follow a hang-glider from Uvat in Central Russia, both the pilot and the plane dressed up like cranes to fool the birds into following what they would think was their own kind. Bob said the technique had been adopted with success for the hooping crane in the US and I thought it was colossal cheek, as if the land of Salim Ali had been waiting for a black Jew ornithologist from America to resolve its bird crisis.

With Bob away in Bharatpur *everyone* became more at ease. They now had the mental space to deal with the real reason they were in Delhi. Sujata went on a tangent first. 'I hope you're looking after your money, Ma,' is how she began.

'Kya matlab?' said Beatrice.

'No *matlab,* Ma, I just get worried about you sometimes. I hope you're keeping your money properly and not just dumping it in the bank.'

'Where else should I dump my money then?' said Beatrice. 'Under my gadda?'

'No no that's not what I mean. I mean *investments.* I hope you've invested your money wisely.'

'A few fixed deposits I have,' said Beatrice proudly. 'Do you mean that?'

'Yes yes,' said Sujata, sitting up, and then, like she were a high-powered consultant arrived straight from Wall Street, 'and I hope you've staggered them properly. Spread them out a bit,' she said.

'Yes yes don't worry,' said Beatrice.

'But I *do* worry, Ma. There's no one really to help you with all this.'

'Why, Gudda's here. She goes to the bank when I ask her.'

Sujata turned tense. 'Of course of course...,' and then turning to me and smiling, 'I'm *so glad* you're here, Gudda...,' and then back to Beatrice, '...but she'll go back to Bombay some day, Ma, and then what'll you do?'

'What'll I do? I'll go to the bank myself—what d'you mean what'll I do?'

'No, I was thinking, Ma...you might consider having one more signatory on your FDs so that someone else can go for you if need be.' Then looking at me, 'You've been looking after Ma's deposits, I hope?'

'Not in that sense,' I replied. 'I just encash her cheques for her when she asks me. I had no idea she had deposits.'

'I don't mind if you use my name, Ma, it's no problem at all,' said Sujata quickly, making it sound like I hadn't been looking after Beatrice well enough.

'Really?' said Beatrice, looking grateful, not registering that Sujata lived in London and that what she was saying made no sense.

'Let me have a look at them, Ma, and I'll sort it all out for you. We can go to the bank tomorrow morning.'

'No no, just now everyone's too busy. Let the wedding be over then we'll go,' said Beatrice.

But Sujata made it out like Beatrice came first in the list of everyone's priorities and so they went to the bank the following morning and I have no idea what transpired there but they both returned looking secretive.

After that episode Beatrice ignored me, gave me the cold shoulder almost, with Sujata looking oddly triumphant, gentle too, so when Beatrice said to her at the dining table, 'Will you say grace?' she replied sweetly, '*You* say, Ma, and also say a prayer for our dear Neha.' Everyone shut their eyes.

'Thank you Father,' Beatrice began, *'for this spread table before us. And for giving us this opportunity to celebrate Christmas together when you arose from the dead. Help us to know your will and the purpose for which you died on the cross of Calvary. So that we may have everlasting life Amen.'*

Neha began to giggle, and then snort, her mouth full of food for she wasn't the one to wait until grace was said. Bob, back from Bharatpur, shocked everyone into silence by planting a kiss right on her mouth.

'Ma, it isn't Christmas,' I said hastily, 'and it's Easter when he rose from the dead and *why didn't you pray for Neha?'*

'Shut up, Gudda, leave her *alone,*' said Sujata, sealing my reputation as a bitch. That same fertilizing of ground that Aditi had done.

Encouraged by Sujata's support, Beatrice came out with a fond anecdote from the past, about Sujata as a little girl reciting a radio commercial when she was asked to pray. Sujata knew no prayer so she said *Din mein do do baar malo, Mac-leans, Mac-leans!* 'How we all laughed,' Beatrice said, 'stuffing our napkins into our mouths.'

Napkins? Now she didn't even have quarter plates. She had virtually nothing, thanks to Malini, Sujata and Aditi who had long back taken whatever they could get their hands on. Of course they had generously gifted Beatrice things in return. Hitkari mugs to replace the bone china, plastic tulips in a Yera glass vase on the mantelpiece where Beatrice's old Belgian cut glass vase had once stood. There was just one nice thing in that house now, an old English bowl with faded pink blossoms in clusters that Beatrice used to hide on the topmost shelf of her cupboard and which I dug out and cleaned and placed on that mantelpiece when I heard everyone was coming, I was so stupid.

'Ma, where'd you get this bowl from?' Sujata asked, walking up to the mantelpiece after breakfast.

'Oh that,' said Beatrice, looking up, 'just some toota phoota bowl someone gave me long back. Gudda's the one who keeps taking it out and putting it there for nothing.'

Sujata lifted the bowl to check the hallmark and vintage. 'Good god,' she whispered.

It was long after the wedding was over, after everyone had left, when I was dusting the house one day that I noticed that the bowl was missing. I questioned Beatrice, I questioned the servants, I upturned every single cupboard but I found it nowhere.

Among the hundred-and-one people who came and went from our house that season was the sisterhood, lured by the prospect of wedding khana and also by the fact that Beatrice had suddenly grown a real sister. One of them was Violet, pronounced Vylit by Beatrice. She wasn't much older than Malini but she was a blowsy, aggressive little thing who had spent her life drifting from home to home with an expression on her face like the world owed her. She'd led us to believe she'd been deserted by her family but I think she was another one of those Christians, just like us, no relatives to the left or right of her. Her skin had the patina of years of things not going her way, from the broad structural to the petty. If she had a focus on anything it was her hatred of Hindus. Malini, Sujata, Aditi and I never objected to her, we simply pretended she didn't exist, we had no choice, because Beatrice adored her. She was perpetually hanging around pretending to help but actually eating constantly and then laying herself down on the drawing room divan for an afternoon snooze. It was Aditi who emerged from the fog around her one day and decided to settle the drawing room, upturn Violet's agenda. 'Where have all the cushions gone?' she asked Beatrice. Actually, Aditi didn't give a fig about the cushions. Hers was another problem entirely. She was consumed with guilt at her neglect of her mother.

'Must be there,' replied Beatrice.

'Where?'

'There only.'

'But *where?* Once there was a cushion on every chair.'

Violet spoke up. 'I know where all the cushions are.'

'Where?' said both Aditi and Beatrice.

'Don't ask, that will be better,' said Violet.

'What do you mean, don't ask?' said Aditi aggressively.

'Zara socho, what is inside the cushions?' said Violet with the expression of someone whose moment in time had arrived.

'What?'

'Inside the cushions! Cushions *ke andar!'* repeated Violet.

Aditi looked baffled. *'But where are they!'*

'That's what I'm telling you. First tell what's *inside* them.'

'Stuffing,' said Aditi obediently.

'But what is the stuffing made *of*?'

A stillness came over Aditi. 'Cotton you mean?'

'Yes cotton,' said Violet triumphantly, as if the mystery of the missing cushions had been solved.

'So?' said Aditi.

'What is cotton used for, I am asking,' said Violet, extending the precious moment of having six eyes riveted on her.

'Don't talk nonsense!' said Beatrice. 'Utter nonsense this Vylit is talking.'

'*Not* nonsense, sister!' said Violet. 'What happened to the cotton when there is a young girl in the house?'

'What girl?'

'*Arre baba,* young girl, servant girl. Do you think if it is a servant girl it will not get her menses?'

'What!' said Beatrice.

Aditi's hand flew to her mouth. 'Mama, she's saying Lajo used the cushions as sanitary napkins!'

'Utter nonsense!' said Beatrice.

'*Not* nonsense, sister! Do you know what is the price of the sanitary napkins?' She picked up a cushion then and leaned forward into Beatrice's face, jabbing the cushion with her finger. '*Iske andar ghusair ghusair ke* she is taking out the cotton!'

'Chheeeee!' said Aditi.

'She is a *robber* this means?' said Beatrice.

Aditi's syntax which, unlike Violet's or Beatrice's, was perfect, collapsed completely. 'But you mean she straight puts the cotton there?'

'No, she is first wrapping it round sister's bed sheets. Where are the bed sheets, tell me?' she said, moving her hand like a bandar-wallah playing his dumroo. 'The dubble-dubble bed sheets sister had? All gone! When this dirty girl is washing them now we have to lie down on the gaddas till they are dry. Plain gaddas. Specially in the monsoon—two-two days we lie on the gaddas!'

Aditi contemplated the vast sociological implications of this for India. The theatre of past–present–future, the never-ending karmic cycle of being Indian, the impossibility of exercising any control over her mother's life. Then she asked that forbidden question, the one you never ask in India without receiving a horrific reply. 'But where does she throw them?'

'What where,' said Violet. 'In the nala! From the window!'

Aditi shut her eyes and took a deep breath.

'I am going to visit Sister Nirmala now that there's no place to lie down,' said Violet standing up, smoothening the front of her dress, picking imaginary threads from her shoulders.

'Who's that?' said Aditi.

'You don't know,' said Violet.

'Then why are you telling me?'

'I should not tell you?'

'No, but you are telling me as if I know who that is.'

'No no no, you don't know.'

'Then why did you tell me as if I did?'

'Because I have already told you about her.'

'When?'

'Yesterday I told you she has cancer.'

'Oh *that* one? Then *say* you are going to visit the lady WHO HAS CANCER!'

I looked at Aditi in astonishment. Then I turned to Violet and said, 'She's dying?'

'Why dying? These days nobody's dying. Her stomach was swelling so they took out twenty litres of water.'

'With cancer you get twenty litres of water in your stomach?'

'And when *iggzaman kiya,* it was oily,' said Violet, rubbing a thumb against two fingers.

'*Cheeeee!*' went Aditi.

'*You* only asked,' said Violet on her way out of the drawing room.

'*Who* is she I want to know,' Aditi said to me as soon as Violet had left the room, 'and why is she living here?'

'God knows,' I replied, 'ask Mama.'

'That's no use,' said Aditi. And then, 'But *when* did she arrive? Who *saw* her coming?'

'God knows,' I said again, delighted.

'Because I don't *like* her,' said Aditi. 'She's not *right* for Mama.'

'But she's Mama's best friend.'

'Who said?'

'No one. But she acts like that.'

'Exactly! How do you know Mama even wants her around?'

'Be reasonable, Aditi,' I said. 'Mama's quite capable of shutting the door in someone's face.'

'Maybe she doesn't realize...'

'Doesn't realize what? That that woman is living here? How can you not realize someone's living in your house?'

'It's possible,' said Aditi. 'So many people coming and going that maybe Mama got *confused*.'

'Give me a break!'

'But anyway I think she should go.'

'*Why?*'

'Because she's so *morbid*. It isn't good for Mama to be around morbid people. Besides, you never know, maybe *she* stole the bed sheets.'

'For what? She doesn't have a house.'

'Could be giving them to that cancer lady for all you know...has she left?'

'No, I think she went to the loo.'

'Then wait here, don't *move*,' said Aditi. 'Keep watching the door. Have you noticed how she never says Bye before actually leaving? See if she has anything in her hands before she goes.'

So I sat looking at the door while Aditi looked at me. That was her style of delegation.

Fifteen minutes later Violet emerged from Beatrice's bedroom and marched towards the door with two large plastic bags, one in each hand.

'Look!' Aditi hissed.

Both of us stared dumbly at Violet who turned briefly to look over her shoulder at us before vanishing down the stairs.

'Do something!' Aditi hissed again.

'What can I do, Mr Naidu?' I said, just to irritate her.

Bob, who was passing just then, went, 'Who's Mr Nye-doo?'

'I'm going to tell Mama,' said Aditi, rising. 'This is daylight robbery.'

Beatrice entered the room just then, face dripping, towel in hand. She always did that—washed her face and then couldn't bear to stay in the bathroom a minute longer, went dripping and talking all over the house.

'Mama, we have to talk to you about something,' Aditi began.

'What?'

'We want to know who's Violet. Why's she here?'

'Why? What happened?'

'We think she's a thief. We think she's taking things behind your back.'

'Huesht!' said Beatrice. 'No servant of God would do that.'

'I haven't seen her do any servanting, I've only seen her eating.'

The devil got hold of me then and I began to sing at the top of my voice:

Where have all the cushions gone?
Long time passing
Where have all the cushions gone?
Long time ago
Where have all the cushions gone?

Gone into Vylit's chaddies every one
Oh when will they ever learn…

'Can you please be *quiet!*' said Aditi coldly.

I sang louder.

'Have you gone out of your mind?'

Louder yet.

'Buss karo!' shouted Beatrice. *'Both* of you have gone mad. Do *not* in future say anything about a servant of God. And please remember, *Vylit is my friend!'*

'What are her qualifications to be your friend?' shrieked Aditi whose voice had gone really high-pitched now. My ears were ringing.

'What *nonsense* do you talk,' said Beatrice. 'Does she need a degree to be my friend?'

In desperation Aditi turned on me. *'Why did you do that?'*

'What?'

'Sing like that. So I couldn't hear anything she was saying.'

'Sorry,' I said laughing, 'but you heard every word. Every single word. If she wants to be robbed let her be robbed.'

'No one *wants* to be robbed. What are you *saying?'* Tears sprang into Aditi's eyes.

'It's a deal she's made with God. *Leave her alone!'*

'What are you *talking* about!'

But I didn't know what I was talking about. I think it was two different things but most of all that IT WAS WRITTEN. That we had a mother like Beatrice, that Beatrice had a friend like Violet and that we all had a god called Jesus who one day wept. So what was Aditi talking about, was the real question. Why was she trying to make sense of Beatrice's life *now?*

A Wedding and Four Funerals

Once on the rampage Aditi could go on and on *and on,* in that shrill voice of hers, and so I fled, went for a walk to the nearby Deer Park. It was crowded that day, children everywhere, and mothers, shapeless, hopeless-looking mothers in tired chappals and wild hair, faces stuck against the deer fence, fingers entwined around wires. I had a brief thought of electrifying the fence, watching a hundred clutching bodies go into rigor mortis. I turned away from the fence and took the path to the historical monuments, sat on the ancient wall that ran around the lake and looked at the old stone, the dilapidated balconies and staircases. The last time I had been here they had smelt of musk, of old parchment, of running water and hidden streams but now their capillaries were bloated and they stank of pus.

Sitting there on that wall the thought came to me that I could bridge the barrier between me and Malini–Sujata–Aditi by telling them about my marriage. Pour my soul out to them so we would end up friends. But they were so self-absorbed that it would have been like making an announcement in thin air. They would listen for a while and then they would carry on with whatever they were doing, leave me standing. Besides, when would I say it? At the breakfast table so they'd have the energy to summon up enough respect for me to react somewhat, tell me what to do with my life now, or over dinner when they were falling over their food in exhaustion? What if they got up and went to bed straight after listening and fell asleep? Because that's how tired everyone became in that house, and I would be wide awake, tossing and turning because telling anyone anything never helps, it only creates a barrier between the teller and the listener.

Besides, what would I tell them? Sitting on the parapet I began looking for words, precise, pure, uninventive words that meant only what they were meant to mean and couldn't be tossed around in the literary imagination, in light or in shadow to deliberately deceive. Economical words that stayed where they were, in a cell their own size, but Anand had confused me so terribly by coming to Delhi that those words hid behind other words that hid behind more words, all so artificial and contrived and I was afraid that if I began talking I might need a hundred years, which nobody's stupid marriage merits.

So I never told them at all and if anyone asked me in passing if all was well with me, I answered Yes and No and that was fine, because they all heard the Yes; no one pursued the No.

'D'you think Anand could have a word with Ram Bhajan?' Malini said to me one day.

'Why?' I enquired. 'He's not Anand's cook.'

'So that he knows there's a man around somewhere in this house full of women,' she said.

'Does Anand look like a man to you?' I replied, cashing in on the buzz about his job, a matter I'd overheard them gossiping about behind my back the previous evening. *Nothing escaped them.*

'Honestly, Gudda!' said Malini, fingers flying to her mouth, turning to Sujata and Aditi for support, as if *I* was the bitch.

So that was the maximum I revealed about Anand, which was no revelation at all, not in the face of the dreadful things they'd revealed to me about *their* husbands by then, the pigs they'd married in front of whom Anand began to appear to me to be carved in god's own image.

That was the essence of the confusion I faced, and that was why those three read my situation all wrong, said to me that evening that what on earth did I want Beatrice's house for when I had a beautiful one in Bombay.

But I had never wanted Beatrice's house!

But I didn't say it.

I didn't say it because the way they looked at me, the way they said it, implied that *I* had got Beatrice to change her will. I heard thunder and lightning. I saw the sky split wide open. I sucked deeply on my cigarette and I blew the smoke at them. I blew it right in their faces.

Malini didn't bring up the matter of Ram Bhajan again. No one did because the matter was small in the face of everything else that was wrong with us. When I look back on the matter now, what appeared to be wrong with Ram Bhajan? Four things that are wrong with everybody's cook: he wasn't labouring over the gravy, he wasn't frying the masala enough; he was diluting the milk; he was beginning to answer back; and he was beginning to look like a buffoon, taking a kitchen jharan and tying it around his head for no rhyme or reason, not like a bandanna but from the chin upwards like a Sardarji, with the knot on top of his head.

So why would I have listened to Malini? What was a knot on someone's stupid head compared to what appeared to be looming over mine?

It landed the following evening, not like the birdshit I had been viewing it as thus far but like an alien rewiring my brain so that I hit back with a fury that astonished me.

'Jin jin ko gin peenee hai gin peelay' is how that evening began, Sujata entering the drawing room with a bottle and four glasses. Whenever she got silly there was trouble ahead. 'You do the honours, Gudda,' she said, dumping the tray in front of me aggressively.

'Why *me?'* I said. I was the youngest for one, and hardly a drinker.

'Why *not* you, dear?' she said. 'It's *your* house after all, we're your guests.'

'Shut up, Sujata,' Aditi said.

'But isn't that true?' Sujata shot back.

'What's the problem?' I said, sitting upright, trying to look bored and weary.

'You don't see a problem?' said Sujata.

'No, I don't,' I replied.

Sujata smiled a wife-of-a-diplomat smile. Then she poured the drinks. 'Here, Gudda, let's drink to you—you have no problem at all, *only we do!'*

'Why did you do that, Gudda?' leapfrogged Malini, unnerved by Sujata's foreplay.

'What?' I asked. 'What is it I'm supposed to have done?'

'Okay,' went Sujata, 'if you want to pretend, *let's all pretend!'* Then, *'You* begin,' she said to me. 'Tell us how Mama's will magically changed while you were...let's say...while you were minding your own business...or while you were at the movies...'

'Why don't you ask Mama, why are you asking me?' I raised my voice.

'Don't use that tone with me, Gudda, I'm warning you...we're all trying to be civil here.' Sujata's glass was trembling.

'No, I don't think you're being civil at all, you're insinuating some horrible things to me. If you're upset with Mama why are you taking it out on *me?'*

'No, we're not upset with Mama at all,' said Malini. *'Who* said we're upset with Mama?'

'In other words,' I said, 'are you saying *I* wrote Mama's will while *she* was minding her own business? *What are you saying?'*

'I'LL TELL YOU WHAT SHE'S SAYING!' shouted Sujata, slamming her glass down on the table. 'That none of us knew till now what a sly little conniving *bitch* you are!'

I had two choices. To pull her hair out by the roots or pretend I hadn't heard her. 'If I was sly,' I said to her slowly, 'would I have sent you the will? Does that make me sly or the opposite?'

'Yes,' said Aditi, 'and why did you do that? I mean how could you be so brazen, I mean what were you trying to show us sending us the will like that?'

'I shouldn't have sent it to you? I should have waited till Mama died and *then* shown it to you?'

'Look at her,' said Sujata, 'she's already killing off Mama. My god, you're really something, Gudda.'

'I mean I feel so bad…' said Malini looking down sadly. 'I mean sometimes I think…'

'Just shut up all of you!' I shouted. *'Just bloody shut up!'*

There was stunned silence. 'Okay let me understand this, Gudda…' said Malini in a controlled voice.

'You understand nothing, NOTHING!' I yelled, grabbing the bottle of gin and pouring it into my glass like it was water.

Malini reached out and grabbed the glass from my hand. I grabbed it back, gin spilling all over her and the carpet.

'But that's how she's always behaved,' said Sujata, 'and now I suppose our mother's only *her* mother.' The two things were totally disconnected but that was Sujata, she had you-know-whose genes in her.

'Okay,' I said threateningly, 'you want to really know why she changed her will?'

'Bloody drama she's creating,' said Aditi, looking disgusted but clearly nervous inside.

'Because you can't talk about the reason, can you? And SHALL I TELL YOU WHY?' It was the boulder in my knapsack and I was going to hit them with it right between their eyes.

But of course none of them wanted to hear it. 'Gudda, you know you're not only sly, you're bloody psychotic,' said Malini.

'Let her be, she's half-mad,' said Sujata.

'No, I'll let you be,' I snapped back, 'like I've always let you be, like you've in any case been.' My boulders were descending in a landslide.

'What shit is she talking?' said Malini.

'I know what she's talking,' said Aditi. 'She's trying to tell us she's been taking care of Mama and we haven't and so the house should be hers.'

'So if you've been taking care of Mama that makes us nobody, does it?' said Sujata furiously. 'And what about the fact that you've been bumming off Mama forever which we certainly haven't! I don't suppose you've been paying Mama rent, have you?'

Aditi, gentlest and vaguest of souls, inspired by Sujata, turned strident, hawkish. 'And where was she for twelve years?' she said, looking at Malini and Sujata. *'Ask her, ask her,* I had to come *twice* all the way from the other end of the world because she dumped Mama in between just like that, *ask her, ask her.'*

I looked at Aditi in astonishment. 'What are you saying? It was *Mama* who...'

'Mama *what?'* said Aditi. 'When you found she wasn't giving you the house you just *dumped* her...so don't make yourself out to be superior...'

'And what care have you taken in the first place, Miss?' added Malini. 'Gone up and down the stairs a couple of times to give her her tablets? For that you think you're owed a whole HOUSE?'

'And what if you went up and down the stairs?' added Sujata. 'Doesn't seem to have done that ass of yours much good!'

'There's no need to be rude, keep quiet,' said Aditi, not so much in my defence as getting ready to chuck one of her own little boulders at Sujata.

Sujata stared at Aditi incredulously for a second and then slammed her glass down. '*And who the fuck do you think you are, telling me to keep quiet?*' she said to her between clenched teeth.

'Well, it's a fact that Gudda's taken care of her in the last few years which you certainly haven't,' replied Aditi.

This was *it*. 'And what the *fuck* have *you* done for her all these years, Miss Intellectual, dropping by only when your conscience starts pricking you? *You* don't tell *me* to keep quiet, understand?'

'Shhh!' said Aditi, glancing nervously at the door.

'Don't *shhhh* me!' Sujata snapped.

'Ssshhhhh!' said Aditi again. 'Lower your *voice!* Mama'll wake up.'

Everyone stared at the door.

'Look Gudda, NO ONE is telling you you haven't take care of Mama but the house should be divided equally in all fairness,' said Malini, frustrated that no one was getting to the point.

'So divide it,' I said.

Malini was stumped. 'Yes...but...'

'What we thought,' said Aditi, 'what we thought is that...look, Gudda...the pie has to be cut *equally,* no one's telling you you won't get your share....' She made a round with her hands. 'No one gets a piece larger than the other.'

'Pie?'

'*The house, the house*—we're just trying to make you understand.'

'Okay,' I said.

'Okay?' she said incredulously.

'Sure,' I said. 'Go ahead.'

'Well, that's just it,' she said, turning to Sujata for help.

So Sujata said, slowly, as if I were a retard: 'Well, that's the problem, Gudda. The house has just two floors and we're four of us.'

'Go on,' I said.

'So what we thought is,' intervened Aditi, 'there's no other way of doing this but to sell the house, to a builder maybe, and that way we could divide the money.'

'Mama…?' I said.

'Well, let's face it,' said Sujata. 'Mama isn't going to be there forever and Aditi's too far but Malini thought she could come next year and I'll fly down from London too and we could organize the sale.'

'Mama'll be dead by then?' I said, taking immense care to keep my voice steady. I had to hear this. I had to hear it *all*.

'Not necessarily,' said Malini, 'but as a contingency plan what we thought was that Mama could move to a rented flat. And you of course would be back in Bombay by then.'

'What she means,' added Sujata all in one breath, 'is that David's going to Toronto on work for about a month in July next year and it's convenient for her to come to Delhi then, and that's just when *our* posting in London's over too, and after London we're being transferred to Brazil so it's convenient for me to come *before* Brazil, you know Gudda I'm growing older too and I really can't take these long flights, I mean it used to take me two days to recover and now it takes me ten, god knows coming from South America will totally kill me.'

'Really?' I said, looking sympathetic.

'Yes,' she said, 'so that's what we thought…'

'One small problem,' I interrupted.

'What?' said Malini.

Four heads turned simultaneously as Beatrice entered the room just then. No teeth, her mouth like a cave, breasts hanging against her stomach like two laukis. Through her nightgown you could see two spindles supporting the misshapen bulk of her hips. *'Kya baat hai, itna shor kyun macha rahe ho?'* she said.

'Sorry, Mama,' I said, 'we were just talking.'

'Ab Good Night bolo aur so jao,' she said.

So the four of us got up, not because we were obedient but because we were uncertain and terrified as to how much she might have heard. 'Good night,' said Malini, Sujata and Aditi hurriedly to each other, and to me. I didn't answer.

They dispersed to their rooms. I looked at my watch. It was five to midnight. I sank back on the sofa. I tried to think. I tried to sink my head in my hands in an attitude of despair. It wouldn't happen. Into the silence of the night I tried to whimper, hoping it would make me cry but the stillness in the air that night was strangely peaceful. So I got up and went to the balcony instead and looked up at the stars, and I began to think about Iqbal, whether he was alive or dead, and about all that I hadn't been able to tell them and now wouldn't. *Yes, the two issues were connected!* Everything in the world was connected that night, one end of the world to the other, Iqbal to me, the globe to the sky, sky to earth, but nothing, *nothing* wide enough, or deep enough to contain my anger.

The next morning I awoke to a terrible noise. The kind legitimized in primal therapy when the victims of frustration and madness are invited to break plates or fall to the ground in apoplectic screaming. It was Aditi and Beatrice fighting. Not in the silly manner they had fought over Violet, but seriously, and that was odd because Beatrice and Aditi never fought like that. Aditi had always been favoured by Beatrice for her fair skin and her foreign husband. It was to her that Beatrice poured her heart out on Aditi's four-yearly visits, complained bitterly about everything including me, all of which might have passed off as a bit of family flotsam had it not been for the fact that Aditi always took on the role of Beatrice's solicitor. Where there's a solicitor, there's a victim, where there's a victim there's a victimizer, all of which usually suggested an opposite sort of crime was taking place in that house. So when Beatrice turned the barrels on *her* she was shattered.

I heard doors banging, footsteps on the staircase and suddenly Aditi was standing in front of me, her hair having grown dimensions suddenly, some in a bop pin, some tucked behind a ear and some that flew like the last flourish of an artist on a dramatic portrait. And for all her height she looked small, partly because the roof blanched up as she entered, like a child diving into its mother's petticoats, keeping one eye glued on the terrazzo as it metamorphosed into a stage.

She sat down on a chair, crumpled tissue in her fist and looked around, first at the bookshelf, then at the lamp, then at my bed as if she was desperately seeking new affiliations there.

'Water?' I asked. She'd always done that to me when we were small, abandoned me when I cried to fetch me water so she wouldn't have to put her arms around me.

'Yes, if it's no bother,' said Aditi.

'Of course not,' I said warmly.

Look at it this way, Aditi. With the nala at our door we could be dying of bubonic plague. Let's not blame Beatrice for everything.

'You okay?'

'I suppose so,' said Aditi, giving me a crumpled smile. 'I really shouldn't have lost my temper like that.'

Why? Why can't you lose your temper?

'I mean it's really not her fault, is it? She has no memory.'

Beatrice's memory slipped through dead meat like a butcher's knife. Every two pice you owed her.

'Where does her memory come into this?' I said sharply. 'What happened?'

'No, what I mean is, I think everything we do or say is based on some memory. I think she's completely forgotten everything.'

So everything Beatrice said or did was invalid? Aditi had turned Beatrice's brain into the mist that followed us as we walked up the mall of a hill station where Beatrice had taken us one summer. We were walking along when Beatrice stopped dead on an incline, shone her torchlight on our faces and said something shocking. She said we were walking through a cloud and I looked up at her with difficulty because she had knotted my muffler under my chin and asked her how that could possibly be. But she said it could. Now Aditi was saying it couldn't though when we returned to Delhi it was she who'd looked up at the clouds in the blue sky and said to me, 'There's Nainital, there's Mussoorie, there's Simla!'

But the cotton wool in Beatrice's brain wasn't quite like that. It had been taken out from an old razai so through gaps in the muffle you could hear the sound of her screams.

Aditi, do you remember those summers we spent together in the hills? The funny man who gave us green pastries and chikki toffee out of a tin trunk?

'Yes, it's become so terribly difficult,' I said.

'Yes,' said Aditi. 'She says one thing and then a minute later the opposite. I mean she told me only this morning...' Her hand flew to her mouth. She held the tissue over it and looked at the bookshelf.

'I know I know,' I said, 'and then she must have contradicted herself totally.'

'Yes, and then she denied that as well.'

'And you felt like a fool, I know I know.'

'But that's not the point really. It's just that...well...she wouldn't stop talking...went on and on...I just had to stop her.'

'Yes,' I said, 'but what was the issue?'

'But that's the whole point. There wasn't any.'

'Then what was all that noise about?'

'But that's just it. There's always some noise about nothing.'

'Can't be nothing.'

'I'm telling you, nothing. That's what I'm trying to tell you. It's her memory. She invents things.'

'But having no memory means you forget things, not invent them.'

'Yes, but she begins by forgetting and then I suppose she can't bear it so she starts inventing.'

But when you forget you also forget that you've forgotten.

Forget that you forgot to forget.

Like the whole world depended on your memory of it.

Like the cloud that wasn't a cloud until you looked at it from afar.

Like the shudder that ran through Aditi that morning wasn't a shudder until four days later, after the wedding was over, when that visit of hers came to an end and I watched her plane take off into a twilit sky, into the colours of despair.

Two days before the wedding Beatrice had a tantrum. 'The wedding shimmers like a jewel in the distance,' she said like an orator, sitting on her bed, legs hanging down, nightie hitched up to her knees, tears rolling down her cheeks. 'I don't know when it begins and when it ends, nobody tells me *anything*.'

I looked around me at the walls, distant hills from which help cometh. 'Hush, Mama, that's not true,' I said. 'Show me your clothes.'

'She didn't buy me anything nice,' she said in her little-girl voice, reserved for just those times when you couldn't afford that kind of tantrum. The wedding was almost upon us and for all the things that Malini, Sujata, Aditi and I had been doing, nothing appeared to have got done. I hadn't even looked at my clothes and now here was Beatrice making a fuss about hers. It was unfair, specially because we hadn't followed any of the rules for ourselves, about Malini giving us all new saris, we'd let Malini off the hook on that one, but we'd made an exception in the case of Beatrice. So, in the midst of all sorts of mayhem, Malini had taken her shopping and now god knows what Beatrice was complaining about.

From behind me Malini burst into the room wild-eyed. *'Bloody bitch,'* she said between clenched teeth, throwing a cheap plastic bag on Beatrice's bed.

'What happened?' I said.

'I bought her these two saris with love and affection and now she says she doesn't like them. *Tell her to fuck off.*'

I could see the lines of tension on Malini's face. I calculated fast whose side I should be on but sums don't always add up when you're terrified and so I just looked at Malini and at Beatrice and at the plastic bag.

'Look at them, *look* at them!' Malini said, upturning the bag in a frenzy. *'You* tell me, what's wrong with them?'

As nylon tumbles out fast from cheap plastic bags, Malini didn't get her money's worth of shaking. The saris emerged in a slither on Beatrice's bed—one a pale blue and the other white with yellow flowers on it. Simply not for a wedding.

Malini's eyes had tears in them now and her fingers were trembling as she turned the saris this way and that. *'What's* wrong with them, *you* tell me!'

Beatrice stood upright, her face with a No Comment writ large on it. Queen Lear, Machiavelli, none of those names were appropriate for her suddenly, for without her brassiere on she looked no more evil than an old rooster. Coat hanger for shoulders. Sheer drop from her shoulders to the floor. Tears that bypassed her sunken cheeks to fall at her feet.

'Very pretty,' I said tonelessly. The immediacy of the scene confronting me began to fade. A chiffon curtain dislodged itself from my mind to fly over a troubled ocean. Malini's clutching and declutching fingers reminded me of something. They were the same fingers that had torn bits of chapati years ago and stuffed them, without dipping them in curry, straight into my mouth until I had gagged and let it all out over my chin and onto my frock, part masticated, part whole. Malini had screamed and I had screamed and Beatrice had come running and I had turned to her and buried my face deep into the pleats of her sari, sobbing. *'Demented kid,'* Malini yelled. *'Takes one hour to chew!'* Beatrice led me into the kitchen and shut the door. Then she picked me up and placed me on top of the counter. 'We won't tell Malini, all right?' she said, taking a little box out of the kitchen cupboard from which out came heaven in the guise of a chocolate pastry with icing on it, on top of the icing a dreamy Charmis-creamy swirl. I put my finger forward but she placed the whole thing in my hand with a kiss on my forehead. *'Why must she feed me, why can't I eat myself?'* I asked, but Beatrice was looking out of the kitchen window as if there were miles and miles of ocean there.

'What? *What!'* Malini shouted at either me or Beatrice, I wasn't sure.

'I'll sort this out with Mama, you go,' I said to her quietly.

But Malini didn't go. She launched a tirade against Beatrice, about things way beyond saris and we listened to her silently and at one point I wondered if I should take courage in my hands and slap Malini across her rude face but it would be a lie to say that either Beatrice or I were shocked because that was how Malini was and that was how Malini would always be. *Half-mad.*

If every family has its acoustics it has its quality of silence too. Beatrice wept for a while and then she stopped and that was worse because every other sound in that house got magnified, the sound of Ram Bhajan's children from the back of the house and the sound of kitchen clatter from within forming two parts of a misaligned cage in which she sat, dry like a pillar of salt, sculpted by an angry wind. In such an attitude a ray of sunlight on the floor or across her cheek would have lent her the required poignancy but there were three 100-watt bulbs on in that airless room of hers and they showed up the map marks on the old distemper instead.

'Nylon,' said Sujata to me on the morning of the wedding. 'She wants Mama to wear *nylon* for the wedding?'

'True blue nylon I swear,' I said.

'I think I'll buy her a sari, let Malini go to hell,' said Sujata.

'Don't do that,' I said. 'You know how Malini gets if you make her look small.'

'And that temper of hers, baba, she'll say something to me you're right...*chalo chhoro abhi*...but I must say this is sick. Maybe I'll give Mama my sari to wear just before the wedding so there'll be no time for Malini to...'

'Then what'll you wear?'

'Something, anything,' said Sujata looking like a saint.

But Beatrice never went to that wedding in the end. That was the week her osteoporosis was detected and she kept wrapping bits of cloth around her arm and switching off fans and eating calcium tablets even though she was told it wouldn't help now. She backed off from every function at the last minute and in the frenzy of dressing up no one really noticed. The cars were lined up outside, taxis honking and the *tik tik tik* of heels echoed through the house and all thought of her was suspended in a cloud of perfume.

It was only after the wedding was over, after Bob and Neha had left for their honeymoon, after Malini, Sujata and Aditi had gone, when the photographs came, that I saw she wasn't in a single one of them. It was as if she had shifted outside the frame of our lives and like the Siberian crane in winter would never return.

What is it about photographs? What evil power do they acquire in dark rooms beyond the image of flesh and blood? I kept staring at them, looking for Beatrice, Beatrice herself circumambulating the railings above, calling out to me in a voice that had a new echo to it, an after-a-horrible-wedding echo, a half-mad relentless so-tired emphysemic sound...*Gudda Gudda Gudda*...I had to get away from that sound, away from the mess the house was in, unwashed clothes everywhere, the smell of stale perfume, calcium, the sight of Violet collecting bits of ancient food in katoris, Anand, who was there for no rhyme or reason.

He looked like I'd thrust a steel rod up his spine when I told him I was off to Mugair, leaving him in that house with three old women. I almost felt sorry for him. I tried to look helpless, as if I couldn't help it, as if the nation depended on it and yes, the nation depended on it was the way I saw it, after that wedding my life, my reason, my sanity depended on it, so three days, is what I said to him, and I'll be back, *three days is nothing.*

Three days isn't nothing if you consider that God created the whole world in seven so I shouldn't have been surprised when I returned from that trip and saw that three days was all it took for Anand to demolish mine.

The Second Journey

These stories are as much about dislocations between histories and presents, and as much about the failure of the past to coalesce into a comprehensible 'now', as they are about the necessity of history to a meaningful sense of self and place.

—Debjani Ganguly

Should we thank the British for the trains they left us? Yes, of course and yet I know it's those trains that made my ancestors dream dreams beyond the possibility of their fulfilment, made them move around quite unnecessarily at times, shuttle between towns for no rhyme or reason. Just look at the way that network expanded under the British, its route mileage increasing from

288 in 1857
to
1599 in 1861
to
3373 in 1865
to
5077 in 1871
to
7322 in 1877,

a marvel of engineering and at the same time a curious phenomenon of geographical connectivity destroying a deeper, more valuable one. Did the railways come to India too soon? Had they not been there would the Dahiryas, the Bhils, have been scattered the way they were? Would Beatrice have been who she was? It's stupid to question progress, I know, and yet…

Post-colonial India is full of stories like the one dadi tells me, about once proud races who can't be traced beyond sad figures on railway platforms of small-town stations, sitting on hold-alls waiting for the next train to come in. Waiting, waiting for a new life to begin…

It happened like this: Shortly after I arrived in Mugair, Maddy developed a toothache, fed Uncle Billy in a bad-tempered way, shoved a clove between her teeth and went off to sleep. Then Milly announced she had indigestion, was skipping dinner, which left Daniel, a crazy, grumpy sort of fellow who doesn't seem to like me and so there I was, left to spend the evening alone with dadi. I tried chitchatting with her at the table, quite expecting it to be a monologue, I took a couple of shots and suddenly hit bull's-eye. Dadi's dark world is lit by fireflies. Maybe it was all the jogging of memory caused by my constant questioning, it might have evoked some nostalgia in her but she began quietly, so quietly you could have almost passed it off as an old woman's mutterings. 'Like a ping-pong ball she was,' she said, and it wasn't so much the sentence that caught me as the expression on her face—there was no drama to it and she was staring at her curry bowl just like Beatrice did, like there were miles and miles of ocean there.

'Who?' I asked.

'Beatrice,' she said.

What emerged was a patchwork blanket, quite peculiar, and I'm sure she added her own imaginings to it and Maddy got up in between and joined us with a pile of sewing, looked like she was about to protest every so often and return dadi to the path of truth but I silenced her quickly, nodding at her to let her know *I knew*. They were wisps of images from a fading film you could hardly catch before they melted away and sometimes just words that didn't connect with other words and sometimes her story lost its sequence entirely, moving along railway lines between towns in a manner that I could hardly distinguish one from the other. It was no Ramayana or Mahabharata that emerged but something about how Granduncle Billy became a tidda, about my grandaunt Harriet wearing her brassiere backwards, about a Rajput prince called Dandelions and finally, something quite sad about Beatrice not owning any knickers.

What I'd hoped to piece together from dadi's ramblings was quite different—who lived and died when, what they did for a living, how the Dahiryas metamorphosed from poor peasants to owners of colonial houses and hunting lodges and Wedgewood dinner sets but none of that happened. I learnt nothing about that vortex of history beyond dadi's fireflies—here one second, gone the next, here, there, everywhere, nowhere. It's what happened to the Jews, general knowledge of whose fate at the hands of the Nazis doesn't extend beyond the concentration camps, from there frog-leaping to the Nuremberg Trials. What happened to those who survived? Their homes had been occupied by strangers, they'd lost their belongings. How did they rebuild their lives?

Later it dawned on me that it was my inacceptability, my unwillingness to lend credence to anything beyond the parameters set by history books—those unidimensional accounts written by people who weren't even there—the fear of stepping into that blurry but no less legitimate domain of old women's memories that had wrongly made me look upon it as a mere story. Because if dadi had such people inside her head it meant they existed, in part if not in whole, and if they existed, then surely I existed too, not in the manner of the lizard's tail that continues to live in a gasping fashion for a few minutes after the rest of the lizard is dead but with dignity and wholeness and with the comfort that all that while when everyone I knew in the world had gone around referring to this relative and that relative, I too had not been alone.

In between, dadi scuttled off and returned with a letter. It chilled my bones to the marrow for it was proof that she wasn't entirely lying. How she got hold of that letter is anyone's guess, another firefly.

Here's what I understood from what she told me, including the parts where I never understood whether what happened happened before or after what happened next:

> Rose, not Hubert, was the legal owner of Grace Place, so after Rose died and the title deed was transferred to Hubert's name he decided to show the world exactly who he was. But Grace Place had a way of wringing your dreams out of you, hanging them out to dry so you spent your life either flapping in the wind or feeding the tiddas, making whirring sounds at them like Billy did.
>
> Billy was a genius in his youth but there's such a thin thread between genius and madness and Billy's thread broke. He'd gone to Oxford with the help of the missionaries, returned three years later with trunks full of books that lined the walls of Grace Place, went around with the air of being the only literate around, quoting Walt Whitman and Lord Byron left right and centre at the oddest of moments, bringing everybody's conversation to a dead halt as they sat around trying to decipher what he meant. As if he was saying something but telling them something else. Deliberately out to make them look stupid, so the first time he got down on his haunches and started whirring like a tidda they thought it

was just another one of his rude messages to them. Hubert said it was a terrible waste, sending the bugger to Oxford.

To keep out of Hubert's way, Billy took to feeding the tiddas that hovered over Grace Place, went to the backyard with chanas in his hand and then ate one, threw one, ate one, threw one, so the tiddas had a permanently expectant look in their eyes. He got so obsessed with chanas that every time a meal came on the dining table, a large bowl of chanas would be placed in the centre and Hubert and Andrew and Harriet would keep throwing them at Billy while they ate. Billy would fly around their feet grabbing them, and *leh Billy, leh Billy, leh Billy* they would go between conversations and when they were fed up of him they would chuck the chanas to a far corner of the dining room so he would have to whirr all the way there and back and they would get a couple of minutes' respite.

One day Hubert caught him. Billy had climbed up on stool upon stool to the roshandaan outside the bathroom to watch Harriet bathe. Hubert went to the yard and pulled out a barbed wire from the chicken fence and whipped Billy with it, screaming *Tu ne yeh seekha Oxford mein*? *Yeh seekha*? *Yeh seekha*? *Haramzade*! the sound of the whip cracking down on him with each yeh. Then he marched to the dining room, to where Billy's photographs were hung, of his days at Oxford and his framed graduation certificate, tore them off the wall and threw them on the ground, smashing the glass to smithereens. He had finally found a reason to do what he had wanted to do for years.

Billy spent the next few days and nights in the backyard with the tiddas and then one day, was back at the house whirring. Except that he no longer flew around like a tidda but sort of dragged himself along now like a wounded dog. A week later he was found dead in the yard, a lump of tidda shit on his forehead.

'But dadi, Granduncle Billy's alive!' I interrupted.
'You call this alive?' she replied.

Harriet's dream meanwhile was to become a doctor, to wear a white coat over a Murshidabadi silk sari that would rustle when she walked, stethoscope hanging from her neck. All the nurses would flatten themselves against the walls of the hospital corridors when she passed and she would nod at them briefly, sometimes not at all. When Harriet summoned up the courage at the dining table one day to say she wanted to study medicine there was hushed silence. A grim sense of foreboding entered her but she was a determined woman so she brought up the subject again and this time Hubert looked up from his plate and said: *'Utter nonsense!'*

'Why?' said Harriet bravely.

'Because you can't have your cake and eat it too!' thundered Hubert who like all thick-headed bullies knew no rhyme or reason.

Harriet didn't bring up the matter again. A few nights later she simply packed her things and walked out, leaving a note for Hubert that she didn't know where she was going but that she was definitely going.

Twenty years passed. Harriet became Chief of Surgery at Chandanpur's Lady Hardinge Mission Hospital. The Murshidabadi silk took longer to materialize than the white coat and the stethoscope so she made do with drip-dry saris for a while which was all right if you consider Hubert's theory about the cake—the one you can't eat and have too.

Back at Grace Place, with Harriet gone and Billy dead, Hubert was left alone to bring up his daughters Flora and Beatrice. Andrew was no help, he was obsessed with food, wouldn't stop eating. Larger and lazier he grew until his jaws became huge and flappy and hanging like the ears of a

Basset Hound, turning the corners of his eyes downwards with their weight, at night splaying themselves across his pillow like two shivering steaks.

While Flora spent most of her time curling her ringlets, Beatrice ran wild, playing gulli-danda with riff-raff.

Flora eventually, with the encouragement of the missionaries, became a teacher, moved to the House of Chandrakund to tutor a foreign-returned brat called Minx who kept dropping jewels in her lap in return for Flora letting her poke her fingers up her ringlets, yank them loose and then watch them spring back like yo-yos. Flora had been hired to teach Minx Hindi but she didn't know how, so she invented a novel method her own that skipped the alphabets to go directly into sound. It didn't matter what things meant as long as they sounded right. So, for 'open the door' in Hindi she didn't tell Minx to say 'darwaza khol de' but 'there was a cold day' which she said was one and the same.

Minx's uncle fell in love with Flora. He married her, shortly after which he had a stroke that turned him into a quadriplegic so Flora brought him back with her to Grace Place where she tucked him away in one airless room of the house, did nothing for him but change the flowers in his room daily, hoping their cloying scent would choke him. *Dandelions*, Beatrice used to call him. Do you want to see Dandelions? she would say to her riff-raff friends, going skipping towards them and they went skipping along with her as she led them to a part of the house very few knew existed. Spat on a windowpane clouded with age and grime and wood polish, rubbed the spit in with her fingers round and round until it formed an oval of light, then catching hold of their heads from behind she pushed their faces to it; it stank of her spit, and they saw him lying on a bed looking up at the ceiling.

It became a ritual, watching him, like a band of anthropologists who'd discovered a new strain of mankind, an exclamation mark without a sentence, a candle in a crypt that they waited upon for the slightest flicker, waited and watched until the night something horrible happened: they saw his eyeballs move, his lashes flutter and they followed his gaze to the ceiling where they saw a lizard making its way directly above his head. Suddenly he screamed, his eyebrows two mad seagulls. Beatrice and riff-raff screamed back, flew down the corridor, leapt over banisters in search of Flora, the sound of his screams hot lava at their heels except that when they found Flora they had to do an about turn, tyres screeching, for Flora was walking naked in the moonlight, Chandrakund jewels slung from forehead to ankle, dragging herself down misty corridor after corridor in the opposite direction, *away from the sound!*

Hubert, livid with Beatrice for fraternizing with riff-raff, decided to punish both her and Harriet together, never mind that their crimes were twenty years apart. He packed Beatrice off to Chandanpur, hoping it might destroy Harriet's career.

Here dadi switched from telling a story to directing a film, my heart began to thump, I heard the shunting and clanging of bogeys, one chasing another of an entirely different vintage.

A cold winter's evening. The Aravali Express pulls up at Chandanpur station. Hubert, seven feet tall with a middle parting, emerges from a compartment. He looks up and down the platform imperiously. Holding on to his hand is little Beatrice in an ugly nylon frock, hair pulled back tightly into two braids. The rubber bands at the ends of them have been wound round and round so many times that despite the oil in her hair, the braids stand stiff as if whoever made them for her was ensuring she would never have to make them again. If you look at her shoes carefully you will see dried splatter marks on them, as if she hadn't kept her feet nearly wide enough apart when urinating. And if you look at her lips they're going up and down—she's making the sound of a moving train: *Chandanpur ke che che paise, Chandanpur ke che che paise, Chandanpur ke che che paise…*

'Chupp!' Hubert says, slapping her hand but she doesn't stop. She'd begun her muttering soon after the train pulled out of Mugair Junction and kept it up through the night like a mantra, moving her hands round and round in the air like the wheels of a train. Looking closer you will see lesions on her body, ring-shaped patches with white pustules at the edges. The one on her neck glistens like a diamond pendant and as if by auto-suggestion she pulls her hand out of Hubert's grip and her fingers fly back and forth scratching like a tarantula dancing in the deep.

A coolie materializes from the mist. He heaves the trunk on top of his wobbling head, the brown hold-all over his shoulder. *'Nazareth Square ke liye do ricksha,'* Hubert says imperiously. The luggage is piled on to one and they climb onto the other. As the rickshaw starts moving the expression on Beatrice's face is that of a princess with an entourage. She doesn't notice the newness of the roads or the unfamiliar trees that line them. It's only as the rickshaw begins to slow down that she gets a frown on her face, a frown that turns to open alarm as the wheels stop turning and the large white wooden gates of Lady Hardinge Mission Hospital loom in front of them. Hubert picks her up by her armpits and puts her down on the road roughly, making her nylon frock fly up briefly, giving you a glimpse of her knickerless state. She starts picking at her sores again.

The gate creaks open. They enter a square where a group of children stop their game of gulli-danda to stare at them. The girl is scratching violently at her sores now, on the verge of drawing blood. They walk towards the converts' hutments. Hubert indicates to the rickshaw-wallah to put the luggage down outside the door of the fourth house on the left, casts an imperious glance around him and then turns to ring the bell...

'Phir darwaza khula...' *said dadi in a whisper, making daraoni ankhen, as if she'd been telling me a small-town ghost story all this while. Then her teeth went askew in her mouth and, as if I had accused her of lying, said,* 'I tell you Harriet was a churail. A dayan!' *Shortly after this she confused me completely, turned the clock backwards and arrived in Chandanpur herself, a week before Beatrice, peeping through a window at Harriet, displaying unexpected empathy with her predicament, in between returning Harriet's soul to hover like a bat over Grace Place.*

One afternoon, a week before Beatrice arrived in Chandanpur with her hair in two rods, the rain fell at a clean forty-five degree slant so the khas-khas on the windows of Lady Hardinge Mission Hospital needed no watering. But they waved at the wind like so many joyous sailors spotting shore so the rain entered from the sides of them and the orderlies had to run around banging windows shut and lighting hurricane lanterns along the corridors. Such was the darkness that came upon Chandanpur town.

Chief of Surgery Dr Harriet Lawrence had bolted the door of her office from inside so she wasn't aware of what was happening inside the hospital, or outside, where the rain was a great-coated stranger in a hat, beating a tattoo on her window. He wiped the fog on the glass in order to look in on her and he saw through the pattern his fingers made that Harriet was running, her arms and legs not coordinated, but wildly flailing, as if all hell were pursuing her. Behind her the yellow walls of Grace Place receded in a downward slope like they were at the corner of a fisheye lens and Harriet rose up a dune to the centre of the frame and down again until she fell out of the frame forever, leaving the bats to encircle the silver moon over Grace Place, crying *Harriet's gone, Harriet's gone.*

The reason Harriet had bolted the door of her office was that she couldn't let the hospital staff witness her loss of composure. Composure was what it was all about and it was a grand conclusion she'd come to, in the manner of Scarlett O'Hara picking up a clod of earth in her blistered fist, swearing to the sky that she would never go hungry again, except that twenty years ago, the day Harriet had announced she would never be bullied by Hubert again, she was seated on a trunk, addressing the galvanized-iron roof of a railway platform, digging her fingers into the folds of a brown hold-all.

Now at her desk, not looking at the rain, she wondered whether Hubert's bulemic nonsense would follow her to the ends of the earth. She could spit his theory right back in his face saying 'I ate it, now you can have it' which would make no more no less sense than the theory itself but she was afraid he would grab her long hair by its roots and entwining it around his fingers drag her back across the dunes to Grace Place. He would leave her there with the tiddas and she would turn around and look at them and see that something terrible had happened to them. They had blood on their whiskers and a wild look in their eyes because Hubert had forgotten to feed them all these years and so they had eaten up Billy, knowing their chanas were in there!

All these years and Hubert had lain in wait of her, dropping on her like a lizard from the roof. Drawing his letter out of her handbag now, she began reading it again, slowly this time.

To Dr Harriet Lawrence
Lady Hardinge Mission Hospital
Nazareth Square
Chandanpur
15 December, 1933

My dear sister Harriet,

I trust all is well with you. You have not been in touch but then a woman of your achievements would have a great number of things to do.

Harriet I cannot deny (and God forgive me for not bearing my burden lightly) that life has been hard since Rose died. I have decided to move to England for some years with the hope of starting life anew. The Mission has found a placement for me as well as quarters and I will be departing from the shores of India on January 15.

You might be aware that Flora lost her mind after the death of His Highness. Berty and Beulah, God bless them, have offered to keep an eye on her provided I find another home for Beatrice. The reason they make this distinction is that Beatrice has been running wild since her mother's death and Beulah, as you know, suffers from arthritis and cannot keep running after her. Beatrice herself has been keeping indifferent health having recently recovered from whooping cough and now appearing to have some kind of skin ailment. We all felt that with your experience in the medical profession you would be the most suited to care for her.

I trust you will not refuse your brother in his hour of need and will by now have forgiven him for not having been more understanding of you.

I will be arriving in Chandanpur with Beatrice on the Aravali Express on January 4.

I look forward to our reunion.

Your loving brother,
Hubert
Grace Place
Hakra Cantonment
District Mugair

After the rain the lemon sun sent its slant into hidden corners. A vaporous light emanated from the stone walls of the hospital and the smell of drenched khas-khas filled the air. Harriet rose from her desk, tucking the letter into her handbag, and turned to leave the room. At the door she looked back briefly.

A bottle of Quink ink.

A neem tree outside her window.

A mahagony desk.

She looked at these things as if she were looking at the whole of her life for the first time. Because Hubert had disregarded it. Then she walked swiftly down the corridor, seeing no one, the tunnel swallowing her up floor after floor…

'Then what happened dadi?' I asked, my heart going out to Harriet, but dadi looked up sharply at my tone and swiftly reverted to her earlier thesis of Harriet being a churail.

She beat Beatrice with her stethoscope, so all the years Beatrice lived with her she stayed under her bed, peeping out at Harriet and one day she saw Harriet wrapping a hospital bandage round and around her chest. So tightly that the blood sprang into her eyes and her breasts vanished. Jumped out from the other side of her, one after the other, nipples erect, singing like bugles. So she had to wear her bodice backwards. Got thrown out of the ladies compartment on her way to Hindoli once for the ladies thought she was a man and they screamed for the tee-tee saying *mardua aa gaya, mardua aa gaya!* Harriet stood up outraged and slapping her breasts said, *'Kya yeh dikhta nahin, moorkhon?'* but her arms wouldn't go all the way back so she ended up slapping her shoulders instead so the ladies thought she was threatening them with her manhood so they screamed even louder until the tee-tee came and threw her out of the train and they fell upon their aloo-poories in relief.

'One minute,' I said to dadi, 'churails have their feet backwards, not breasts!'

But dadi didn't answer, she looked tired and bewildered, so I looked sadly out of the window at this terrible denouement, at my grandaunt Harriet dismembered forever for posterity, a lone figure on a railway track in the midst of nowhere, picking up her pieces, her brain from her shoulder, her bun from the nape of her knee...stumbling off in reverse-forward or however you'd describe the stumble of a wounded churail.

Sadder...

Harriet never made Beatrice's plaits ever again, left them as Beulah had made them so Beatrice's hair grew into and around the rubber bands while the rubber bands themselves melted into her hair like treacle.

The years passed playing gulli-danda at Nazareth Square. When the missionaries of Chandanpur strung up their badminton nets, Beatrice and the other children turned spectators, watching them reverently or picking up their shuttlecocks for them. Beatrice never bent from her waist when she did that but descended into herself, wrapping her frock around her knees first because she'd run out of knickers long before she arrived in Chandanpur and Harriet didn't make her any. Told her they were an unhealthy English habit, that airing your private parts set your soul free.

So that was Beatrice for posterity: soul, breasts, private parts blathering in the wind…

Sadder still…

As soon as it was announced that the first medical conference in India was to be held in Chandanpur, Harriet put Beatrice back on the train to Hakra and then as soon as Beulah heard the conference was over she put her on the train back to Chandanpur and then Harriet found another excuse a year later and then Beulah did the same until finally Harriet put her on a train for good when she heard that Hubert was returning from England.

'Like a ping-pong ball she was, your poor mother,' repeated dadi, wiping an imaginary tear with a gnarled and trembling finger coated with cold curry.

Morning: Maddy hijacks my plan to go to Hakra. We go, but to attend the funeral of a woman called Dora. Dora isn't a relative or even a family friend but something in between. Why am I going to the funeral of someone I don't know? Nor do I want to go anywhere near Grace Place with Maddy. She's becoming aware of the power she has over me by virtue of my ignorance and she's enjoying that power, telling me stuff in bits and pieces, leaving out essentials. Look at how our conversation about Dora went:

Maddy: *Dora mar gayi.*

Me: Who's Dora?

Maddy: *Arre Dora bua*!

Me: She's a relative?

Maddy: No no no.

Me: Then?

Maddy: You won't understand. She knew your father. She's an orphan. (*What's the connection between knowing Iqbal and being an orphan, I don't ask, nor how an old woman can be referred to as an orphan.*)

Me: What happened to her?

Maddy: Legs.

Me: What happened to her legs?

Maddy (*efficiently wrapping bun-omelettes for our journey*): Arre baba, how many times did I say to them that this is not a good sign but did they listen? (*Who is 'they'*?)

Me: But what happened to her legs?

Maddy: So fat (*holding her hands two feet apart*).

Me: She had elephantiasis?

Maddy: Why do you always use such big words?

Me: But what happened to her legs?

Maddy: *Kanjoos makhee choos saare,* that's the problem! Took a tonga!

Me: Why are you wrapping so many bun-omelettes?

Maddy (*making two packets out of a mountain of bun-omelettes*): *Yeh tera hissa; yeh mera hissa!*

I give up.

Maddy wants to go to Hakra by roadways bus and I like the idea, rattling along munching bun-omelettes, except that I'll be at her mercy then, so I pull out the card Babu gave me last time, summon him from the Prithvi Palace and now we're leaving, armed with bun-omelettes for the funeral of a woman who died of either fat legs or stinginess or tonga.

As the miles fly past on the Mugair–Hakra highway I find myself thanking god for the English, for the magnificent roads they gave us, for their extraordinary ability to cut a metal swathe across impossible terrain. Thanks to the highway that terrain is not as impossible as it would have been a hundred years before. There's been a green revolution since, wheat fields and bajra and mustard on either side and even the hills around appear to have softened from how I imagined they would be, mellowed the way women do with age, sprouting a few hair on the chin, or is it that short period before they die, when they assume the manner of adolescent girls? Of course I know there are other harsher parts of the desert where the Aravali flaunt their age like tyrants.

An hour into the drive we pass a milestone reading 'Hakra'. My head spins. The place exists. Beatrice exists. *I exist*. The air changes at this exact spot and it's not my imagination. There's a clear divide between the rest of the world and the Thar, no fence to tell you that this is where the world ends and the Thar begins, only a certain virginal wind, the same one that travels all the way to Delhi in the months of May–June, sullied by then through all it picks up on the way. If winds have a source like rivers do, this would be it.

We hit the cantonment first. It's completely deserted. Deep in the heart of its burning acres stands the beautiful ochre and white St Paul's Cathedral in perpendicular Gothic with an elegant spire that beseeches the heavens and a ten-ton bell that resonates for miles around. We get off the car briefly at my insistence. Within the cathedral, along the walls on either side, are marble plaques commemorating officers and soldiers of the 89th Field Battery who'd died in the 1857 Mutiny and if you read the inscriptions you'd begin to believe the cantonment contained men of flesh and blood although, Maddy tells me, on account of the temperatures here, you'd have to wait till twilight to see them because like the legendary witches of the Thar that's when the battalions emerge. No blood on their fangs but heat boils suppurating inside their fatigues, running and marching and doing their drill.

Where is Grace Place? You would imagine Maddy would do me the courtesy of pointing it out to me but she doesn't and I don't ask because she's cultivated an air about her like we're passing through one of the hundred cantonments across India.

Dora lives on the opposite side of the highway, in a place with the quaint name of Bethlehem Square, in British times headquarters of Rajasthan's powerful Scottish Presbyterian Mission. Up ahead in the distance where the highway ends you can see the ramshackle outline of old Hakra, the part that existed long before the British came here. Before that, lining the same side of the road as the cantonment, is a row of dhabas and further ahead, a bus stop complex. We pass a shop called Ghantaghar Sweets, no ghantaghar in sight, only flies cruising over acrobatic arrangements of burfees and laddoos. As we near the bus stop I find it impossible to tell Maddy I want to stop here, spend a moment at the place where my father was seen last so I tell her instead that I want to stop for the famous Hakra milk-cake and she screws up her nose and goes *'Cheeeeeee!'* Just then we plunge into a kacha road on the left, next to a bicycle shop where tyres are being washed, the Ambassador dipping violently into an oily black pool that splashes our windows and obliterates the view. With Maddy chattering and Babu cursing I hardly focus on the bus stop and then it's too late.

This kacha road is the entrance into Bethlehem Square. I screw up my eyes for the place is enveloped in a haze of dust, looks at first glance like it's grown out of the hills around. It baffles attempts to give to it a perspective in the landscape. You can hardly say it nestles at the foot of the Aravali, which it does, for that would give an erroneous picture-postcard impression, nor can you position it in barren desert for the sake of austere beauty for it lies only at its fringes. There's no colonial column and arch here, only the flat roof and yellow wash, against which the magenta bougainvillea of the desert would have stung the British like an open wound upon the memory of ivy and greystone, for it was only the Himalayas they really understood, its red-roofed cottages and beds of hollyhock and hills with peaks to them, peaks upon peaks into a snowy horizon so unlike the foothills of Hakra that from a distance look like lumbering bison in single file.

Unlike the cantonment there are no real roads here, only dirt paths that seem to have established themselves through time. The ground is hard and dry, layers upon layers of petrified dust, harder than those hills, a thin powdery layer on top making tentative attempts against the tyres of our car to turn into a storm. Somewhere in that cloud of dust is where the disintegration of the Dahiryas began, new beginnings arising from it, some that will never come to my notice now, caught in the fine dust that weighs down the leaves of trees, lives in the cracks between the stones here. The layout of the place is angular, strict and at the same time you see all the buildings at a glance on account of the large spaces between them. To my right is the Lawrence Memorial Church, smaller than St Paul's but equally beautiful, its stained glass panes glowing like burnished jewels turning colour with the passage of the sun. It has a gory history, Maddy tells me, named after two missionary brothers, John and William Lawrence whose eyes were gouged out of their sockets and delivered on a plate to the British Resident in Mugair by the mutineers of 1857. To my left are six large bungalows, once the homes of the officers of the Mission. At the centre of the Square stands the double-storeyed orphanage, to its left the single-storyed Mission school, yellow-washed like the orphanage but while the walls of the orphanage have faded to cream, the school has been freshly painted a bright urine yellow. Imagine it in that dry field under a noonday sun, then picture a hand of kindness showering bougainvillea on that landscape, transforming it magically to ease the pain in your heart at such bleakness—those flapping weightless leaves and the particular strain of wild fuschia of the region hangs over walls, it picks up its skirts and then falls in a heap over fences and sometimes it grows in the midst of nowhere in uncontrollable clusters masquerading as trees.

Everything at Bethlehem Square appears to have maintained its original layout, with even the sun here appearing to be a nineteenth century one, nailed to its cross overhead. No encroachments, only neatly apportioned areas dictated by the need of the hour, a need frozen in time so that even if lives changed, people changed, they couldn't alter the original structure laid down for them. Far in the distance stand the converts' hutments, twenty-four of them cheek-by-jowl, set in two rows facing each other. As our car moves towards them my heart begins to thump.

We park along the side of the hutments and walk up to Dora's house. It's overflowing with people. The drawing room furniture appears to have been shifted around to create space. Her body lies on a bed in the middle of the room, covered with a white lace sheet. A young girl removes the sheet from her face as we near. Dora's mouth, nostrils are stuffed with cotton wool. I stand there and look at Dora, whoever she was, and then I do an astonishing thing, I begin to cry. There are about a hundred people in here, including the 'warlords' of Christianganj—Wilma and Satya Paul's family—everyone seated on plastic chairs extending across one more room. They're singing *Abide With Me* softly, mournfully, in Hindi. I had no idea there was a Hindi version. I wonder if Mahatma Gandhi whose favorite hymn it was knew. I settle down on one of the chairs next to a woman who instantly stretches an arm forward to share her hymn book with me so I am forced to sing, my voice breaking every so often in grief, just like hers and I realize that grief at funerals is as infectious as a low-down thing like yawning. I am embarrassed in case Maddy sees me crying but she doesn't. She'd abandoned me the moment we entered which is just as well because right after the hymn when people begin to get up and move around several come towards me, touch my arm or briefly lay an arm around me. It's enough for them that I seem to know Dora and so it feels like I do. This brings on some more weeping until I am fairly submerged in grief.

I cannot tell who the Dahiryas are among the crowd and since the ones I've met so far don't know it themselves I can hardly ask. Many have rugged faces although the men are wearing suits and ties—Rajput peasants masquerading as English gentlemen, definitely not daredevils opposing Alexander the Great which indeed their warrior ancestors would once have done. There are farewell speeches for Dora who was clearly loved. At least two refer to her as an orphan just like Maddy had done. I am perplexed and then something even more perplexing happens. An argument begins about which eight people should carry her coffin and one man says it has to be orphans, no one else, as if it were a caste literally, after which he begins singling out some very old men.

While everyone rustles about in the ghastly effort of shifting body from bed to coffin I look around the room. Ancient warped and rusty room cooler, the white light of the desert sneaking in through worn-out khas-khas pads in laser beams, Sunmica coffee table with the corners of the Sunmica curling up to display cheap plyboard below, plastic blue daisies above a TV set, a ceramic plate above the fridge with those ominous three lines the British left behind:

CHRIST IS THE HEAD OF THIS HOUSE
THE UNSEEN GUEST AT EVERY TABLE
THE SILENT LISTENER TO EVERY CONVERSATION

I see a stack of photo albums on a windowsill full of dust. I sneak up to the window and flip through them. Small black and white photos, rows of women posing together with oblong faces, the pallus of their saris tightly covering their heads up to the hairline, all staring twenty degrees away from the camera to offer three-quarter profiles, soft untroubled eyes and a look of self-containment, of 'not seeing' that a modern-day model tries so hard to emulate.

I pick up a pamphlet from Dora's Sunmica table. Beatrice's pamphlets are Shakespeare next to this. Here it is, word for word, letter for letter:

Rajasthan is in two great parts. The Aravali Hills and the Great Thar Desert. Here three great religions of the world meet. It is a hard rock well. In 75 years hundreds of god's servants brought living messages and the wilderness shall rejoice the desert shall bloom. One Church one faith one Lord and soon the Church in Rajasthan merge in century and in Enternity.

With simple beginning and simple faith in 1922 with borrowed tents, no electricity, no conveyance, the small village churches came in carts dancing and singing. I was six year old and used to come with my father a great excitement, love and joy in that tent.

So intense was the spirit of the convention that Christian Endeavourers' came on cycles in one night when there were no proper roads between the village and town. I enjoyed that nights pleasant trips. 1922 was God's appointed time. Rajasthan awakened for the political and social awakening just after the 1st world war. Side by side this small assembly grew and now a big plant of Spiritual Freedom.

Sing with Reginald Heber's spirit,
Waft waft ye winds His story,
And you ye water's roll,
Till like a sea of glory,
It spreads from pole to pole

Zinda Iman Buzurgon Ka Musibat Men Tha Fatehmand.
Now when in sessions of sweet silent thoughts I sum up the remembrance of things past, then I drown an eye unused to flow for precious friends 'Hid in death's darkness night' and weep afresh love's long since.

'But if a while I think of thee dear friend all losses are restored and sorrows end.'

I hear a terrible heaving, wheezing sound behind me. I swing around and see the coffin being lifted into the air, toppling and swaying in a most undignified and dangerous manner and so Dora's last journey on earth begins on the shoulders of eight geriatric orphans who look like their livers will burst with the strain. I wait for the crowd to file out and take my place at the tail. Three cars are waiting outside. One offers me room which I refuse and which I regret later as the walk to the cemetery takes a good forty-five minutes and the sun is killing.

When I'd heard the cemetery was just behind the Mission I'd imagined it to be nearer but it's almost as far as the road to Doom Dooma that runs a good two miles away along the outer periphery of Hakra. It's situated in the middle of nowhere really, camouflaged by tall brambly bushes that keep scratching the sides of cars that have no choice but to move as slowly as the walkers. After a point cars can't go, and this is well before the cemetery so the smart ones have to join the walkers, with the last ten minutes along a dirt path so narrow that you have to go single file, plucking deadly branches aside to prevent them from lacerating your face, the crackling sound of bone-dry twigs under your feet accompanied by the distant sound of cars and trucks speeding along the Doom Dooma highway, all oblivious of Dora's death. Finally the path opens up at a slight incline and you see a ragged old brick wall in the distance, the same colour as the hills, a miniature great wall of China. This wall encloses the graves.

Inside, the graveyard is as wild and unkempt as that path. No one maintains the place. I see dry flowers here and there on a grave, bleached by the sun, looking like they had been placed aeons ago. There's another graveyard at the cantonment, Parveen Paul informs me, where the English are buried and is somewhat maintained by the cantonment staff while this one's officially dependent on the missionaries long gone. The graves are fairly simple here—no flying angels or open Bibles carved in marble, only crosses, some keeling over, some broken with iron rods sticking out of them.

As the preparations for the funeral begin I wander around. The graveyard is divided into two sections, one strictly for the orphans of the famine, for it wasn't only the Dahiryas who found their way here but hordes of devastated peasant families from the neighbouring villages. Here the graves are even simpler, some not even proper graves, only mounds of earth overgrown by weeds. At one end of this section are forty graves in five rows, not even mounds of earth, just small oblong tombstones like milestones standing close together as in a war memorial. This is where the eighteen Dahiryas lie, the ones who died soon after their arrival in Hakra.

The other section is given to the families. At the head of the dead lies Hubert, next to him Rose, below Rose, Andrew. A shiver runs through me. Here are My People finally, Beatrice's people, under cold, cold marble. Their graves are the largest, most elaborate here, complete with birth and death dates and verses from the Bible, although much of the ink in the engravings is gone. I stare at them, unable to break through the marble in my mind, unable to comprehend that these were people of flesh and blood once, my blood, so I turn around and look at the graves next to them, names I do not recognize but the majority of them have the same surname—Lawrence. Why are my family's graves larger and grander than the rest? Where is Iqbal's mother? I see Maddy waving to me frantically. The preparations are over; the funeral is about to begin. I start walking across to the orphans' section.

Just as the 'dust to dust and ashes to ashes' part is over and everyone begins picking up clods of earth to throw on Dora's coffin we are hit by a hailstorm. It happens without warning, without the sky growing dark at all and I think maybe Dora was someone special and it's a sign from heaven that she and God have met up until someone tells me that's the way hailstorms happen here. If the light changes at all it becomes even more fluorescent. We stand around the exposed grave, pelted from above by rain and hailstones as large and hard as pebbles. There's nowhere to hide, not a leaf or bush in sight, only those brambles, so everyone shrinks into himself, eyes tightly shut, heads lowered, hair plastered, soaked to the skin in minutes. With the hailstorm comes an icy wind that rages through the graveyard, making my teeth chatter even in that heat. I'd heard about the extreme temperatures of the desert, burning days and freezing nights, but this flip happens in broad daylight within minutes. I see Maddy giggling, helplessly attempting to hold a limp georgette dupatta aloft like a roof, huddled with a group of women she appears to know well, and a loneliness as sudden and as huge as that storm envelops me and I begin crying into the rain, not so much on account of Maddy as an awareness of the years and the people I've lost and can never regain. Just then I see a man staring at me from across Dora's grave in a manner as though he knew the difference between tears and rain, as though he knew my tears had little to do with Dora.

Funerals make you hungry. There's meat back at Dora's house, big chunks of it floating in oil. Thick rotis from the market, rotlas I should call them, coin a word. I have three, chomping and chewing, after which I help myself to water from a ghada placed in a corner of Dora's verandah, I haven't the expertise, the water spills all over me, I wash my hands from a low tap awkwardly, it splashes all over my shoes, I wipe my mouth gingerly with wet fingers for there's no towel around. As soon as the feast is done the men light up furiously and I see that in Hakra smoking is still considered a wonderful thing to do, cigarettes dangling from lips rakishly, even while conversing, even while hands might be busy, so you could include a bit of James Dean there in that image of Rajput peasants impersonating Englishmen. Is that how Iqbal might have looked once?

I amble towards Dora's gate. The sky is a lurid pink. I look across the dry field of the Square when the man who stared at me at the graveyard comes up from behind and introduces himself as Philomen, the one Maddy said worked in a mandi in Hatundi and knew everything about Rajasthan. Turns out he's a gentleman farmer, grows aloe vera in the desert, has a government contract to supply the plant for medicinal purposes. Not at all the sort of farmer his father would have been, sitting under a peepal tree puffing at a hookah. Philomen laughs as I share my thoughts with him about how like the Sarasvati the peepal tree is becoming a myth, how even the traditional village square has become the e-choupal.

Like Maddy, Philomen says he thought Beatrice and Iqbal had only three daughters. It seems wrong to be chitchatting like that after a funeral so I ask Philomen how Dora died and he grinds his cigarette under his shoe just like James Dean and tells me she had diabetes, that her legs got gangrene and that even then she could have lived except that instead of taking her to the Drummond General Hospital down the road they took her all the way to Mugair, that too in a tonga instead of hiring a taxi. By the time they arrived in Mugair, she was dead. *So Dora did die of fat legs and stinginess and tonga!* Then Philomen points to the orphanage. 'That workhouse is where Dora grew up,' he says, 'and where your father grew up too.'

My blood turns cold. Iqbal an orphan? What happened to my grandmother Nanhibai?

'She died when he was seven,' Philomen tells me, 'of tuberculosis. Your father was transferred to the orphanage then.'

I am unable to digest this immediately so I change the subject. 'And where's Grace Place, where my mother lived?'

He looks surprised. 'Didn't you see it on your way through the cantonment? It's right there on the highway.'

I am silent. We start walking then, towards the orphanage, on close view almost Dickensian, as if it were enveloped even in that sunlight by a phantom English drizzle. Half-broken old-fashioned eaves tipped over its windows like brooding eyelids.

'Why do you call it a workhouse?' I ask.

'Because the orphans were put to work here by the missionaries, trained in crafts like basketry, carpentry, embroidery, things the missionaries sold at cantonment fetes for the orphans' upkeep.'

Iqbal made benches and tables? He embroidered handkerchiefs for Englishwomen? The image burns into my heart like acid.

I change the subject again. 'And why do so many graves have the surname Lawrence? Everyone's a Lawrence here?'

Philomen laughs. 'It's a long story,' he says. 'It began reasonably, with the naming of the Lawrence Memorial Church after John and William Lawrence although it wasn't after them that all of us were named but after the very first missionary to set foot on Hakra soil, a man called Lawrence Lawrence. With so many deaths and so much devastation around, the poor missionaries must have grown exhausted. Mass conversions meant a mass changing of names and how many names could they think of?'

'What a lot of confusion it must have caused,' I say, 'everybody with the same name!'

'Not at all,' Philomen says. 'Your granduncle Andrew was Larens Sahb, somebody else was Lawaris, or Lalloo, and the people of Hakra found a million more ways of saying the name so if you introduce them to a new Lawrence tomorrow they'll manage to look as if they're hearing the name for the first time ever!'

Philomen is an uncomplicated man, philosophical, non-judgemental, belonging here and yet not. He seems to have broken away from that nineteenth-century cross nailed over Bethlehem Square, and yet stayed. Minding his own business, growing that aloe vera somewhere while continuing to be involved with everyone here. Unlike Maddy, with no side agendas, and so I ask him why my part of the family appears different, including their graves, why they lived in Grace Place and not in the hutments here, and then the question that dadi never answered, about how a bunch of ganwars turned into English-speaking sahibs. This is what I gather from things he tells me, things his grandfather told his father, understanding in the process why Maddy was so dismissive of Grace Place, why she reduced Hubert's hunting lodge to a heap of rubble smelling of dog-piss:

Two decades after the Dahiryas arrived in Hakra, Hubert, Rose, Andrew, Billy and Harriet hit the big time, moved out of Bethlehem Square and into Grace Place after which they began to behave like Bethlehem Square never even existed. Turned the rest of the Dahiryas, including Maddy's forebears, into the notional Chamars of Manu's first order, declaring they would have no truck with them. The reason why the move occurred is unclear. Some say Bethlehem Square was bursting at the seams, others that Rose manipulated the shift through her bootlicking of the missionaries who, without a by-your-leave of the cantonment, sanctioned their occupation of Grace Place. Hard to believe now, not then, for even though the cantonments always appeared to be in the forefront in British India, the Missions was where real power lay. The Dahiryas never liked Rose; she didn't care. Sat herself down among the sofas and antimacassars at Grace Place, modelling herself on the Great Queen.

Who was Grace Place built for? No one knows. Its last British occupant was a Colonel Pierce who after suffering six bouts of dysentery fled to England.

As nothing succeeds like success, or a better address, there was no looking back. Done with the Mission School at Bethlehem Square they entered Mugair's Glenmore Public School, modelled by the British on Eton and Harrow. Then, as reported by dadi, Billy after Glenmore, went to Oxford. Simultaneously, two good missionaries called Miss Drummond and Miss Glass, to Hubert's horror, proceeded to ruin the women of his family. They began a zenana group at Grace Place in which they not only held sing-songs and Bible studies but filled Rose and Harriet's heads with nonsense about equality between men and women. It was under their encouragement that Rose took up the study of medicine, eventually taking up the reins of the Drummond General Hospital. She took over Miss Glass's pets too, two murderous Rottweillers that guarded Grace Place, kept the riff-raff Dahiryas of Bethlehem Square firmly at bay.

Harriet, satellite of Rose, followed in her footsteps, ended up Chief of Surgery at Chandanpur's Lady Hardinge Mission Hospital.

Hubert, meanwhile, got suspended between the past and the future. The one person at Bethlehem Square he stayed in touch with was his childhood friend, Philomen's grandfather, to whom he kept muttering about women having forgotten their place although he didn't appear to remember his because as the years went by he became more English than the English, reading *Blackwoods Magazine* and *Tatler*, ordering rumble-tumble eggs for breakfast, insisting that his vegetables be washed in potassium permanganate, ordering everyone to dress up for dinner, hiring a khidmutgar to stand behind his chair to flick away the flies while he ate. Unfortunately, Hakra with its one corrugated-iron cinema hall and twenty shops hadn't much to offer a man in his position. There was no life beyond the bazaar in the old town nor was Hubert allowed into the British officers' club so to compensate he shifted from the Lawrence Memorial to St Paul's at the cantonment for his Sunday worship, largely for the tea and fellowship that followed the service. For the benefit of the English he returned to his warrior past, told the officers colourful stories which appealed to them much more than his peasant origins would have, aware that they considered the warrior castes of Rajasthan to be the most warlike and manly of the Indians, the physical characteristics of which Hubert certainly bore.

At some point he acquired that hunting lodge in the village of Ranigaon nearby after which he began to believe he was an English fox-hunting squire, an aristocrat of sorts. He became brazen to the extent that he began inviting British officers to join him on his shoots. Hunting was the commonest diversion of officers at the Hakra cantonment who found time heavy on their hands and Hubert had much to offer

> them, for behind the lodge was a lake that extended into marshland abounding in game and wildfowl. It was here at this hunting lodge, on velvet nights, when the hills around had grown dark and you could barely see their outline against the sky and the trees were lit by flashes of fireflies that he sat on his porch guzzling port wine with wild boar sausage, listening to the night sounds of India. 'If ever, during my lifetime,' he told Philomen's grandfather once, 'the British quit India, I'll quit too. It would be no place to live in, no law, no order, nothing but chaos.'

'What about Dahirya?' I ask. 'Why did he, why did no one think of going back to reclaim their land?'

'But that was a long, long time ago,' says Philomen, 'who knows where it is?'

Back at Dora's tea is laid. Plates of Britannia biscuits are being passed around, namak para and pastries. Big hogs, that lot, but so genuine in their grief along with the bonhomie that collective grief engenders that I guess they didn't need to pretend that with the loss of Dora they'd lost their appetites too. I take my chance then, thinking they'd be at it for a while. I tell Maddy I'm not hungry, I'm going for a walk and Maddy nods back vaguely, not having noticed I just returned from one.

I sneak up to the car, tell Babu to return to the highway at top speed, back towards the cantonment. At the bus stop I ask for directions to Grace Place. Everyone seems to know it, everyone but I its owner. It isn't more than five minutes away from Bethlehem Square and I see that indeed we'd passed that bit of road on the way here except that Maddy had begun to chatter like a maniac just then, waving her arms about in the opposite direction to turn my focus. Growing in front of me now is a grand two-storeyed neo-classical Georgian mansion straight out of *Gone With the Wind*, fluted Doric columns supporting a barrel-vaulted portico, both wings of the house decorated with a florentine pediment, large French doors up above opening on to colonnaded terraces, verandahs, more porticos. Lining the winding gravelled driveway is the majestic dhak like a guard of honour, its orange blossoms from a distance appearing to set the house ablaze. I am stunned. How could a peasant have lived in such a palace of a home? How could Beatrice have lived here? *How could I own something like this?*

Except that I don't. A well-polished brass nameplate at the gate reads 'Major Hanumant Singh'. I don't need to ring the bell. The Major is standing at the portico, four dogs around him, barking and salivating.

I introduce myself. 'I'm Hubert and Rose Lawrence's granddaughter, Andrew Lawrence's grandniece.'

'I paid Mr Andrew in full,' is the Major's rude response.

'I'm sure you must have,' I say, taken aback.

'I also have the papers to prove it,' he goes on to say and I should have demanded to see them but how could I, although I knew he couldn't possibly have the papers as Andrew's letter said he was leaving them with his lawyer.

I ask to look around the house, and that's the other thing, if I had shown the least interest in his papers he wouldn't have let me in and at that point I was more keen to see the house than stake a claim to it. So I tell him I'm on a sentimental journey, not an acquisitive one, after which I put him further at peace by telling him I'm visiting *all* the places my relatives lived in once. Then I walk past him and into the house and he has no option but to follow me.

It hits me right between the eyes: the interior of Grace Place is a replica of our house in South Delhi, on a much larger and grander scale of course. Before me is that wretched courtyard, quite magnificent here, staircase on either side, carved railings all along and above. Why would Beatrice have carried the past with her like that? You don't run away from one world and then build a new one on exactly the same architectural plan as the first. Was she stupid enough to believe she could achieve the same effect in a space a hundred times smaller?

Taken aback by my boldness the Major makes an attempt to recover his dignity, starts acting like he invited me in and is now showing me around. He leads me to the gol kamra, a stately room with a high roof, the Major's sofa set below diminutive and far too modern. Where could Hubert and Rose's furniture have gone? Two chairs are with that thieving broad with big breasts but what about the rest? Could the ones at Bethlehem Square have stolen it? I saw nothing of value at Dora's. Could some of Maddy's furniture, including her antique Chinese screen have belonged here? Am I surrounded by thieves? On either side of the gol kamra are bedrooms so large that the beds are placed in the centre of them. We go up to the first floor that opens on to a terrace from where I see a small lake in the distance, long-legged white birds on its shores. There's also a view from here of the road to Doom Dooma, a band of gaily dressed women in ghagras and odhnis walking along in the distance, silver jewellery glinting in the sun, a reminder of that other Rajasthan, so far removed from my one. Right behind the house roll acres upon acres of cultivated land, wheat stalks swaying in the breeze. We descend through a spiral staircase at the back to a row of outhouses, a motorized well and a dozen bullocks standing around doing nothing. There are empty chicken pens too. Tiddas, the Major says, killed all the chickens.

So many parts of the house I don't get to see at all, the Major is in a hurry to get rid of me, I of him, particularly at the well where a thought crosses my mind of pushing him into it which I could well have done with the strength of the blinding rage that comes over me. It's he who takes my leave finally, almost hustling me out of the house. I mutter my thanks, promising to return, which by the expression on his face doesn't please him at all.

How do you take a whirlwind fifteen-minute tour through something that's haunted you for so long? It shatters me, not the house or the Major as much as the reminder of the nature of time, that relentless moving finger Gibran wrote about.

By the time I return to Bethlehem Square everyone knows who I am, courtesy Maddy and Philomen. There hadn't been occasion earlier to introduce me. They're full of questions, and having Beatrice's genes in me I answer them with the expertise of a born liar. They refer to me as Hubert and Rose's granddaughter or Beatrice's daughter. There's no mention of Iqbal, as if he never existed. Then the subject of Grace Place comes up. I act like I'm interested but not enough to go see it. What stops me in my lying tracks is two old women and a man who begin talking as if Grace Place was theirs. To one woman I say, 'I thought my grandfather owned it' and she says, 'Yes, but he was our brother!' The other one is more truthful. 'Had Hubert and Rose been alive,' she says, 'they would never have come to Dora's funeral.' She's pleased that I'm different. Then the first woman waves frantically to a young girl who comes running. She introduces her to me as her granddaughter. 'Do you know of a boy for her?' she says, 'a Delhi boy?'

After that I get a sense that several people are dusting and settling up Dora's house and I think how kind of them, specially since the woman's not there to thank them and then I realize that, tea over, they're on a robbing spree, grabbing Dora's things. I catch Philomen's eye. He gestures to me to follow him to the kitchen. He lifts a thick curtain that hides a cemented shelf high above on which I see a beautiful old English vase and some other antiques that Philomen says Dora stole from Grace Place just before it was sold. 'They're your things,' he says, 'take them.'

'Let it be,' I say.

But he doesn't let it be. He pulls out a Bible from that shelf, a leather-bound one with fine line illustrations and he opens to the title page where I see the signature 'Iqbal Lawrence'. Wilma creeps up behind him. 'I was looking for this!' she says, grabbing the Bible from his hand. 'Dora told me long ago I could have it after her.'

I am outraged but I don't need to express it as Philomen does it for me. *'Do you know who this man is?'* he shouts at Wilma, jabbing at the signature after which he hands the Bible to me. My eyes fill up with tears. I leave the room.

'Yes I know,' I hear Wilma shouting back at him, *'as well as I know who he wasn't!'*

Five minutes later she walks up to me and asks for a lift back to Mugair, she's so shameless. Maddy meanwhile has been on her own robbing spree and emerges with another British relic, a pewter bowl and mug in her hand, decorated with pink roses, quite possibly mine too. The three of us pile into the car. Wilma sulks throughout the journey, sits stiff as a poker, fuming. Maddy clutching that bowl and mug as well as a large plastic bag full of things, god knows what all, in her lap, I clutching that Bible, my first tangible proof that a man called Iqbal lived once, no indication in the dead Quink ink of his signature that he lives now. Growing indication that he wasn't who he was, or was who he wasn't. What on earth could Wilma have meant? A horrible suspicion moves in waves to my stomach. I call out to Babu to stop the car at once. He swerves to a screeching halt as I open the door, lean my head out just in time for the meat, the rotlas to come hurtling out.

Evening: I head for the station. It's transformed. Light bulbs draped over Mugair's mini Big Ben, a grey stone colonial clock tower that stands in the middle of the road outside the station, serving no other purpose today beyond causing traffic jams, the station itself spruced up and banners everywhere announcing Glenmore Public School's Annual Day. The train is late. Another arrives. Hordes alight, all smartly dressed, women in starched saris with matching blouses. City women, and I think they must be mothers, here to attend Annual Day, dressed to the nines to make their children proud and I try and remember if mine ever made me so, hanging around in nighties all day and I worry that nighties might be my only inheritance, I could label them for posterity after their smells...*vinegar, mango, urine, grief*...

I sit on a bench and wait for the train. I pull out the one trophy I've acquired on this trip, Iqbal's Bible, I open it and stare at the signature as if it might say something to me, I follow the loops and curves of Iqbal's handwriting but it says nothing at all, like everyone else it doesn't even hear me.

The Convent of Hermaphrodites

Natasha had been leaping about our house like an over-friendly gazelle that entire wedding season, sometimes in shorts, sometimes in pink sequined salwar kameez. She was showing no inclination for finding her own husband and so I'd begun looking around. 'You really think I'll agree to marry a stranger?' she said to me one day. 'They're all strangers,' I replied. 'If you marry someone you know, you'll have to un-know him eventually. He'll change. Ten years down the line you'll wake up one morning and find that the grumpy old fart in your bed is a stranger.'

There's no touchstone in the case of a city but the feeling of displacement when I returned from Hakra was the same. Delhi had changed. It had already changed while I was in Bombay but now I began to notice it, it began to bother me. Alankar Cinema had gone and in its place stood a shining multi-storeyed mall called 3Cs on the top floor of which was an open-air restaurant with nylon grass for a carpet. I shouldn't have been resentful because I hadn't seen a film at Alankar even once but it had been a sort of landmark in my mind's map of Delhi. The way things were going there was no guarantee that 3Cs wasn't a fly-by-night operation, that it would be there the next time one looked. Teksons bookshop had moved from ground floor to first floor in the mad juggle for space that South Extension had become and Cottage Emporium had shifted from its mouldy barracks behind Janpath to a spanking five-storey monstrosity opposite the Imperial Hotel. One could no longer find what one was looking for. The display had changed, the fabric had changed, the staff had been juggled around and, worst of all, their cafeteria Bankura, instead of expanding in tandem had shrunk to the size of a coffee counter and was selling stale sandwiches wrapped in cellophane.

Summer went, winter came, Anand stayed.

Delhi was crisp with cold that year and I with a nameless fear. The amaltas and gulmohur had gone and each barren branch appeared to be splayed against the sky without volition of its own. A taut thread of resistance was growing between me and the city and it seemed to be extending itself into a triangle to include Natasha and I had no clear idea why. I began to feel strangulated by that thread so that everywhere I looked I imagined it to be a last glimpse I was having of something. Buses were switching to CNG. Construction of the flyovers had begun and though one was told it was something to look forward to directions were getting muddled up. There were road diversions everywhere and secretive tin sheet walls that had sprung up along the sides of roads with the sign 'Metro under construction'. So while cars would be flying overhead there would be trains hissing underfoot, spewing smoke up manholes New York style except that Delhi's manholes were always choked, so trains would arrive with a deep rumble, the doors of compartments would slide apart and no one would emerge, they would keep sitting there because they would all be dead, asphyxiated. Meanwhile, because Delhi had so many municipal authorities that the left hand seldom knew what the right was doing, the dead and dying and bandaged including the ones blown up in those CNG buses would emerge at the crowded AIIMS crossing, throw off their crutches, put on stilettos and march smartly towards subway stations. Some would march straight into garbage bins because there was a remarkable resemblance between the new ones and the entrance to those subway stations.

I responded to several matrimonial ads behind Natasha's back and, one day, received a call from a Mr Bakshi. He said he was a retired army officer. He assumed I was a relative.

'No,' I replied, 'I'm a family friend.'

'Where are the girl's parents?' he asked.

'Unfortunately neither is alive,' I replied.

'What happened?'

'They died in a car accident,' I said.

Anand wasn't particularly concerned with my doings. He appeared to be quite indifferent to Natasha on the whole. On one occasion he passed a negative remark though. Natasha was expected for dinner and she went off with some friends instead, leaving Anand and me who'd put aside our plans for the evening feeling foolish. 'Don't you think she should treat you with a little more respect?' he said. 'Doesn't matter,' I replied good-naturedly but I began to wonder. Was it Natasha who needed me more or I her? Did my guilt arise from the fact that I hadn't been friend enough to her mother? People around a suicide case are apt to be stricken by feelings of inadequacy and I got the feeling that somehow Natasha knew that. She could hardly have known what had transpired between Mona and me, leave alone Mona and Anand, but her eyes accused me constantly. On the other hand it could have been my guilt that drew the accusation out and this conundrum was something Natasha and I lived with, dodging each other now and again but on the whole letting the affection between us, and my concern for her, rule.

Mr Bakshi said he, his wife and his son would like to meet me, Anand and Natasha at the Gymkhana Club at 7 p.m. for a drink. Anand refused to go. I wore a pink georgette sari and was examining my jewellery when Anand said, 'Don't do that, they'll ask for dowry. Keep your wedding band on, that's all.' He had started exercising suddenly and had just got off the treadmill and was pouring sweat. He had a towel around his neck and for a fleeting moment looked the way he did when I first met him.

'No one asks for dowry any more,' I replied.

'No one believes in arranged marriages any more,' he said. His disapproval bothered me. I had wanted us to stand up together like surrogate parents.

So in retaliation I told him I was taking his Mitsubishi instead of my Maruti 800 because I knew he hated my taking it. 'They might see us off to our car.'

Natasha entered just then, giggling. That was the other thing about her. She had a habit of walking straight into our bedroom without knocking. Anand handed me his car keys. As we were leaving she looked over her shoulder and gave him a wink. He didn't respond. There was an expression on his face I couldn't quite fathom.

On the way Natasha and I chatted about this and that, about the mother of a friend of hers who had Parkinson's. 'I think she's pretending,' Natasha said.

'How can you pretend at Parkinson's?'

'Of course you can,' she said and proceeded to tremble and twitch, distracting me from driving. I didn't think it was funny at all.

'And why would she do that?' I asked coldly. 'What a way to live.'

'A weapon,' replied Natasha, 'she uses it as a weapon to stop her daughter getting married. Every time she finds a boyfriend her mother's trembles get worse.'

'How awful,' I said, wondering suddenly what Natasha was really like. For all the rehabilitation work she appeared to be doing with the victims of the earthquake that had hit Ahmedabad earlier that year I had never seen compassion in her. She was always cruel, always imitating someone. 'Don't tell the Bakshis you live alone,' I said, changing the subject. 'They'll get the wrong impression.'

I looked at her sideways. She was suddenly contemplative, almost depressed. 'This isn't going to work,' she said.

'Of course it isn't,' I replied. If I had said it was she would have argued.

The Bakshis were waiting for us at the bar. The boy was short and his legs were spindly. He was probably the age his father'd said he was but he was balding. I didn't look at Natasha. The trio was rising from their seats to greet us. It was too late to run.

Mr Bakshi was an exuberant, friendly man. He ordered drinks all around, paneer tikkas, chicken tikkas and aloo chaat and then proceeded to talk non-stop, as did his wife, their sentences crossing each other like two trains hurtling from opposite directions and since she was seated opposite him it gave Natasha and me something to do—turning our faces this way and that. Everyone ignored the boy, including his parents, and I began to wonder whether the ceaseless chatter and the excessive food was a deliberate attempt to deflect attention from his obviously bad looks. There's a way of looking at someone without actually looking at them and during the process of such selective hazing I saw that his nose was long and greasy and like a chhalni, with a multitude of open pores. I felt sorry for him. Unlike his parents he seemed to know from the start that it was no-go. Natasha was way out of his league.

I felt a depression coming on and at the same time curiously began to feel snug and content in the company of strangers whom I knew I would never meet again. As if we were all together in a train compartment, licensed by the impossibility of getting off to exchange familiarities. I think I had a kind of sixth sense too, a feeling that something was about to go horribly wrong and that I needed to extend the evening. Through the hazing I saw that the club had deteriorated. The sofas were lumpy, the chicken tikkas undercooked. The paneer were better although they had ageing lumps of chaat masala stuck on them. I began to feel like two people in one because at the same time as I was writing off the Bakshis I was feeling more and more at home with them. Mr Bakshi was two drinks down and shards of paneer were flying out of his mouth as he talked about army life, his brothers and sisters and uncles and aunts, none of whom appeared to have done anything spectacular. At the other end of the hall, Rocky Fernandez and his band came on and several people, all on the wrong side of forty, began to dance.

I thoroughly misled the Bakshis. That they were impressed with Natasha was obvious. Then the topic of her parents arose. I explained again, about the accident. My lines were practiced by then and I had almost begun to believe them myself when I realized it was the first time Natasha was hearing them. She looked stunned.

'That's all right,' Mrs Bakshi said sweetly. 'We're very broadminded people. My sister-in-law even married a Muslim.'

Natasha lunged for a tikka, suppressing a choke.

Finally the boy spoke. He asked Natasha whether she would have a coffee with him some time if he called her. She nodded. He asked for her mobile number. She gave him Anand's.

Back in the car Natasha exploded. 'We could have come in a phatphat and they would still have wanted to marry us!'

I didn't respond.

'Why did you lie about my parents like that?' she burst out.

'I'm sorry,' I said. What had she expected me to say? That her mother committed suicide and her father was a sex-maniac?

She burst out again. 'You seemed to be *genuinely* enjoying yourself. What is *wrong* with you?'

I didn't reply. She was appearing as brittle as glass.

On the way home I was silent. I didn't encourage her to talk. I didn't want to hear her voice.

Anand grinned as he opened the door. 'So how much dowry did they want?'

'Oh we couldn't afford them in a hundred lifetimes,' I said, brushing past him. He appeared like glass too. Tears stung my eyes. I had no idea why.

'Don't know what's the *matter* with her!' I heard Natasha say as I fled to the bedroom.

I didn't emerge for dinner. There was a smell of carcass in my mouth from the chicken tikkas. The quality of my skin didn't feel right.

Natasha stayed on, talking to Anand in the drawing room till quite late. I thought I heard raised voices once but it might have been my imagination.

A lot was, those days. And it wasn't to do only with things immediately around me. I saw cosmic connections between Lutyens Zone in Delhi coming down to the ground and Buddhist sites in Ayodhya rising up from under the ground. The papers were full of both these—Delhi's vulgar new master plan and the archaeological discovery that was threatening to alter political perspectives on the Babri Masjid issue. Something was escaping my understanding and it was causing a discomfort so deep that I found myself rushing towards windows in the middle of the night for deep breaths of air.

Maybe my ears were too finely tuned. Not in the manner of being able to place my head on the ground for the sound of distant hooves but an operatic thing that started with the breathless drone of a single locust. And then several, until they smothered me with their angel wings, crawled up my legs and dived through my sleeve into my armpit.

'It's probably hot flushes,' Anand said knowledgeably one night when he awoke and saw me leaning my face out of the window. I had an urge to slap him.

'It's the city,' I muttered, 'it'll go up in flames with all that CNG, I'm worried,' but I don't think he heard me.

A few days after we'd met the Bakshis, Anand left for Bombay to bring the rest of his luggage. When had we decided this was going to be the new order of things? I felt helpless, as if someone else was running my life for me. It felt as if there were ten of Anand around me. Sitting in that house I was overcome by claustrophobia.

I was stricken by the smallness of our life together, the smallness of life with Beatrice, the smallness of everything down to the size of my bedroom and my teacup, the smallness of that dustbin called history, mostly stricken by the manner in which I had been magnifying it all. I suddenly wanted a brand-new story, outside my own, larger than my own, larger than anybody else's and what better than the story of Delhi itself? Delhi had seven avatars, seven histories. I decided to go on a history walk through Mehrauli.

I went across to Natasha's house to find out if she would come with me but I found a lock on her door. On my way out I bumped into a neighbour who said Natasha had gone to Ahmedabad on work. I was taken aback. We led independent lives mostly but she always informed me if she were leaving town. She would give me her keys and I would water her plants. Was she annoyed about the Bakshis?

Two days later Natasha rang me. I tried to keep the coolness out of my voice. When she began to say something about a sudden trip having turned up I pretended I wasn't even aware that she had gone. 'Listen,' I said interrupting her, 'I have this great plan.'

No, she said, she hadn't heard of Phoolwalon ki Sair. Yes she knew about Qutb Collonade because of Jessica Lall's murder. Her level of general knowledge astonished me but, anyhow, she agreed to accompany me to Mehrauli over the weekend. Anand returned from Bombay on Saturday morning and on Sunday Natasha and I put on our keds, packed some sandwiches, a bottle of water, tea in a thermos and left.

'Are you sure I didn't bully you into this?' I said to her in the car. I was in high spirits.

'Not at all,' she said with an artificial brightness. She looked gaunt and pale.

'You know sometimes I think I go overboard about history,' I said, not wanting to focus on her, feeling complexed and at her mercy.

She didn't respond. I thought I saw her blink back a tear.

'Is the wind getting in your eye?' I asked. 'Do you want to roll up the window?'

'No no it's fine,' she replied, her mind clearly elsewhere.

'What happened in Ahmedabad?' I said then. 'You haven't told me anything.'

'Nothing,' she said, suddenly looking alert. 'Why should something have happened?'

'I mean, what did you go there for?'

'The earthquake,' she said, as if I didn't know that.

'Complicated earthquake, huh?' I said stupidly.

'Yup,' she said, and then clammed up.

I wanted to know. I genuinely cared but I could tell by her profile that she was in a dungeon.

'In an Adivasi dialect, *Mehr* means green and *uli* means bitter mango,' I said in an attempt to move on.

'What?' she said, swinging her face around angrily.

'MEHRAULI,' I said, 'that's the meaning of the word. Bitter green mangoes.' We were at the Qutb crossing and I gestured towards a clump of trees near Lado Sarai. 'In Mughal times there used to be a vast mango orchard there, did you know?'

'No,' she said, 'and so?'

It was clear that the trip was going to be a disaster. Then several minutes later she answered my old question as if I hadn't said anything in between. 'No I don't think it's wrong to go overboard about history if at the same time one isn't resistant to the present.'

'Who, me?' I said, 'I'm not resistant at all, when was I resistant?'

'Oh you carry on about this and that *all the time,*' she said, 'as if you're in a time warp, as if you're not there at all, as if just by pretending something doesn't exist, it'll cease to exist.'

It didn't make sense. Not then.

'Your seven cities,' she went on, as if they were *mine,* 'they don't exist, it's the one *now* that does but you don't want to believe it. I think it's a weapon you use, like Parkinson's.'

I was stunned. Anand was right. I had been too familiar with the girl. She didn't know how to talk. 'Do you want to go on this trip or not?' I asked quietly, threateningly.

'Yes of course, that wasn't my point,' she said.

The point of it all hung like vapour on a misty morning in December. I had gone for a walk on my own once, too early, down Shanti Path and found that I couldn't see a thing. I had wandered around like a lunatic until I saw a dark shape growing in front of me. It turned out to be a tamarind tree. I sat below it, leaning against its trunk, letting the dew seep through me, waiting for the vapour to lift. When it did, I didn't know where I was. In that mist I had crossed the road and gone to the other side and then wandered into one of the side lanes. What if a car had hit me?

Anything can happen to anyone. Jog Maya was caught in a storm while fleeing from Kamsa. Her body began to disintegrate in the lightning and thunder. Her torso fell on Mathura, her feet on the Vindhyas and her head on the spot where Natasha and I were now standing 5000 years later, in front of the temple that Yudhistira, the Pandava king, built for her. Within the temple were shrines to Shiva, Vishnu, Ram, Sita, Lakshmi, Ganesh, Hanuman and Kalki, beyond which stood the sanctum sanctorum to the dismembered goddess. A self-appointed guide attached himself to us and began babbling. Emperor Aurangzeb, he said, tried to destroy the temple but his troops were attacked by a swarm of bees when they reached the spot.

I was mortified that the man had seen us for what we were. My original thought had been to just wander around aimlessly but because of Natasha's stupidity I had felt obliged to focus, to visit the historical landmarks first. The absurdity of descending on Mehrauli in Reeboks, eyes round as saucers, hit me. The body language was wrong. 'Let's have some tea,' I said, as soon as we emerged from the temple. I had never hated the smell of incense before.

'Should I get the thermos from the car?'

'No,' I said sharply. 'We'll sit *right* here.' There was a dhaba a little way ahead and I began walking towards it determinedly, not giving her a chance to protest. Over tea I ignored her, cultivating a faraway expression on my face to keep her at a distance. I was still recoiling inside at the manner in which she had spoken to me. I tried to remove my focus from her and turn it towards the awesome knowledge that Mehrauli existed, beyond the broken bits of wall visible from the road on the way to PVR, beyond the fancy Qutb Collonade and Ambawata Complex—red herrings that had led me to believe that Mehrauli was a lost city. Days, weeks, months would not have been enough to take it all.

But we had half a day, and so we saw the tomb of Adham Khan, the Rajon ki Bain baoli, Metcalfe's house and then beyond the gates of Metcalfe's Estate, near the Mehrauli bypass, the tomb of Balban. What struck me more were the parts en route where there was nothing specific to see—the run-down havelis and smaller houses, the web of wooden balconies, arched verandahs and gateways obscured partly by electricity wires and telephone lines and people and cows walking past unaffected by the enormous history that lay around them. Homes that were clearly of Mughal vintage had been casually divided up into smaller residences, all dimly lit, probably due to the number of unauthorized connections. This was life stealing from life in the manner of an amoeba and a part of me rejoiced at this visible proof that there was no last page to history; it was a flowing river, a moveable feast.

The main bazaar was choked with scooters, handcarts, trucks, motorists and garbage. Somewhere in that mess I recognized a garish tiled doorway with minarets on either side. I had seen it in a coffee table book once. It was the Hijron ka Khanqah or convent of hermaphrodites dating back to the time of Babar. 'How creepy is that!' was Natasha's response when I told her what it was. I looked up just then and saw an eagle perched on top of one of the minarets. My spirit soared. Like the eagle I was king of all I surveyed. Ignoring Natasha, I walked up to the door and pushed it open. Inside was a spacious courtyard with a stone floor swept remarkably clean. On either side were rows of rooms with another floor above overlooking the courtyard in the manner of an old haveli. There wasn't a soul around.

'Let's go home now,' Natasha said, and just at that moment two hijras emerged from nowhere.

'What do you want?' they asked aggressively.

We were saved, literally by the bell. Several bells. They began chiming in unison, accompanied by a discordant chanting of voices that emerged through a door at the far end of the courtyard. The two hijras forgot about us and began rushing off in that direction.

'Come *on!*' I hissed at Natasha.

I left her no option. We followed them through that door to enter a shrine where we saw about a hundred hijras praying. They had their backs to us and were concentrated on a little statuette up front that didn't resemble any of the gods one knew. There was a circle of diyas around it casting an eerie glow from floor to ceiling in that otherwise dark and dingy room. The two hijras who had accosted us slipped into the group and instantly joined the chanting and wailing. Holding Natasha's hand firmly I lowered us both to the floor behind the last row of hijras who were oblivious to our presence.

When the bells stopped, cymbals and clapping began and the voices began rising in tempo, mostly an incessant wailing with intermittent babbling. This carried on for about fifteen minutes, with Natasha and I in hypnotic shock. Then suddenly all hell broke loose. It started with a few hijras swaying and shivering as if they were having a fit and then one by one they began to stand up and dance, stamping their feet and clapping their hands, skirts twirling, plaits flying. It was the right time for Natasha and me to flee unnoticed except that the noise that appeared to be reaching a crescendo ceased sooner than we expected. The ceremony came to an abrupt halt and suddenly we were in a room with a hundred hijras wholly in their senses. My legs turned to water.

'Who are you?' one of them yelled and the entire group swung around to stare at us.

They surrounded us even as we began backing out through the door and then one of them pushed Natasha. I had a glimpse of her terrified face as she stumbled to the floor. Another one boxed my arm.

'We're going, *we're going,*' I said, bending down to help Natasha up. 'We came here by mistake.'

'No mishtake! No mishtake!' one shouted.

Natasha began to cry.

'Hush up!' I said to her fiercely, nearly in tears myself.

'What did you come here to see?' another one demanded ferociously. *'This?'* With that he raised his skirt and flapped it in my face. I got the unmistakable whiff of unwashed genitalia.

'Oh my *god,*' Natasha whimpered.

'Here,' I said to the smelly one, opening my bag, 'take this and let us go.' I held out a hundred-rupee note.

'What is *this?*' he said.

'Take it,' I repeated, riveted by the cheap maroon lipstick on his thick lips.

He began to abuse me in foul language, clapping his hands on my face. 'Do you want the child to come out looking like a snake?' he said.

'What child?'

He gestured towards Natasha. 'The one in her stomach.'

I looked at Natasha. 'There's no child,' I said. 'You've got it wrong, she isn't even married, *I tell you we just came here by mistake!'*

'No mishtake,' he said, 'hijras make no mishtake. The child is here for our blessings.'

'Crackpot, bastard,' I whispered under my breath, partly to Natasha who had turned to stone.

Suddenly she opened her bag and took out a thick wad of notes and handed it to him. 'Let us go now,' she said to him firmly.

'Thank you, shishter,' he said, waving the bunch of notes around her head in blessing and then cracking his knuckles against his own.

It was Natasha who took my hand this time. 'Let's go,' she said calmly.

I was stunned. Was Natasha, the girl with no boyfriends, pregnant?

Was I to focus on that or hold on to the fact that we were standing where Babar, conquerer of Hindustan, once stood? The two together were more than I could comprehend fully. History came out of the core of the earth to stand at the edge of a cliff along which Natasha and I ran stumbling, holding hands.

As we reached the car a terrible sense of foreboding came over me. I opened the door, I turned around and looked up at the minaret and saw that the eagle had flown.

We drove back in silence. Natasha refused to come in for a cup of tea. 'I have cupboards to settle,' she said and then as I waved to her from my gate I got that feeling again, that I was looking at something for the last time.

Anand was sprawled in front of the TV, watching cricket. But he was dressed as if he was about to go out. 'How was the trip?' he said.

'Great,' I replied. I didn't want to tell him anything. It was dark and dank inside the house, as if *this* was a moth-eaten pile of history and that not. It never used to be that way, not in the Delhi I knew but over the last year builders' apartments had come up all around and they had stolen our sun. Anand had been muttering on and off about buying that plot of land in Gurgaon and I had successfully changed the subject each time. Gurgaon would have been worse with its malls and multiplexes and slippery movie theatre floors with blue lights glinting under them. I switched on a light.

Anand turned off the TV. 'We have to talk,' he said.

'Should I make tea first?' I didn't want tea. I wanted my hands folded around a circle of warm ceramic.

'No,' he said.

I sat down before him.

'I'm leaving,' he said.

'Again?' I said, 'but you've just returned.'

'No, I'm leaving for good,' he said.

'What?' I said.

He looked me in the face then, something he hadn't done in a long time, and said, 'I'll be honest with you, Nandu, there's someone else.'

But there had always been someone else! What was new?

'I'm sorry,' he said, going towards the bedroom. Fifteen minutes later he emerged with a suitcase and went out the door.

I didn't know what to do. I told myself I should pick up the phone and call someone but I didn't know who to call. So I called no one. I said to myself that perhaps Anand had gone temporarily mad. Perhaps he was taking revenge for my having gone to Hakra. Perhaps he'd return by morning.

But he didn't.

I couldn't tell Beatrice because she would have piddled with joy. So finally I dialled Natasha's number. There was no response. An hour later I dialled again. And again. At 8 a.m. I went across to her house. There was a lock on her door and scrolled into the lock an envelope in my name. The note inside was short:

Dear Guddamaasi,

You cannot imagine how sorry I am. But somewhere you knew and you chose to be silent. Anand and I had no choice under the circumstances but to leave town. If I love him it doesn't mean I never loved you or that I'm not grateful to you for all that you've done. Forgive me if you can.

Natasha

Forgive me if you can.

Tell your children their father's dead because he had a roving eye.

Forgive India!

Forgiveness isn't easy in December. You could start the day with everything seeming small and you feeling big and forgiveness and understanding pouring like nectar from your soul and then by evening the tightness and the lines around the mouth return. The thing about deceit is that you survive it, and you don't. If you learn to sleep again, you wake up in the morning remembering.

Then December turned to January and the wind began to blow and the very act of pulling my coat together tightly as I walked down a street made me feel wretched and alone. Even though the coat was of superior leather. Anand had got it for me from Germany and I was thrilled with it because it was so unlike the Indian ones that squeeze you at the bust and then flare out at the hips, and so odd was that marriage of ours that even through that wretchedness and aloneness I found myself heaving a sigh of relief that he had given me the coat *before* he left.

When a Man Is Gone

Things that slither and whirr in your kitchen in the dead of night. Dead light bulbs cleaving to their holders. The motors of washing machines transmogrifying into diesel trucks racing down a highway. Couriers who ring your doorbell in the afternoon. Neighbours on balconies. *Sisters' husbands*. They all know when a man is gone.

Shortly after it became public what Anand had done, Sujata's husband sent me a message saying he would take me to the cleaners if I tried usurping the family property.

He? Not Sujata?

After all those years of acting like it didn't exist, it was *family* property?

Beatrice's home, my home, was *property*?

Left to ourselves, Malini, Sujata, Aditi and I might have resolved the issue of Beatrice's will but they went and reported our conversation to their husbands. I never got a chance to tell them what I had really meant, that I never wanted the bloody house, I just wanted them to say they were sorry, take back their filthy accusation. It would have been a bonus if they apologized for the decades too, for traipsing around the globe while I took care of Beatrice but I never really expected the latter and it was too late for the former because soon after I got that message, Malini's and Aditi's husbands joined the fray too. Suddenly it was full-blown war; not two but six against one. That's when it dawned on me that not one of the six had uttered a squeak when Beatrice had produced her first will.

So I sent Sujata's husband a message back saying I would tell the world the size of his penis and to Malini's and Aditi's that I would chop off their balls and feed them kofta curry.

Then I grew frightened because they were powerful men. Sujata's husband was High Commissioner in London, Aditi's practically king of Silicon Valley, and David by then CEO of a multinational investment banking firm.

So I hired a lawyer.

Ashwini Luthra was his name but Luthra & Luthra said the board outside his chambers. Lawyers do that, I discovered. Increase their name to the power of two on the basis of a long dead father or uncle to give you the impression you have two batmen with flying black robes on either side of you to protect you.

I was introduced to him by a friend. He looked up briefly at me as I entered his office and then his eyes went back to his files that were open before him but in that fleeting moment I got the feeling he'd sized me up completely. Lawyers must be like that, I thought, they have to keep their radar on high alert.

He had an odd sort of sex appeal that ugly men sometimes have and he also looked like a criminal but I brushed that off with the thought that people do begin to resemble those they mix with. I had a horse-lover friend who began to look like a horse and I know any number of men who look like their wives.

'Yes,' he said after a minute, without closing the files. I had seated myself by then on one of the two chairs facing him and had finished looking around.

'What a lot of books,' I said. That's the other thing about lawyers. They line the walls of their chambers, floor to ceiling with a huge, impressive leather-bound, gold-embossed library of obese books but if you try and take one of them out you discover the truth because they're all stuck together.

'Yes,' he replied.

'I'm Anandita,' I said. 'Anandita Bharti, I spoke to you on the phone this morning?'

'Yes, yes, your mother's will, the family property dispute. What can I do for you?'

'Well, it's like this,' I said, retucking the strap of my handbag over my shoulder. I felt my voice catch. How much are you supposed to tell a lawyer? How do you interpret the pain in your heart in legalese? Why was he calling it a family property dispute? How could I tell him I didn't give a hoot about things like property? But then why was I here? Should I have been on a psychiatrist's couch instead?

I took the easy way out. I burst into tears.

Ashwini looked at me silently for a while. Then he swivelled his chair around, picked up a box of tissues from a shelf behind him and placed it in front of me. 'Take your time,' he said. There was no alarm on his face, no revulsion, no compassion either.

I took several and bunching them around my face, sobbed and heaved into them as if I would vomit. Then I blew my nose violently. 'I'm so sorry,' I gasped, looking around for a waste paper basket.

'Here, give it to me,' he said, and to my amazement I placed the sodden tissues on his palm.

'I don't know where to begin,' I said.

It really was the hardest part. *A thousand years*.

'When did your mother pass away?' he said gently, prompting me.

'But she isn't dead,' I said.

'Then what's this about?' he said. 'You said to me on the phone your sisters were fighting with you over your mother's will. A will comes into play only after someone's dead. They can't fight before that.'

I was flummoxed. 'But they're accusing me now of forging her signature,' I said.

'Ah!' he said. 'But she's alive you said.'

'Yes, of course she's alive,' I said, 'I just *told* you that, I'm living with her in that house.'

'And you *haven't* forged her signature, you say?'

'Of course not!'

I showed him the will.

He didn't read it but as soon as he saw Beatrice's photo he said I would need a certificate from a doctor that she was sane.

But Malini, Sujata and Aditi had said she wasn't! How would you know? I had asked, never dreaming that my question would be amplified legally, that I would have to run circles around doctors, lawyers, seedy touts to procure certificates to prove her sanity in a court of law.

'No, there's no *of course not* in the eyes of the law. If she's alive why isn't she standing up and saying it's her signature?'

Because she can't stand.

Because she can't stand without me supporting her and then everyone'll say I forged her standing.

Because I wouldn't put it past her to deny it's her signature now.

The law has a funny way of subverting the truth. Even if you say *that is the way that it was* you can't always back up your statements rationally. It's like the story dadi told me about churails and brassieres. Leave alone their direction, you can't always remember whether what happened happened before or after what happened next. So you superimpose beginnings on ends, ends on beginnings and sometimes let the middle breathe.

That's lethal, scratching the paint off walls, watching them take in great gusts of air while the parts that are too high to reach hang you to death.

I looked at Ashwini like he were the headlights of a car. He was approaching the truth head-on. He had found its nucleus.

'Because I haven't even told her what they said.'

'You haven't even told her?'

How would you like to be told a thing like that?

'No.'

'Then Mrs Bharti, I suggest you do. You do that and *then* you come to me.'

But I didn't tell Beatrice. You don't tell someone who's dying to get on with it because you've hired a lawyer. You don't tell them that while they were sitting on the potty and crying their children were calculating the worth of their property.

The trouble is, nor can you tell them after they're dead.

Between Beatrice and Ashwini my life began draining away into the gutter, I'd only been to Mugair and Hakra by then, I hadn't even begun to look for Dahirya. I kept telling myself I'd go between hearings but Beatrice began to conduct something similar within the house, the house itself began to resemble the Tis Hazari courts, she started quarrelling about the smallest of things, stretching a two-minute exchange into hours of useless debate. One day she told Flora to *get out.* The matter was a long drawn out and complicated one but I traced its origins to Violet and politics. So Flora returned to Mugair where she had come from and my plans to go fell apart once more because I couldn't leave Beatrice with Violet alone, Violet might have starved her to death, eaten up all the food, and then Beatrice made me write Flora a letter telling her to come right back, and who told her to go off like that? So Flora arrived once more and this happened repeatedly, the *get outs* followed by my pleading letters and her returns. Flora was like the sand dune she'd emerged from, ever willing to make its pile elsewhere, ever blowing in the wind.

So I went nowhere.

The terrible thing about home is that sometimes there's nowhere else to go.

Equally terrible the space between old age and death. In Beatrice's case it stretched forever. At some point she gave up what she used to call her Quiet Time, her private session with God that she used to hold on her bedroom balcony at six every morning, shutting everyone out. Did she give it up or did she simply forget?

And she was turning smelly too, not washing after No.1 and god knows maybe after No. 2 too, because every time I entered her room those days I felt I had overstepped, gone straight into the nala. I'm not sure when exactly it was that she began slipping into dementia, disappearing into the good night, because initially I put that down to a dream, believing in the manner of the relatively young and cruel that you could tick off your brain cells if you really wanted to. It began with her losing her memory, and her keys. She could never find them. I thought it was a simple enough matter, of fixing a permanent place for those keys but she kept changing the permanent place so we were forever looking for her keys.

She drove me mad with her shenanigans that summer, for once she got a taste of the power of amnesia, the derivative power to build and rebuild worlds at will, she exercised it to the hilt, sometimes pretending she'd lost her keys just to get me to stop thinking what I was thinking and start lifting mattresses instead, diving under beds as she stood there wringing her hands, making big round innocent eyes. For a while I got misled into thinking it was Violet and Flora who were up to tricks, hiding her keys and then whacking her money which began disappearing too but sometimes that money would appear from under her mattress, limp as muslin, wads of tenners, fivers folded in no order the way cooks giving you hisaab do after running that money through the hands of the diseased and TB germ-spitting millions. So then I began to think it was she herself who was robbing herself, *purposely,* just to drive me crazy.

Then she stopped sleeping. Initially I thought it was simply greed, a desire to clock up a greater number of waking hours before death, a devilish manipulation of time itself, making it stand still, or go backwards by pretending night was evening, fooling the cosmos into giving her bonus minutes on earth. But then she began stealing time from *me.* She began sneaking into my room at dawn to turn my fan off so the last few hours of sleep were spent in a stupor of disbelief. Sometimes she would shine her torch right in my face. *'Can you move the torch!'* I would shout. *'Why do you have to shine that thing on me when you talk to me? Why don't you shine it on yourself?'*

'Why can't you dress properly?' I shouted at her once, pulling out a pretty pink sweater from a trunk that I had bought her many years ago. It had pearly beads on it and she loved it. Those nighties of hers had become a two-edged sword for me; not only did I have to look at her in them but I'd begun to fear that anyone else looking at her would then look at *me* accusingly, like I hadn't been looking after her well enough.

'Put it back!' she yelled, grabbing the sweater from my hand, folding it lovingly and returning it to the trunk.

'That's right!' I said. 'Keep all your nice clothes away, wear only rags, *what sense does that make?'*

'But that's my going-out sweater, Gudda,' she said. 'I'm saving it for when we go out next.'

And where do you think you're going? I wanted to shout at her but didn't, because it struck me just then that the next time she went out it would probably be for her funeral.

Then she began pacing the floor at night with a pole in her hand, the extra long one you remove cobwebs with. She would thwack the sleeping servants who would let out blood-curdling screams. One night the screams didn't stop. Stumbling towards her room I found Lajo sitting on the ground in a pool of blood. Beatrice had smashed her nose. She was looming over her, white hair askew, looking like Oliver Cromwell. God knows how the mind works in a crisis because instead of doing something I stood there wracking my brain as to how I knew what Oliver Cromwell looked like.

That was the night I realized she hadn't been manipulating the cosmos at all; she was simply turning crazy. That was also the night I touched her after a long time. Didn't grab her shoulders and rattle her teeth which was more my style but placed my head against her bent and bony shoulder, stayed that way for a long time, smelling her old woman smells and feeling the bump of her ball and socket joint against the cartilage of my ear, the physical discomfort of it drowning out a growing fear that I was losing her.

At other times she wasn't crazy at all but hugely watchful, almost uncanny with her remarks. As if she'd pinned the whole world on to the wall in front of her bed with her gaze while the rest of us perceived it helter-skelter. A shrinking woman with a history as big as the universe, the history she wasn't telling, the only one who understood the mystery of history itself. How do I put the whole thing in perspective? *We* were the fumblers on that wall, the ones in a cosmic daze, Violet, Flora and I. I specially, rummaging around like a scavenger in the dustbin of that history. Trying to get to the source of Beatrice and at the same time making every attempt to get away from her.

One night *I* thwacked *Flora.* I woke up in the middle of the night to the sound of Beatrice shouting, the sound of a door being pounded, and I found that that miserable little sand dune had locked Beatrice into her room. The door had no key so she'd taken the trouble to drag a table from the living room to jam against the door and was refusing to let her out. Beatrice was terrified, falling into my arms when I let her out. She was trembling.

'Why did you do that, you stupid bitch?' I yelled at Flora.

'But she wasn't letting me sleep, Gudda, *what could I do,* she kept shining her torch on me when I kept telling her *I want to sleep, I HAVE A RIGHT TO SLEEP WHEN I AM FEELING SLEEPY.'*

So I picked up that pole and hit Flora in the legs with it, *I don't care what posterity will say of me.*

The Gang of Six took full advantage of what was happening to Beatrice. After establishing all sorts of powers of attorney which they needed since they weren't there themselves, they further conspired *with* Beatrice through those powers of attorney. I'm not sure Beatrice even knew what they made her sign every now and then. Sujata's papers always arrived by Diplomatc Bag which impressed Beatrice no end; she thought she was being called upon by the nation no less to sign. So *with* Beatrice they put a case on me for eviction. I told Ashwini I would like to sue them right back for not having paid me to be her nursemaid all those years but Ashwini said this wasn't the United States of America where people went around suing people for sitting down and standing up besides which, when they filed their case they also put a caveat in court barring me from suing them.

'What's a caveat?' I asked him. It was one of those words I knew but had long ago placed in a drawer called 'not needed' and thrown away the key. Ashwini explained and didn't explain. That was the pattern of things with him. I nodded constantly while he was talking, to encourage him to go on, but within a minute I'd lose the thread of what he was saying even though the speed of my nodding would increase and he would catch on because my follow-up question to him would be a dyslexic attempt to connect the pain in my heart with legalese. It was a hopeless mismatch of minds, exploited thoroughly by Ashwini who instead of attempting to come down to my level went higher and higher above my head and then suddenly even lower than me when he said things like *Relax, you don't need to understand, just leave it to me.*

Leave me the money and fuck off was what his demeanour gradually began to indicate and that money I lost track of. I paid and I paid and I paid. Lawyer's fees, court fees, stamp papers, affidavits, couriers, endless photocopying that even at Re 1 per page amounted to a fortune, touts that Ashwini claimed to have hired to push my papers through and then the mother of them all, 'out of pocket expenses'. Every time I tried to enquire what those were, Ashwini turned cold. At some point I toyed with the idea of suing *him* but I was too embroiled with him by then and it would have been like suing the devil after handing him all your suing equipment. He had all my originals with him, in a file he kept far from me—Beatrice's will, the perpetual lease deed of the house, ground rent receipts, property tax receipts, my passport etc. He had my whole life in that file. I was paranoid that if I dismissed him he wouldn't return that file to me. Or that he would sell it to the Gang of Six. I heard that lawyers do that sometimes. A friend said I could report him to the Bar Council if that happened, but he *was* the Bar Council, he was its secretary.

I didn't know what to do. By the time I realized I'd landed myself a lemon, a vast amount of money had gone down the drain and I had two choices before me: to cut my losses and run or hang on to Ashwini with the hope that, given my ignorance of legal procedure, it was I, not he, who was the idiot. Unfortunately I chose the former; in any case it was too late to choose the latter. I entered a terrible cycle of debt but I kept reminding myself that Beatrice's house would soon be mine and that the nightmare that Ashwini was spinning around me would soon be lifted, gone like those monsoon clouds that never actually break over Delhi, just cause a bit of darkness at noon and then float away to some derelict village where they descend like the Ganga, wipe off a thousand hapless souls or two. This is how I imagined calamity would strike, not quite over my own head.

Like a lot of old people, Beatrice grew addicted to signing, as if every time she signed she was announcing she was still alive. If there was too long a gap between papers she was asked to sign she invented some herself so that in the middle of that mess she wrote one more will making Malini, Sujata and Aditi co-owners of her house *during her lifetime,* with a codicil that *after her death* the house would come to me. Ashwini laughed when he saw those papers. 'What's this rubbish?' he said. Yes, it *was* rubbish, a combination of what Malini, Sujata and Aditi were trying to get her to do, her not wanting to anger them further and at the same time sticking to what she wanted to do. She stood Ashwini on his head. 'You know this is not even legal this rubbish,' he said but it multiplied his work and with it, my bills and my confusion.

What it also inadvertently did was cause Malini, Sujata, Aditi and me, out of sheer disgust and fatigue, to start speaking to each other again. A kinder soul than I would have credited Beatrice with some kind of genius for having orchestrated such a thing but the truth was different. Beatrice had always been a mischief-maker, revelling in creating differences between people, but now she was a *senile* mischief-maker who never understood half of what she was doing. In the process she sunk us to the greatest depths man can sink to, in which he carries on fraternizing with someone he's suing in a court of law, and this happens, I learnt later, especially with long-drawn-out cases. You divide yourself in two. Let your lawyer deal with the dirt, the plaintiff side of you, pretending all the while that you don't even know that devilish character in order to heap affection on the defendant. That was how things came to the astonishing pass that even while the three witches of Macbeth were boiling their terrible brew, I dropping into it the occasional lizard, I suddenly found myself calling them up to ask them whether they knew anything at all about Dahirya, or if they remembered anyone, apart from Maddy, from the days of their youth who might.

Of course they knew the past somewhat, not that I hadn't known throughout that they did because they had Hakra clearly inscribed on their birth certificates, but who said to me that when they could hardly visualize Delhi any more how did I expect them to remember a mofussil town in the back of beyond? They were too little, they said, but I also suspected they suffered from that other sort of amnesia, different from Beatrice's, the one that was exposed when Sujata expressed her rage at those photos of tribals splashed all over the media, her terrible fear of someone thinking she was one of them, someone not seeing the high-class Rajput bark under her exfoliated skin. They didn't want to remember the past. They didn't want to be associated with the dregs of society.

One day though, a year and a half after that case began, Sujata relented, after which she got carried away. 'We'll make a film, can you just see it?' she said to me on the phone.

Me: No.

Sujata: We'll get a crew together, a cameraman, I know one cameraman.

Me: What'll the film be about?

Sujata: Us…the family…the old warrior clan…the stupid Brits…

Me: Warriors? I thought you said we were bandits…

Sujata (*Angrily*): Yes, yes, and you can do all the research, I'll handle production.

Me: And how d'you propose to film something that's disappeared? Who'll you get to play the Brits? Tom Alter? And where the fuck is Dahirya?

Sujata: This isn't a joke, Gudda. How can a whole village walk off just like that? Anyway, haven't you heard of stock footage? We'll get Skinner's Horse sort of riding past in clouds of dust and then through those clouds we'll sort of zoom in to a close-up, a face, somebody's face, a relative's face, a Rajput warrior's face. That's how we'll begin, can you just see it? Or maybe the house where Mama lived...it was a beautiful house...

Me: But Skinner's Horse wasn't even around then. And whenever it was, it was somewhere else.

Sujata: Well you know what I mean. Whoever there was if it wasn't Skinner's Horse. You do the research, I know nothing about history.

Me: Neither do I.

Very long silence

Me: Why do you want to make a film in the first place?

Even longer silence

No, Sujata wasn't trying to help me at all. She was intrigued by the possibility of a last-ditch attempt at manufacturing a rolling pin to hit India on the head with the next time it humiliated her. No small bonus would be a mint-fresh view of her world on a platter. Never mind if it upturned mine, sent me on a wild goose chase, for by the time that happened Sujata would have grown bored of the whole game and would be spinning some brand-new yarn about having known all along that that psychotic, ancestor-worshipping sister of hers would one day fall off the edge of the world.

Such was my bewilderment and guilt at this unforeseen twist to our relationship that I never mentioned those calls to Ashwini. I didn't fully understand lawyers. Later I learnt lawyers are used to such infidelity in clients but then at that time I thought he would fall apart in contempt of me. I also thought that with all that *Don't talk to me you bitch, talk to my lawyer* that had gone on between them and me, it was illegal for me to be talking to them at all. Miranda loomed over me Hollywood-style. Anything I said to anyone those days—to lawyers, to bitches, even to Beatrice—could and would, I thought, be held against me in a court of law. Just like the relationship between Ashwini and me, my right to remain silent and my desire to speak weren't coinciding at all.

How can someone who's disappearing assume the dimensions of a colossus? How can your house, so full of sounds, turn into a chilling void? On account of Beatrice's dementia Dahirya began to recede into the distance, and in the face of the power breakdowns that summer *everything* began to appear futile. Those breakdowns didn't bother Beatrice at all; she lay on her bed fanning herself with her hand fan, looking triumphant—not those Japanese ones but those cheap reed ones shaped like a Neanderthal butcher's axe.

Our invertor stopped functioning because its batteries didn't get a long enough period to recharge so most often we lived with one dim light and a fan that you could have moved faster had you stood on a stool and turned its blades around yourself. When I suggested to Beatrice that we get ourselves a generator she was outraged and so I told her I was getting one for myself, for the ground floor, and this declaration that my life was separate from hers turned what could have been passed off as another bit of family flotsam into full-scale war. Such are the complications life heaps on you when your days are empty and your nights spent chasing mosquitoes in the dark.

'Move that thing from the staircase!' was how it began, the first time I switched it on. I had fixed 'that thing' in the stairwell thinking that if I put it in the front or at the back of the house

she would have to run around shutting a whole lot of doors and windows to avoid the noise. *'The whole house vibrates, my head vibrates like an earthquake, I cannot sleep. Move it!'* she screamed and I saw that inadvertently I had found something in the world that could drown out her voice, the sound of her pissing, the *smell* of her pissing, for the diesel fumes that emanated from the generator first smothered the stairwell and then slowly permeated through every crack in the house.

'What?' I shouted back at her from the courtyard, knowing full well what she was saying but my rage against her had achieved awesome dimensions by then and the thought of her swirling round and round like a whirling dervish with her fingers in her ears brought joy to my heart.

It was vicious, it was moronic and it was followed by deep remorse. Precisely at the same time she was overcome by defeat but never being one to admit so, she twisted it around to appear like she wasn't past compromise. She quietly got Lajo and Ram Bhajan to shift her things to the room at the back of the house. Simultaneously, I shifted the generator to the back too, neither of us aware of what the other had done and so that night when the electricity went off I turned the generator on and a few seconds later a piercing shriek ran through the house. She was leaning over the courtyard railings in her nightie, screaming like the house was on fire. *'Put it off, put it off, PUT IT OFF!'*

'What is it now Mama?' I looked up wearily.

'How dare you,' she screamed. *'You have put it right below my bedroom. Do you want me to die? Are you trying to kill me? Do you want me to have a heart attack? I cannot breathe, those horrible smells are coming straight on to my bed. PUT IT OFF!'*

'That is not your bedroom,' I said, 'your bedroom is in the front side.'

'No, no, no, it is not, it is now in the back side!' and so the next day I shifted the generator to the front of the house and she

screamed about not being able to sit in her drawing room any more and that was how that war was conducted, that was why she hid the electricity bill when it came and that was how she won because a few weeks later two men from DESU came and cut our connections off and the whole house was plunged in darkness.

Of course she denied it, pretended she had never seen the bill and I was on the verge of believing her when I found it, scrunched under her mattress in the same spot where she'd hidden Anand's letters. So I stopped talking to her. Meanwhile I did the needful, three trips to DESU where the lifts never worked, a dozen applications to restore the electricity, addressing the clerks as Sir, telling them things like *My sick old mother will die* and finally bribing them an arm and a leg from my meagre savings.

Every time I saw Beatrice's face those days I wanted to come out with a string of abuses which was why I decided that it was far better that I cease to speak. But throughout that period she followed me around, sick as she was, upstairs downstairs, room to room, using every trick in the book to make me open my mouth. She never knocked, entered slam-on, so I began locking the downstairs door but she would get Ram Bhajan to climb over the railings and open it for her, he would let her loose on me behind my back, and this happened again and again and I began to wonder whether this was what was happening, whether it was a law-and-order situation, that Ram Bhajan had no respect left for me or whether Beatrice possessed powers that let her enter through shut doors.

'As God is my witness...' she began one morning.

I was standing in front of the refrigerator when she crept up behind me. In the brief second before turning around I toyed with the idea of falling in, locking myself in. She was closer to me than was tolerable. Her armpits and the plateau between her breasts stank. Her faded blue dressing gown had papita stains on it and her sleeves were rimmed with dirt.

'As God is my witness…' she began again.

'God will never be your witness!' I turned around screeching, banging the refrigerator door shut, side stepping her quickly before she touched me. After days of silence the sound of my own screech frightened me and I turned to run, just as her hand shot forward to grip my arm.

'Leave me alone!' I screamed, taking huge strides towards my bedroom door, catching a glimpse of her disordered, undignified mien as I turned to shut it.

'Open the door!' she shouted. *'Listen to me!'* The sound of her arthritic knuckles hitting wood made my face pound. I stepped backwards, staring at the door in horror. Then I walked up to my bed, picked up my pillow and covered my face.

She continued knocking, a persistent, even-paced *tak tak tak*, on and on, and then suddenly she stopped. I put the pillow aside. I heard the sound of the front door opening and a few seconds later, the sound of her ascending the stairs, her plastic slippers going flip-*chipak*-flop. I examined my middle finger. The flesh had got caught in the door. I sucked at it. I debated whether to open the door or not. She was capable of simulating an exit while standing behind the door silently. I stood staring at the door a long time, trying to sense her presence when I felt a movement near the floor. A slip of paper was emerging through the gap. I recognized her spidery old-woman scrawl. *Gudda,* the note began:

> *Please believe and have that much faith in me that I will never NEVER lie to you. You have got it all wrong and in your emotional way shouted at me when I am neither guilty nor evil as you call me, I am old and confused in my memory. I can NEVER NEVER EVER do this thing you accuse me of. I am sad and grieved over the misunderstanding, so forget. I am leaving the amount you have spent on those electrician cheats on the dining table. Please*

come up as soon as you can because I would like to show you my finger. I suspect cancer.

I wish I could say that I wept. I wish I could give the impression I had a shred of humanity left in me but my heart felt like flint that summer and if I began talking to her it wasn't because I forgave her but because it came to me that there was nothing to forgive.

It was a day I look back on now as the beginning of the end, not just in terms of one woman's rite of passage but of a larger history, the one that fits all the small stories into the big one, the one that tells you when the harvest's done and when it's time for you to pick up your little bundle of hay and wend your way home.

Except that I had already done that, I was already home.

Not Mugair, not Hakra, not Dahirya – *this* was my home.

But it no longer felt like home, with Ashwini on my head it felt like a piece of real estate and since I had already been feeling I had no country either, it was as if there was nothing left.

The newspapers didn't belie that, for even as the most powerful Christian in the world, George Bush, began smoking Muslims out of their holes in Afghanistan, the Krantikari Manuvadi Morcha emerged in India to send Christians diving deeper into theirs. It was around then that Dara Singh announced his intention of entering the assembly election fray from Muzaffarnagar and Ghaziabad. It didn't matter that he was the prime accused in the murder of Graham Staines. The KMM saw nothing wrong with that. As far as they were concerned the man was a hero. Jhabua, meanwhile, was back in the news with three lakh tribals congregating at a Hindu Mahasangam. Their purpose: to force the forward-inching foot soldiers of Christ into retreat. The Rapid Action Force, the Special Armed Force and about 1500 additional security personnel were being mobilized to protect the thirteen lakh Hindus against the lakh-odd Christians in the district. And what about the four nuns who'd been raped there some years before? One newspaper referred to them as 'The Nowhere People', something *I'd* become, 'unfit now for both the outside world and the world in which they lived.' A nine-year-old girl was brutally raped that season, strangled in a toilet within a church compound. The RSS declared it was Christian priests who had done it so along with the Mahasangam, rallies were out to protest against the very existence of churches.

The house by the nala had moved on to another plane by then, a cross between the sci-fi and the metaphysical, Violet and Flora reading or watching the news and then running to Beatrice's bedside excitedly to report the latest atrocity, Beatrice not caring so much about the individual incidents as the fact that the signs were growing, of Christ's Second Coming. The imminent Rapture. It was the Rapture she was particularly enamoured of, the rising up into the skies of the born-again, the not rising up of the rest upon whom would visit a fate as terrible as Hiroshima, Chernobyl and Bhopal combined. Sometimes I worried about the Rapture too, just in case there was a one per cent chance Beatrice wasn't making it up, and it was a terrifying thought, waking up one morning and finding myself alone in that house with Beatrice, Flora and Violet perched high on a cloud each. It was a pretty neat way to die actually, so when I thought of it like that it wasn't terrifying but consoling because Beatrice would then never have to take that horrible thing called the dying breath, I would be spared the sound of her death rattle, of picking her up in her growing smallness and placing her inside a coffin and sometimes I wondered if Beatrice was scared too which was why she was hoping the Rapture would happen soon, why she had begun looking almost pleased every time someone gave her terrible news.

There was the morning I found the three of them poring over *Tehelka*, a photo of six bald Oriya women captioned 'Fanatics enforce their agenda with brute force'. The heads of the women had been shaved because they had refused to reconvert to Hinduism.

'The end is nigh, sister,' said Flora.

'Praise God,' was Beatrice's response, both hands held up to the sky.

Women on the Moon

Winter came and went, summer returned and with it that bunch of women creating all sorts of *gadar*, subtexts. After that furore about the generator the question arose as to what speed the fans should be. Beatrice didn't like ceiling fans, even in summer. Maids who look after old women do. There was a perpetual battle on between Beatrice and Lajo over the issue. Flora was on Lajo's side and so was Violet. I, growingly, was on my side alone except that equally growingly I didn't seem to have one.

'Remove that rubber band!' Beatrice shouted at Lajo one day. It was a blinding fluorescent yellow and Lajo purposely wore it to irritate Beatrice. A girl with *one* garment, *one* rubber band that she wore day in and day out, god knows if she ever changed her knickers. She danced off, out of the door into the corridor singing, as if her flippancy would create a vacuum between her and Beatrice wherein Beatrice would diffuse.

'What's wrong with her rubber band?' I said.

'Feeling *hot hot hot*,' said Violet.

'You're very modern,' I said, swinging around, 'knowing such songs!'

'What song?' said Violet, looking bewildered.

'What song?' said Beatrice, getting up—ever since the wedding got over she had been perpetually getting up and sitting down or sitting down and then standing up again for no rhyme or reason. She swooped into a deep dark corner of her cupboard, emerged with two of those Neanderthal fans, handed one to Flora and they both started fanning themselves vigorously. It was a miracle *something* moved, with all the farting that old women do you couldn't be sure it was plain air. Violet, meanwhile, lay ignored on her bed, an Egyptian mummy embalmed in sweat.

Flora said to me, 'So was there electricity last night?'

'Wasn't there?' I said, trying to remember how it was last night. My intelligence quotient had reached an all-time low, you couldn't get me to fit two Montessori blocks together.

'How would I know,' the Egyptian mummy spoke, looking up at the fan and down at Beatrice sarcastically. *'How would I know?'*

Beatrice looked guilty. 'You can put on the fan if you like, Vylit,' she said, 'but then cover me with a sheet.' Hearing this, Lajo danced back into the room and lunged for the switchboard. Not only did she put the fan on but she turned the regulator full throttle. Ancient as that house was, it was the sound of walnuts being cracked open with a door hinge. Beatrice sat bolt upright. *'Why did you do that stupid girl?'*

'You only said put it on.'

'But did I tell you to make it faster idiot?' So Lajo turned the regulator round again. This time to zero.

'Can I recite *Daffodils*?' said Flora, fanning herself vigorously, not happy that Violet knew a song.

'Yes *please*,' I smiled at her.

But a sparrow entered the room just then and had the cheek to brush past Flora's shoulder. 'That sparrow sat on my shoulder! What kinds of birds are these?' she exclaimed.

'Never mind, Flora,' said Beatrice. 'When a bird sits on you it's lucky.'

'Not sits, *shits*,' said Violet.

'Gaali kyon bak rahi ho?' said Beatrice.

After two minutes Flora asked again, 'Now can I recite *Daffodils?*'

'No!' said Beatrice.

'Then can I tell a joke from *Reader's Digest*?'

'Okay,' said Beatrice.

'In *Reader's Digest* I read that there are three words you should never *never* say.'

'What?' I said.

'One is No.'

'And...?'

'The other is Yes.'

'Jaldi jaldi bolo, Flora,' said Beatrice impatiently.

'WHAT'S THE THIRD ONE?' I said.

Flora went into deep contemplation. 'I forgot,' she said.

Beatrice and I looked at each other. 'So how's it a joke?' I asked.

'Pagli,' said Beatrice to Flora.

I looked around me at the room. For the wedding I'd spruced up the house a bit—new Bombay Dyeing bed sheets, faux cut-glass glasses from INA Market—but like Cinderella's coach it had gone back to being a pumpkin. The curtains needed dry-cleaning. Up along the pleats were little soft clumps of white floss. The carpet too had acquired a patina—it was almost artistic if you looked at it in a certain way. Gently deepening in colour towards the edges where nobody stepped. One of those thin, inexpensive wall-to-wall affairs that look grand in the beginning and then suddenly die on you. Somewhere in the middle of that carpet at an angle was a tiny fifty-rupee Dilli Haat rug that I had placed to hide a stain. Patchwork everywhere. No permanent solutions. Even the walls had pictures where they clearly shouldn't have been, hiding some mark or the other. Or hiding an old nail from which another picture of another size had hung earlier. Layers upon layers of life in that palimpsest of pain. The smell of pain. Even those curtains stiff with pain.

I tried to create some new smells that summer—the whiff of manure, freshly sliced bamboo, newly mowed grass. I began spending more and more time in the garden. I even stole Natasha's wrought-iron chairs one day, repainted them green and arranged them in a semi-circle to make it appear that I had reason to seat myself here and there to some end or purpose. Sit here and then sit there and then have a nimboo pani and then lie down and then go upstairs to see if Beatrice was still alive and then come downstairs and again sit here or there. So many options, so many ways to move myself round and around to stop from thinking. Those chairs were small payment for what Natasha had done and indeed an unwanted reminder of her but in the face of all those legal goings-on, I slowly became deadened to everything else but that lawyer and for some odd reason, that garden. The garden and I became one. The maali would arrive every morning and by then I would have examined each leaf of every plant lovingly, readying myself to instruct him to cut this, pare that, water this, shift that and I would go to the extent of saying that that garden kept me from dying, dying before even Beatrice who I was beginning to believe would live forever. I *wanted* her to live forever, one of the reasons being that as long as she was there the Gang of Six would keep their distance from me. I couldn't bury my face in her pleats, sobbing, like I used to but figuratively it was the same thing—as long as she lived, I lived too.

But sometimes, only sometimes, I had a thought of stealing the maali's cycle when he wasn't looking and winging away down that road with a lump of manure on my head, allowing myself the well-earned luxury of going mad and, with it, the licence to abandon Beatrice. But I loved that garden and who knows, perhaps I loved her too along with that ugly house I was fighting tooth and nail for, none of which ideas stayed with me beyond those fleeting moments when my bare feet or my hands were in touch with the good earth.

It was long due, a sense of despair, and it was something to do with the view from the drawing room window as well, of the security guard I had hired. It was so hard to accept that I had had to do this in my own country. It called for a building of imaginary worlds within existing ones and somewhere in that twilight zone of helplessness, fear and sadness, I found myself reaching for Iqbal before I had found him, for pieces of a jigsaw puzzle that were growing increasingly into a picture at odds with the one in front of me. Was it too late to stick someone's shadow back on them? How do you abandon the living for one who might be dead?

A thought came to me that I could take advantage of the rivalry between Flora and Violet, exploit that old British policy of divide and rule. Both Flora and Violet felt they had first claim to Beatrice, Violet having known her much longer than Flora and Flora being related to her by blood. Earlier I'd been afraid to leave Beatrice with either one of them alone but with the *get out*-s having stopped and Violet staying on since the wedding to protect her turf, I realized I had *two* bodyguards for Beatrice, both keeping an eye on each other, if only to outwit each other but in the process hovering over Beatrice like two hawks after the same piece of meat. By default, what could go too wrong with Beatrice behind my back?

But even if I left, where was I going? I tried to pin Beatrice down, in the same manner as Sujata had got her to transfer her fixed deposits in her name before she died. It wasn't nice on the whole, that *quickly-quickly* rummaging through the vault of an old woman's memories, never minding the woman herself, only the memories, dragging them across the chasm between past and present without a bridge to sustain their existence. It struck me that I was worse than Sujata who took only FDs.

But on account of the Gentamycin Beatrice's hearing had grown worse. Was she losing her hearing or was she overplaying her deafness to fend off a changing world? If you asked her a question, she'd reply to entirely another.

Me: Do you remember Dahirya at all?
Beatrice: You want to distemper the wall?

Or, whenever she chose to hear,

Me: Where were you born Mama?
Beatrice: Hakra, how many times to tell you!
Me: Where were your mother and father born?
Beatrice: How do I know?
Me: How can you not know?
Beatrice: I'm telling you Hakra. *Everyone* was born in Hakra… at least it seemed so then.
Me: You mean now. It seems so *now.*
Beatrice: *Then, now,* what's the difference?

What's the difference...history was an accordion whose pleats you pressed whenever you chose to sing your song. It was anything you wanted it to be—a giant cobweb, chinks of light from curtains drawn hurriedly, the swiftest passage of a mouse up a rafter, an old rag doll you kept in your cupboard for those comfortless days…

This time I didn't lie to her, I simply didn't tell her I was going, slipped out the door at dawn with my suitcase, whispering into Flora's ear that Maddy was ill and was calling for me. It was cruel of me, but I had to get away. If I hadn't I would have disintegrated completely.

Once on the train I tried to clear my tired mind, recall why and where I was going. It all began with Beatrice announcing that everyone was dead, Iqbal was dead, followed by the announcement that I was dead for her, she for me, I thinking that if the alive and kicking could be dead, the truly dead must be alive, they *had* to be alive or the whole universe would be dead. This was followed by those knickers telling everyone that Christians, both dead and alive, were traitors to the land, and since they couldn't get the dead they said let's lynch the living, burn them alive, so even if Beatrice had rewritten her will and breathed life back into *me* by then, I still needed the dead to tell me what they had done to make the RSS hate us so much, in the middle of which I found the letter from Andrew that made me believe Iqbal was alive, and that a house in the desert belonged to me, so even though the dead had confirmed to me by then that much more than Beatrice, it was the RSS who feared they would turn into pillars of salt if they looked back at the history of their country, I still had to look for Iqbal and that house, never mind that the house had been taken over by a military man with a moustache and four killer dogs because by then Malini–Sujata–Aditi had taken my breath away. Let's set the clock right, they said, wipe the slate clean by bringing Beatrice's house down, she's about to die anyway, build builder's apartments with marble floors in place of that moth-eaten house, until the whole business began to reek of loss and I should have told them what Wilma and that Bhil woman in her pastel blue sari had amply demonstrated by then, *what happens to you if you wipe the slate clean,* the past is the skin you're wearing, without it you might as well have been dumped into the world from a passing train and if your ancestors had gone and sold their land, their camels and their mansions you'd never find out where that train came from, spend your life wandering in and out of small-town stations in search of them by which time they'd gone in the opposite direction to bury one life and start another except that in the new India no one could understand them for by that time and in all that wandering they'd lost it all, their headdress, their rain-dance, had no watermark if you held them up to the clear light of reason, so *sell the house only if you're truly hungry some day,* who needs knickers when there are suicidal women like you around willing to lynch your own skin, but I never said it because in the midst of looking for Iqbal I never fully understood why I was fighting over Beatrice's house, I remember thinking that if that house came down we'd have nothing left, *nothing,* but where that connected with those marble graves I saw in Hakra, I'm not sure, I kept wondering that just like those old men in knickers who thought they could rewrite the history of India, maybe Malini–Sujata–Aditi were rewriting the Bible, turning *dust to dust* into *marble to marble*...

The Third Journey

I saw myself as a mere observer, properly distanced by time and relationship, solving a puzzle. Now, strangely, I see myself drawn in, by a gravitational force, pulled into the story.

—*The Book of Secrets*

The number of houses abandoned by the British in 1947 would be legion. While those in the bigger cities were bought over legally or taken over by the government, many in small towns like Hakra went unnoticed. People just moved into them. Those houses passed on to the next generation and the next and by then the people living in them had cultivated a proprietary air about them that made it hard for anyone to question them. The six colonial bungalows at Bethlehem Square for instance are now occupied by the converts' descendants, the ones Hubert and Co. called 'riff-raff'. They act like their great-grandfathers' great-grandfathers owned them.

But the case of Grace Place is different. How different I'm not sure, and of course I know there's no way I can recover its fans, furniture or dinner sets now but the house itself, I tell myself, lying in Maddy's house looking up at the ceiling, might be worth fighting for. I could ask Ashwini about it. I leap out of bed for pen and paper. I start writing him a letter, more to clarify things to myself. I try and explain the situation. It's the conclusion that stumps me: '...*As you will see from the attached letter my granduncle Andrew wrote to my mother, the matter is a hopeless one from the legal point of view. I am wondering now whether it is possible to bend the law somewhat—I would be willing to cheat, lie, bribe, commit a bloody crime, end up in jail...*' but this isn't the way to address a lawyer. I am horrified at my childishness. Ashwini's a two-timing bastard. I'd always suspected that in the matter of Beatrice's house he'd sell me to the enemy eventually, make money from both sides. By asking him for help on Grace Place I could be playing right into his hands. I can see him now, both of us seated in a courtroom surrounded by mahogany walls and whispers and sisters. *'And now m'lord,'* he says, waving my letter around, *'I will prove to you that my client with her innocent face has a diabolical mind, that she is capable of cheating, lying, bribing, committing a bloody crime...I hereby present Exhibit A.'*

I tear the letter to shreds.

I am angry. How dare Maddy not point Grace Place out to me? Why does everyone around here obfuscate, skim over things, deliberately deceive? She finally admitted last night that Dahirya existed but 'there's nothing up there' she keeps repeating like a drone, 'no roads,' as if I'd expected any. Beatrice had always done that sort of thing too but hers was another reason, an emotional one in which she'd obliterated a whole world in order to be able to survive the new one. But here they all appear to be deliberately creating some kind of hierarchical disorder now. Hubert's betrayal of them, his attempt to rise above his station through Rose's bootlicking of the English, their own struggle to survive has something to do with it. Grace Place is seen by them now as *their* own memories of a golden age, never mind who among the clan actually owned the house. That's a petty detail. That's no longer a petty detail when Hubert's granddaughter comes snooping.

Is there a law against people distorting your history? Stealing your dinner sets and ceiling fans? Acting like your house doesn't exist, like your father doesn't exist? I'm leaving for Hakra again, not Bethlehem Square but Old Hakra. I don't want Maddy to come with me so I tell her I'm off to Jaipur, then in case she's watching me from some invisible watchtower with a pair of binoculars I make Babu actually take the road to Jaipur, then two miles down take a U-turn and get back on the Mugair–Hakra highway.

Old Hakra begins where the highway ends, right after the bus stop. I hang around at the bus stop, trying to imagine my drunk, despairing father waiting for a bus but I can't because it's such a beehive of activity, buses taking off every few minutes for Mugair and beyond. Through the mayhem of conductors ululating and banging the sides of buses to announce their departure and other buses rolling in through clouds of dust, the people on the tea stall benches look like a study in still life, due maybe to the enormous size of the brightly coloured safas of the men who sip their tea and smoke their bidis, hands moving back and forth without their heads moving in conjunction, a phenomenon unique to Rajasthan and owing to the weight of those safas that render the heads beneath them immobile. Even the humblest of them looks like a king in this stance, bare legs under their muslin dhotis crossed at the knees like women, elaborately embroidered and sequinned mojris on their feet like Sinbad's boats adrift.

Babu accompanies me on foot into the old town. Beyond a point cars can't go as there's just one main lane here with a bazaar on either side, a sea of people choking the lane to make it appear narrower than it is, bright pink, yellow and olive green safas bobbing up and down in their midst, some turbaned fellows cruising along the lane on mobikes, fancy goggles on, gold earrings glinting in the sun. In between the old shops are posh new ones with shining linoleum counters behind which father, son and probably uncle or brother-in-law sit in a row, gleaming white teeth (Rajputs have good teeth), panels of gleaming taps behind them, white ceramic pots and sinks.

Old Hakra was once connected through trade with the sixteenth-century commercial mart of Bhilwara. Its character today is a cross between that of a medieval village and a trading depot but as its two faces are not separated geographically you can't get a full sense of things as they were, or perhaps that's the way they always were, but it's a matter of lingering doubt because there are parts that look like they've come out of a blurred watercolour painting and then less than fifty yards away the harsh overwrought lines of workshops, where old train compartments from Mugair Junction are being hammered and reshaped into doors and windows, speak a different story—a puzzle of mismatching parts of varying vintage that no one seems to question, they simply flow with the tide, moving among cyclists, cows, vendors in happy disharmony.

Deep in the interior stand the old havelis of the merchants of Hakra and though they aren't more than three storeys at the most they loom like skyscrapers in relation to the width of the cobbled paths that lead to them. Life would have been different here before the British came, those havelis hiding women from the world, the sudden intrusion of male guests sending them hurtling into the zenana from where they peeped at them through fretted windows. In between these fairytale-like houses are ugly new ones, some doubling up as hardware and bicycle repair shops, while some havelis aren't really havelis any more because they've given up their terraces, newly constructed rooms balancing on top of old ones. One of them is painted sugar pink and green, railings above embellished with round copper medallions engraved with a portrait of Queen Elizabeth, the same profile you see on English postage stamps.

The bazaar has eaten up most of the demarcating spaces that would have existed once so you can hardly identify the courthouse-cum-post office complex until you're virtually upon it, giving you a feel of having chanced upon a lost aquatint in a mossy godown smelling of piss. Encroachments everywhere, you'd say if you were an Englishman and looking at it the other way round, new walls growing out of old ones including a shiny black granite statue of Mahatma Gandhi in front of the courthouse, layers upon layers of history choking each other to death. Notionally, if not in scale, the courthouse is Hakra's Buckingham Palace. In the calculations of the British was there a terrible misconception as to the significance of Hakra in the imperial scheme of things, or, was Hakra more important once than anyone remembers? What's a magnificent piece of England doing in the heart of a medieval Rajput town? It's the same air that all small towns taken over by the British bear—Batala, Meerut, Lakhimpur, Bareilly, Jabalpur, Jullunder, Jhansi, Beawar and more—all testimony to that odd historicus interruptus, buildings with domes and pillars, arches and porticoes, built along roads and around squares, quite charming when viewed on their own but juxtaposed with the chaotic Indian way, conveying the sense of a bully having rampaged through land that belonged to somebody else, snuffing out its life breath.

I look for the Drummond General Hospital where Grandmother Rose used to work, the one where nobody took Dora. It's along a narrow lane not far from the courthouse and standing on that lane you can't tell whether the hospital came first or the ugly hardware shops all around but it must have been the hospital because it has on either side of it large windows in an attitude of permanent shock as if they'd expected to look out into the blue yonder. They're tightly shut, bolts jammed with disuse, green casement curtains drawn, but as you enter the hospital you see that none of this double barricading keeps out the constant hammering and sawing from the workshops that eventually balances itself out against the slow whirring of hospital fans, slung low on creaking stems that sway drunkenly over airless rooms. It's like everything else in Hakra that appears to balance itself out against something else and this is the charm if you can see it, old against new, ancient havelis against new houses whose windows and doors smell of train compartments, those buses back on the highway rolling in through clouds of dust against old men on benches frozen in time, the white heat of the sun against the cool of the desert nights, the hospital beating its own brave rhythm against the dying heartbeat of an ancient town.

Babu asks me if I'd like to see the railway station. I never knew there was one. I thought Mugair was it. So we circumambulate the old town to its remote end where a small yellow-washed single-storeyed building stands amidst a dry field, quite isolated from the bustle of the bazaar and looking no more important than somebody's house. A single metre-guage track, a single platform along which half a dozen people stand, no urgency about them, no sense of waiting for a train, as if they'd been standing there forever. Could they be here to kill time? Do people still exist on earth who have fun watching trains arrive on platforms? This is how railway stations should be. One window, one sleepy head framed by that window, all the time in the world to be pleasant while answering a question or giving you a ticket. I hang around the platform for a while pretending I have a train to catch. The names of destinations are written in chalk in Hindi on a blackboard. I don't recognize them...*Chaupat Khamb, Bagri, Indauliya*...despair washes over me. Where is Dahirya? Even the station master hasn't heard the name.

I am tired and hungry. We return to the highway, to the bus stop where I look for a bonda. I'm standing at a dhaba, the ashes of history flying all about me, I feel I'm choking on them and then it happens so fast. I ask the dhabawallah where Ranigaon is, whether he knows where Larens Sahb's hunting lodge used to be once upon a time.

'Udhar,' he says, pointing every which way towards the ring of low hills that surround Hakra.

'Udhar kidhar?' I say, not really paying attention. I am simply making conversation, trying to distract myself from the desire to faint. 'Anyway it's not there any more,' I say.

And he says, *'Kyon nahin bai, bilkul hai!'*

Disbelieving, I confirm and reconfirm this with him and then wrapping my bonda hastily in a piece of newspaper, I look around for Babu. He's a few dhabas away, sipping tea. I call out to him, tell him to try and understand what the man means, wave to him to hurry up.

We take the road to Doom Dooma. Within minutes Hakra recedes and fallow fields begin, in between sudden inexplicable patches of lush green. An hour down the road Babu swerves to the right abruptly and plunges straight into a wheat field, into wheat stalks growing higher than the taxi. An involuntary scream escapes me. I fear Babu's lost control of the wheel until I realize we're on a narrow dirt path running right through the fields. The path is bumpy but Babu doesn't slow down; he negotiates clutch and brake superbly with those floppy half-chappals of his and I hang on for life as we plunge and rise and gallop and shudder our way through those fields, dry brown stalks sweeping the windows, wheatdust turning the windshield and windows opaque.

As suddenly as they'd begun the wheat fields end and we're in wide-open space. I lower my window, Babu lowers his, as I turn around to marvel at how we emerged from that giant clutch of wheat intact. All signs of civilization have disappeared. In the hazy distance are the Aravali, dark and low and brooding here, the sky above without a single cloud, like a scene painted by a child without the skills to create nuances. Flat and blank, yet terrifyingly eternal as if time itself began here, light years ago. There isn't a soul in sight, no farmers with aquiline features or safas, no women swishing along in colourful ghagras, only a terrible emptiness in which not a bird chirps, not a leaf stirs, there are no leaves here, only gnarled branches like overgrown bonsai full of silent, deadly thorns. For miles around nothing but an endless barren landscape.

My back hurts. 'How long more do you think?' I say to Babu.

'We're here,' he replies and that could mean anything, for Babu has no concept of time, I've discovered, but I ask him anyway because words seem necessary to break the silence we've entered, a ritual to stir those skies and those thorns to speak, to acknowledge our existence. I turn away from the window and look through the windshield and that's when I see it, a greystone bombed-out shell of a structure in the distance, the vista and the structure appearing to have grown through time to resemble each other, a joining of hearts through shared isolation so that even the outline of the lodge creates hardly a blemish against the sky. Gigantic weeds growing along the boundary wall, one thorny babool leaning against a broken arch. Babu parks six feet away. I get off the car, he swipes the rug off the seat, follows me to the boundary wall where he spreads it out to form a seat. There is compassion in his gesture. It dignifies my sitting on a broken wall looking at an abandoned house.

I try and imagine how Hubert would have conducted his days and nights in this wilderness but it's all a blank. I get off the wall and walk the four steps up to the porch, straining my ears for sounds, for sudden movements. In the quiet of the desert a footfall is magnified a thousand times. A lizard falls pat at my feet, stares at me with its chinless face and marble eyes. Who knows, there might be snakes. Or go-s. On the wall of the porch is an orange palm, the Congress logo. Below it the words 'Vote for Makhan Lal'. Above the logo, cleaving to the roof, a large conical beehive, alive and buzzing. I swivel around on my heel, taking in the roof, the floor, the wall, the broken arches together in the manner of someone making a survey, hiding from myself the truth that I am afraid. One eye on the beehive, I lower myself on the top stair and survey the garden. It's a virus of nettles. They appear to be stacked in dead clumps but that's the way they grow here, hiding their roots, tumbling over themselves in haste. You could kill a man by throwing him face down on one, pick him up with a deliberate jerk so he leaves his eyeballs behind, impaled on those thorns like two shivering hors d'oeuvres.

Dusting my behind I pluck up the courage to enter the house. There are no doors or windows here. Probably stolen a long time ago, making this a house literally blowing in the wind. The ceiling appears strong though, there's no seepage, only splatter marks beneath the spaces where those windows once were. The walls are covered with graffiti, vulgar words, hearts pierced by arrows, Rakesh loves Sonia, assorted penises and breasts. High up are the old marks of mounts ripped off, on which heads of deer or nilgai might have hung. Two large rooms stand side by side, a fireplace each, back to back. On either side, smaller rooms, all with arched entrances, one arch split by a branch of the oleander that blooms within the house luxuriantly. Nature has reclaimed this forgotten house and it's I, not the oleander, who intrudes. It's a small lodge on the whole, barely a two-minute walkthrough but it smells of monument, of old parchment, of a hidden river flowing through its veins. At one end is a bathroom. I know it's a bathroom from its sloping floor, a drainage dyke leading to the outside but apart from this there are no taps, nothing in it. Everything has been stolen.

At the rear of the house an exposed stairway leads to the roof. Several steps are missing. Entwining the strap of my handbag around my neck and under my armpits to form a rucksack I start climbing on all fours. There's no other way to negotiate those terrifying spaces. I arrive at the roof from where I look around hesitantly for I am unused to horizons. The sun is a burnt orange ball. A hundred yards, two hundred, four hundred, the miles fly past in a haze, stunted acacia, tamarix and zizyphus against that ochre landscape, the colours and hues of this vast wasteland to a herd of nilgai in the distance, beyond the nilgai a dry lake bed, the bitter dregs of old marshland. I take a step backwards as I see Babu below looking around for me. He hasn't seen me climbing.

I look down at my feet to regain my balance. The floor of the roof is dark and grainy. I bend down and touch the old stone with my palm and then I lie down and press my cheek to it, stretch my arms out on both sides to enfold the house, the sleep coming upon me akin to death.

Four a.m. I come down the stairs clutching on to the broken wall. I see Babu asleep in the car on the back seat. I poke his leg. He looks annoyed. He'd looked for me all over, he blusters, thought I'd wandered off in the dark until he discovered I was up on the roof. 'Are we ready to return?' he asks.

'We're not returning just yet,' I say. 'We're going into the mountains.'

He is disbelieving. 'Which mountains?' he says.

We return to the highway first. A single dhaba is open at that hour from which we get tea, a packet of glucose biscuits, a jug of water and a half-used soap to freshen up with. I try and understand from the dhabawallah the layout of the hills surrounding Hakra. He tells me if I'm to venture into the high Aravali I need to head towards Nandanghati first, from there follow the pass into the mountains. 'But you musn't go beyond Nandanghati,' he tells me.

Babu is tightlipped. I plead with him, tell him we'll be back in Hakra by noon.

Nandanghati is two hours from Hakra. We pass many villages on the way. Unfamiliar names, impossible to remember so I jot them down...*Herar, Mahiya, Gurer, Humla, Masihon ka Talab*, the last literally meaning Christian's Pond. An hour into the drive the mica region opens up, once upon a time magnificent golden mountains, now ochre, denuded, the odd shard of mica winking at the sun. It was the richness of these mountains that enabled the Rajputs to struggle against invaders so long for they yielded a wealth of minerals as well as silver... an older than old story, for Tod in the early nineteenth century had already found the caste of miners extinct. Nervously I tell Babu I'd like to stop when convenient for him, to pick up a few stray mica rocks as mementoes along the way but he acts like he hasn't heard me.

Past the mica mountains the Aravali begins to grow dense, rolling in several dark layers as far as the eye can see. The slopes are barren apart from cacti as tall as trees. As we near Nandanghati I tell Babu we're not stopping here, we're going just a little further on until the motorable road ends. He brakes furiously. We sit in the car in silence for a minute after which he says I can go where I please, he's returning to Mugair. I leave the car and start walking. He follows me, mumbling something about not knowing what's good for me. I tell him to go back to Hakra if he won't come with me, park at the bus stand and wait for me while I wander through Nandanghati and then catch the roadways bus back after which we could return to Mugair together. I don't give him a chance to argue. I keep walking.

Nandanghati is antique land. It's chief of a tuppa consisting of a hundred villages and hamlets though you wouldn't believe it, so hidden are those villages between crags and defiles. The road on which I stand is strong and beautiful, again thanks to the British. It's the same all over Rajasthan, metal roads where you would have expected no more than dirt paths. The town is poised elegantly over three hills, slopes demarcated into sections with short stone walls forming a steppe like effect. This would probably be to establish ownership of land and I wonder what for, as nothing appears to grow here, nothing but cacti. You can see from the bone structure of the people's faces here, their weather-beaten skin that they've faced terrible hardships. It's there in their eyes, in their stance, in the determination of their profiles although their features bear the nobility of kings and queens. The safas of the men are much larger here and more vivid than those you see in the plains, or do they appear brighter against that dreary landscape?

Everyone and everything here appears to be mixed up in dust. Through the shimmering haze of heat the houses appear to be balanced on top of each other, so steep is the rise of those hills, gaily coloured walls standing out among the more staid creams and greys, some probably centuries old but painted over generously, the thickness of the paint unable to camouflage their vintage, the unevenness of their walls, the lopsidedness of their jharokas and balconies. Most striking of all are the houses painted white with a touch of neel. They shine against that landscape with much the same effect here as stained glass has on Mission territory. Sprawled across the other two hills is an ancient fort built of stone blackened with age, quite clearly belonging to the pre-cement era, thin slates wedged together to hold it up through the centuries, the only sign of vulnerability being that whole sections of it dip in parts as if the fort were gently sinking into the hills. I ask some passing children whether they know who built that fort up there and they say Which fort? so similar in character is that fort to the hills, merging with them not just physically but in the minds of the people who see, and therefore don't see it daily. I rack my brain for the little history I know and I recall that Gurjaras, ancestors of the modern Gujars, had established themselves in these parts in the beginning of the proto-Guler period. In their struggle for survival, the Huns of Central Asia who had invaded the northern plains and the Gurjaras came into bitter conflict and this battle for supremacy started the process of building fortified settlements. Could this fort have belonged to that period?

The glucose biscuits weren't enough. I am tired and hungry and acidic. A pain shoots through my left side. The air is heavy and dust-laden, the sun grows dim, making the entire town appear like it were shrouded in cold on a winter's evening. I walk towards a tea shop and ask for a tumbler of water. The old man at the dhaba asks me what I'm doing here so I tell him I'm looking for a village called Dahirya and could he guide me? He waves to a group of people in the distance. Four men and one old woman leave the group to collect around us. He passes my question on to them.

'Dahirya doesn't exist any more, bai,' one man says, 'nor the Dahiryas. There was a terrible famine in these parts in 1868 followed by a cholera epidemic and the British came and took away a number of people in bullock carts. Some went with them.'

'What about the rest?'

'Try the dunes towards Jaisalmer, at Sam,' one of them says. 'Maybe they returned to where they came from.'

'But they left the dunes centuries ago,' I say, 'I know for a fact that they moved east, migrated to these parts, built their village along the banks of the Sarasvati river.'

'What river?' the old man says. 'There was never a river here.'

'Of course there was,' says the old woman, 'and still is.'

The men break into laughter. One of them circles a finger round his head to convey she's senile.

She lashes out at him. '*Haramzade*, born yesterday so how would you know?'

'And you were born ten thousand years ago by the looks of you,' he retorts.

'I tell you the river's there,' she turns to me, 'but only the pure of heart can see it, not these haramzade disbelievers.'

Raucous laughter again. They begin to move away. The woman turns back and tells me in a whisper, out of their range, 'Yes, it's true, they came to these parts,' so I ask her whether she knows where their village was and she points in the direction of a disordered heap of gigantic rock up ahead on which no one could possibly have lived.

I look around for a tonga. The pain in my side is growing. No one is willing to take me, no one but an import from Punjab called Ram Bhatinda, owner of a ramshackle tonga without a roof. He tells me he isn't a darpok like the rest, I shouldn't listen to their useless chitter chatter and that he's often travelled through these parts which he knows quite well.

'Where's your roof?' I ask him.

'I have a roof, bai,' he replies, looking hurt, 'but it will take me some time to fetch it. It's under repair.'

I decide to do without the roof and without further ado the two of us take off straight into the mountains, the afternoon sun of the Thar beating upon our heads. The metal road ends. We're on a dirt track now. The tonga dips and heaves, causing my head to shoot through the roofless roof. Fifteen minutes later, a melodious twang, the vehicle tilts forty-five degrees and comes to a dead halt. I am horrified but Ram Bhatinda takes the event philosophically. I decide to stretch my legs as he repairs the wheel. I look around me at the wilderness. The rock the old woman pointed to appears to be growing further away. I ask Ram Bhatinda hesitantly whether he's confident of his horse but he looks insulted so, wheel repaired, I climb back into the vehicle meekly and we strike the road again, heaving and galloping and shuddering. 'This is nothing,' he says smiling, 'wait till we get beyond the rock.'

'Is it very bad?' I ask nervously, the pain on my side moving in waves towards my chest.

'I have never been there myself but I hear it is like the road to hell,' he replies.

I am outraged. 'I thought you said you knew these parts,' I say angrily and he replies that no one knew these parts. 'You make sure we're back in Nandanghati in two hours flat,' I threaten him and he replies that he'll get me back much before that or forego his payment.

By now I am powdered with dust and feeling like a dead leaf forced by the wind to take wing. The sun is up like an all-seeing eye that will not shut and I am losing my capacity to think. With nothing around me but rock and stone and the spectre of the high Aravali looming ahead, I enter a dreamlike state. I imagine I see a sea in front of me, foaming billows arising, until I realize we're entering a large expanse of flat ground between two mountains, the wind playing with clouds of dust. An hour later we're in the middle of nowhere. The rock has vanished. It isn't behind me or in front of me. The pain in my side is acute. I begin to imagine I'll die in the wilderness with nobody finding me or claiming my body that would be feasted upon by wild animals. The horse looks unhappy too, its head hanging low and straining at the reins as if it wished to lie down so I order Ram Bhatinda to stop at once but he appears not to hear me. Lashing at the flanks of the animal, he strikes boldly on into the black heart of the mountains. *'Bewakoof!'* I yell at him angrily, even as the tonga jumps into and out of a large hole slantwise, nearly throwing me over.

Signs of life. We enter a narrow ghati on an incline, perpendicular cliffs on either side into which are carved a dozen niches containing figures of Hanuman, little diyas before them, one flickering gently. My spirits lift. Perched high on a cliff is what appears to be the abode of a sanyasi and a little further on the incline, on the right, a flight of stairs cracked down the middle on account of a large fig tree having taken root there. *'Taanga roko!'* I yell at the top of my voice at Ram Bhatinda who pulls at the reins out of shock. I hurtle off my perch before he changes his mind and head towards the stairs, ready to embrace whoever I might find there but there's nothing but an abyss on the other side and a gigantic pile of ruins frozen in time, thorns growing luxuriantly out of broken walls and columns. Weeds crackle under my feet. Magnificent flights of stairs on all sides descend into the abyss and I realize it's a baoli below me, excavated out of solid rock, its high watermark clear evidence that water flowed here in abundance once. But the only signs of life are huge bats, flitting silently past the columns, and stray dogs, the same colour as the ruins, wandering over piles of debris with large dead eyes.

I return to the tonga. Ram Bhatinda is on the back seat now in a half recline, looking up at the thin wedge of sky visible through the narrow ghati, one bare leg poised over a bony knee, smirk across his face. I contemplate yelling at him once more, at the top of my voice, to turn the tonga around but that one lit diya has given me hope so I refrain and off we go again, through the ghati and deeper and deeper into the mountains, past wasted fields, the remains of deserted villages, according to Tod great cities in their day, now a spectre of desolation, a chilling void, the kiner or oleander taking root in walls that stand in every direction but the vertical. The wind is an inferno here, the sun reflecting off from every angle of the chaotic mass of rock, making the hills appear to be in motion, undulating in waves towards the horizon, dark granite merging with rose-coloured quartz and micaceous schist of every hue to give a gilded appearance to the roofs of houses caught by a ray of the departing sun. There are no people here, only honeycombs that adhere to the ragged summits, huge colonies of bees once called upon as auxiliaries in battle, throwing the enemy into a confused dance. And birds, maddened by thirst, their beaks open, their wings hanging listlessly down. The most barren spots are covered by cacti, tightly packed in clusters of hundreds as if the one were squeezing the breath from the other in order to survive, unlike the solitary mimosa, the babool and the prickly khureel, their thorns as sharp and hard as needles entangled amidst the twisted boughs of the amervela.

We're in the womb of the Aravali now, great black mountains of granite and slate behind us and in front of us, splintered pinnacles in the distance soaring to the sky. Forming dark lines along the crests of the mountains are more fort-like structures with bastions and parapets and towers, again quite clearly of the pre-cement era, brushwood scattered over the surface of dead walls, skeletal trees growing out of them. I know that the Afghans long prowled around these regions and would therefore have required some form of defence. Or could I be mistaking them for forts? Could they have been luxury resorts? Religion appears to have been of great importance too in these parts, evident from the abandoned temples we pass and little mosques with elegant, crumbling minarets. More niches and caves too, some Buddhist, some Hindu, some dating back to the time of the Jaina kings. No sign of the Archaeological Survey of India ever having laid foot here. We're on an excruciatingly narrow ledge along the girth of a mountain now and Ram Bhatinda says we must go single file. I climb out of the tonga. My head spins. I clutch a tree to regain my balance. Four hills surround us with a deep canyon of stratified layers of hard rock below. High on a hill in the distance stands a colonial mansion like a holiday retreat, dank and yellowed by age. Ram Bhatinda pulls at the rickshaw wearily. The sun begins to set, gently passing its veil over the roof of the mansion, illuminating it briefly. In a voice that doesn't sound like mine I call out to Ram Bhatinda that I'd like to return to Nandanghati now whereupon he informs me casually that he won't travel by night. I am infuriated beyond belief. I order him to turn back but he says we would be stuck on the road in the dark and that it's wiser to go on and spend the night somewhere, though he didn't know where. But I won't travel by night, he repeats firmly. The pain in my side is worse. Strange new sounds permeate the silence of the desert. My hair stands on end as I remember something about animals and snakes burrowing deep in the ground to survive the heat of the Thar and then coming out around sunset. Finally we clear the ledge and emerge on the other side of the mountain onto a dry open field. 'I won't go on,' Ram Bhatinda announces here, so we ready to sleep on the ground under the stars and despite the growing sounds of the nether world in my ears I drift off.

The next morning I look around me and I see that Ram Bhatinda and his tonga are gone. I watch the sun rise for a while, hoping the two will materialize from behind a rock at any moment but when an hour passes in such expectation I realize I've been abandoned. I call out his name. I retrace my steps, walking back towards the ledge, casting my eye across the vista but there isn't a sign of him or the horse. I start walking along the ledge towards the ghati but an hour later I see no ghati, only mountains around me stretching to eternity. I continue walking in whichever direction my feet take me until I see something strange. The ridge in front of me is changing shape. It's melting and it's growing, it's changing colour and then swinging from its base as if it were as light as a feather and then returning to size and place, continuing to perform theatrics for several minutes. Far in the distance a huge dense wall of smoke rises and begins undulating in waves towards the ridge, covering it completely, turning and twisting over it like a giant paintbrush. The ridge grows peaks now, crowned with icicles; the next minute a dense mass of foliage, a moving collage that keeps changing until the smoke grows lighter and a ray of the sun scatters the image into a thousand parts, each part within a huge lens, dwarfing the shrubs of the desert, now turning them to giant size until eventually the whole scene starts to fade.

I imagine I'm losing my mind. Maddened by thirst, I stumble along in a daze, clutching my side, seating myself down on a rock now and again, sobbing from fear and pain. The sky is a cerulean blue; by noon the temperature well over a hundred degrees. A wind begins to blow, clouds of dust rising and swirling around me. I cover my nose and mouth to stop from choking. After raging and whistling through the mountains for two hours that terrible wind ceases. With a sensation bordering on madness I plod on, past mountain and plain, neither affording relief from the other. Just as I think I can walk no more I enter a cul-de-sac, a barrier of bare dismal rock that encloses my path like a wall on three sides. Bone weary, I lean against the rock, unable to sit down for the pain in my side that now appears to be causing a swelling. I feel a breeze cool my cheek. I straighten abruptly. When all around me is nothing but heat rising in waves, where could the breeze be coming from? I look around puzzled. I touch the rock. I find it is moist. Then I hear a sound, a chattering quarreling sound that appears to be coming from behind the rock. With the last remnants of energy left in me I heave myself up and begin climbing. Halfway up I change my mind but realize that descent would be impossible now for I hadn't thought of removing my shoes and if I lost my grip my head could split wide open so I continue climbing until miraculously I reach the top.

Drawing myself to a vertical position I look around me and I see that the world appears to be divided into two by that rock—the desert behind me, an oasis in front, cool and shady, thick with gigantic banian and mango trees. Far on the right is a rumbling cluster of ancient moss-covered tombs among which black-faced monkeys leap around in gay abandon. Shaking my shoes off I begin to descend, slipping again and again but quickly recovering on account of the new energy amazement has given me. The monkeys grow silent, staring at me with their button eyes until one of them takes a giant leap into the forest, his companions hurriedly following suit. Bleary-eyed now from exhaustion and as a result quite unafraid as to what I might find, I stumble towards the tombs. They appear to be tinkling gently. Again I imagine I'm losing my mind until I near the tombs and see little bells attached to their arched entrances, the only sound in that incredible aura of quietude. On the walls are painted solar deities seated in racing chariots and, carved into a twelve-pillared pavilion, stunning sensuous sculptures. Every surface of the tombs is decorated, domed ceilings rich with elephants and horsemen and dancing figures. The air is hushed here, radiating a sense of eternity. I contemplate lying down, pressing my cheek against the cool stone ground when I hear the sound of water. It appears to be coming from behind the tombs so abandoning thoughts of rest, I encircle the tombs and come upon two large rocks between which flows a stream of water. But the sound I hear is greater than anything a little stream can produce so after dipping my hands in the water and splashing my face I follow the sound to another set of rocks and in the process find I am climbing a rather high mountain this time to which there appears to be no summit. Giant leaves flap against my legs, whisper and rustle against my cheek as higher and higher I go in pursuit of the sound and when I reach a defile of sorts I stop to catch my breath. Utterly worn by now it begins to appear to me almost a welcome prospect were I to fall off that mountain straight but just then that breeze begins to blow again, reviving me, and I stand up tall and survey the strange new world around me, a dense forest echoing with the screams of the peacock and the call of the partridge. I lean forward to take a look below and that's when I see it, a magnificent ribbon of silver hidden altogether among the hills, rushing and winding through a pass to a golden valley below, three miles wide, its margins aflame with the dhak, and through the trees and patches of light caused by the play of the sun I see people.

The pain in my side is unbearable now. I make an attempt to call out for help but my head feels light, my tongue and lips tight and swollen. I grasp the rock on which I am standing and feel myself sinking to the ground.

I awake to the sound of the rushing river beside me, within a hut on a charpai, bathed in perspiration, some thirty live leeches of enormous size chewing upon my left side. I sit up and scream in horror and pain.

'Lie down, bai, you're tired,' I hear a familiar voice.

I'm in the Ambassador, ochre rug beneath me, speeding along the Mugair–Hakra highway. 'Where did you come from?' I ask Babu, sitting up. 'Where did you find me?'

'What where?' he replies. 'Lying on the road in a dead faint, that's where...you must have got heatstroke.'

'But that's impossible,' I say, 'I went into the mountains, I found Dahirya, I found the river.'

He starts laughing. 'You're a very brave bai, and very determined,' he tells me, 'but with too much imagination. In the two small circles I took around Nandanghati where did you go?'

I look down at my feet. My shoes are missing. I look out of the window; it's dusk outside. Babu has his headlights on, they sway and swing like lanterns on the winding road and I am transfixed by their lonely glare. The years compress themselves like an accordion and I wonder whether what he's saying is being said right then or only in my memory. For the rest of the ride I sit stupefied.

We arrive on the outskirts of Mugair. The town looks different this time. I seem to have been here a long, long time ago and as we wing through its lanes I cannot remember when that was. We reach Indra Colony. I ring Maddy's doorbell. Dadi and Milly and Daniel are seated in the drawing room on maroon velvet sofas, huddled around a black and white TV watching Doordarshan. The light from the TV is ghostly, fluorescent. Milly's eyes look huge and distorted through her spectacles. She jumps up when she sees me. She doesn't say hello. She looks nervous. She yells for Maddy who comes in from the kitchen. She puts her arms around me. I hug her back, bewildered. Then she takes both my hands in hers and tells me I need to leave for Delhi right away. Flora called. Our house was raided.

Who's She, Vylit?

All her pamphlets were gone, thrown in a heap into the nala and set on fire. On our entrance door, carved into the wood with a knife was a message in Hindi: *Angrez randi,* English whore. The drawing room furniture was smashed. Curtains had been torn from their rods. Bulbs had been taken out of their sockets. There was glass all over the floor. In the middle of the mess, in the dim light of a single remaining bulb sat Flora, dry-eyed, silent.

'What happened?' I screamed as I entered the house. 'Where's Mama? Where's Ram Bhajan? Where's Violet? Where's Lajo?'

I didn't wait for a reply. I ran towards Beatrice's bedroom. She was lying in bed not looking particularly disturbed but something was wrong with her eyes; they were in a deep dark place, resting from the sun, lost marbles that had rolled under the sofa so you couldn't get at them.

Violet walked in. *'What happened?'* I screamed again.

'The devil came,' she said in full repose.

'What? *Who* came?' I almost hit her.

'The devil and his disciples,' she repeated. 'I saw his staff. Three arrows on top—666 on his forehead.'

I turned to Beatrice. She was smiling. 'What happened, Mama?' I said gently, rubbing her hand.

Her eyes were completely blank. 'Who's she, Vylit?' she said.

'Gudda,' replied Violet to her, then to me, 'I showed him the cross.'

'*What* cross?'

She dived under Beatrice's bed and emerged with pieces of the wooden cross that used to hang over Beatrice's bed. 'Then I hit him on the head with it,' she said proudly.

'Why didn't you dial 100?'

'100?' she said, looking nonplussed.

'Mama,' I said helplessly, turning to Beatrice.

'Have you offered her some nimboo pani, Vylit?' said Beatrice, and then in a whisper into her ear that I could clearly hear, 'Tell her it's nice of her to visit me but I'm not receiving visitors today, I'm tired.' Then she turned on her side and went off to sleep.

I stared out the window next to her bed, at the trees growing out of the nala, and it seemed to me that the whole world was heaving in pain, it was the world that had changed, not Beatrice's face.

The phone kept ringing. Malini, Sujata and Aditi were hysterical. *'Where the hell were you, Gudda?'* Sujata screamed at me on the phone.

Malini and Aditi wanted to know if they should come. 'Wait,' I said, 'let me understand what happened and I'll call you.'

I didn't call. I let them believe what they'd wanted to believe all their lives—that things were never as bad as they sounded. It suited them, and for the first time in my life it suited me too. I didn't want them around. I felt like I never even knew them.

The morning papers carried pictures of our house. Beatrice wasn't in any of them but Flora, Violet and Lajo were. One caption called them (including the twenty-year-old Lajo) 'three helpless widows'. The headline of another article read, 'High

Commissioner's mother-in-law attacked'. Superimposed on the picture of the house was an inset, a file photo of Sujata's husband, making him appear like he were the owner of the house and chief widow-deserter. It was from the papers I learnt that none of the neighbours had come to her aid. From the neighbours I learnt that Ram Bhajan had fled, someone had seen him down the road even while the house was being ripped apart.

Around noon I went to the police station. I told them what happened. I showed them the papers. I said I wanted to lodge an FIR.

'Against whom?' one cop said.

I didn't know what to say. I asked to meet the SHO.

'He's busy,' he said. 'You can put in a complaint, not an FIR.'

I went back home. I rang Ashwini. 'I think this calls for legal action,' I said, 'not an FIR. I'm taking them to court.'

'Who?' he said.

'Well, I never saw them myself but the neighbours would have.'

'But would they be willing to stand up as witnesses?'

'I don't think so.'

'Then we don't have a case.'

'*How don't we have a case?* My two aunts were witness, my mother was witness, the newspapers are witness...'

'*No*, the papers use the word "alleged" everywhere. See, that's not how courts work, on the word "alleged".'

'I could take photos of the inside of the house...'

'No no no that doesn't prove a thing, Mrs Bharti, try to *understand*, the ladies could have broken the furniture themselves.'

'Didn't you see the papers properly? *Do they look to you like they could do it?*'

'No no no *please* try to understand what I am saying, *you* are not lying but only *I* know that you are not lying, how will the judge know?'

I slammed the phone down on him. I stared at the wall in front of me, my face burning.

So no case was filed, no FIR lodged and in any case three weeks later Beatrice herself was on her way to face that other Day of Judgement. I don't know whether it was shock or old age but the change in her over those three weeks was frightening. First she grew emaciated, then her feet and ankles began swelling up, making her legs look like two lengths of salami at a pork shop. It was at the end of those three weeks that I dialled Malini, Sujata and Aditi.

It's only when the tide recedes that we see what the ocean contained. Something like that happened when Beatrice began to die. Like empty tin cans her children howled in the wind, like yellow and pink plastic bags they fluttered and sank into the sand weeping. Aditi came within forty-eight hours of my call, clutching an open ticket and an overnight bag. Malini, who was the nearest, delayed coming in the hope that she wouldn't have to come twice, that she could on one ticket cover both Beatrice's dying and her funeral, but she had always been like that, getting two for the price of one, just like those nylon saris she'd bought Beatrice for Neha's wedding. Sujata took a week, sauntering in with her eyebrows raised in a subtle attempt to convey to me that the only new thing that had descended on all of us was *my* hysteria. Then there was me, bluebottle in the gleaming sand, the nip in their ankles because if Beatrice died and with my having lived in her house so long I might now exercise that awful-sounding thing called squatter's rights.

Aditi kept bending over her, I remember, so from the chair next to Beatrice's bed I could see only her hips. Aditi's hips. Wide one year, narrow the next, depending on the state of her research on Rushdie. I could think only of Aditi's hips as Beatrice lay dying. But look at the history of those hips. You could divide them into ancient medieval modern, that's how old we'd become. When Beatrice's lungs began to fill up, Aditi it was who took the phlegm out of her mouth, dug her fingers into her throat and yanked it out. I watched Aditi to see if she would gag but she didn't. Later it emerged she needn't have done what she did because the doctor said that people rarely choke on their phlegm and that it was okay to swallow. So after that every time Beatrice coughed, Aditi or I simply put one hand on her chest to contain the pain. Beatrice couldn't speak. She bubbled and gurgled and by my calculation there was easily two kilos of the stuff in her lungs. No food in her stomach, because she had stopped eating almost altogether and Aditi and I took turns slipping teaspoons of sugar water between her wrinkled lips which at times would be prised so tightly shut that you wanted to call out for pliers. Luckily those lips had shrunk into the toothless cavity of her mouth, her chin and her cheekbones stuck out like dykes so we were saved the trouble of having to keep dabbing her with a napkin.

Three days passed like that and we had no idea what to do next. Dying is so shapeless you can barely pronounce the word. Death is different but between the beginning of dying and the obituary notice in the papers is a shapeless hell, a sallow light that mesmerizes you into disbelieving both life and death. That's what the mourning period is probably for, less for grief, more for returning things back to their shapes. In the case of Beatrice, they never would. Everything would appear from then on like a moonscape bathed in that sallow light of dying in which we would wander forever. Beatrice would leave behind her awful light.

On the fourth day she took a deep breath and died.

The death of a mother is drama unparalleled. There was movement every which way, I remember, there was stillness, there were few spaces between the movement and the stillness in which one could register the fact of her death, and so I never did. I forgot about the attack, I kept telling myself, *But she died two years ago when her mind went, so what's new*? The people you think will be around aren't. Others arrive unexpectedly. Darla sent me a cold email. She'd been cold with me since 9/11, when I sent her a letter telling her what I thought of George Bush. I half-expected Anand to come but he didn't, but then he didn't know, and I don't know how I imagined some bird in the sky might have thought our relationship was worth something, enough to fly to wherever he was and whisper my loss in his ear. You don't communicate with the people you should most communicate with. And you find yourself talking to others. I couldn't bring myself to pick up the phone and call the people I knew. I just kept sitting there and looking at Beatrice, trying to understand where she'd gone. I kept looking at her eyes not looking at me. They were the eyes of a dead fish at the bottom of the ocean. Then the doctor came and closed those eyes and that's when I knew she would never look at me again.

As I watched her folding up into a cloud I was alone and frightened and I was small and the wind on the moon lashed my sides and I could find no one.

I would cover my face and wait.

I would let my hair fall off in clumps, like seaweed and look at it and look at what went with it.

And I would never be renewed.

I didn't do much, not as much as Malini, Sujata and Aditi. I remember walking from room to room looking for a scream. I remember lifting a corner of her pillow to straighten her face and finding her torchlight there. Summer holidays in the hills came back to me. I remember telling someone not to remove it, to put it exactly like that, under her pillow in her coffin, I remember thinking she might need it up there to shine on Jesus' face to tell him she'd arrived but I don't remember hearing my voice or making a sound. I don't remember the expression in anyone's eyes. As if all of what happened happened in a silent film. All of us making black and white Chaplinesque movements into a camera so no one could catch up with the real pace of things.

The phone kept ringing. There was ice under her bed. God knows why people think they have to push furniture around when someone dies. The whole configuration of whatever remained unbroken in that house was changed for no rhyme or reason. Someone took Beatrice's photo and placed it on the mantelpiece and surrounded it with flowers. It happened so fast. Two candles on either side of her face. I couldn't focus on that face. I could only remember the pleats of her soft, over-washed saris. We skip decades when someone dies, I'm not sure why. I couldn't remember her nighties, only the saris.

Malini's and Aditi's husbands arrived too, all sorts of comings and goings occurred and I remember thinking, would anything emerge from this family gathering over Beatrice's death? Does grief put relationships back on track or destroy the little that's left? Someone went rushing around organizing the funeral, I don't know who it was. I opened my cupboard and took out Beatrice's white silk sari. Then I opened her trunk and took out her pearly pink sweater. I put my face in it, it was reeking of mothballs. The coffin arrived. Space was made in the drawing room. It was placed on two chairs. It was huge. Beatrice was small.

How the hearse rattled. How my teeth chattered. I kept my hand on her coffin. It wasn't Beatrice inside. *Beatrice had gone two years before.* At the cemetery four men came forward to lift the coffin out. The long walk to the grave. The thick ropes, the descent. The nailing of the coffin, the placing of the stone slabs that shut her out of our lives forever. The 23rd Psalm. I tried to sing but couldn't form a tune.

Very few came to her funeral but of the spirits that arose from her there was no counting. After eating her flesh so that at the age of eighty-six and a height of five-two she weighed thirty-eight kg they did a last tango and departed. But they don't entirely depart, one is told, but enter the one who knew the secrets of the dead the most, so I did a strange thing. Went around after the funeral telling everybody I had never known what Beatrice was *really like* so that the spirits would turn on their tails and go elsewhere. Into Malini, Sujata and Aditi ideally. And there was so much silence, I remember, when we queued up to go round and round and up to her forehead, to kiss it before that lid came down that you could have heard them, Hubert, Rose, Harriet, Andrew, come out of their graves, hands linked, swinging their arms backwards and forwards in chorus, saying,

Beatrice is dead

Beatrice is dead

Like a witch's plot fulfilled. Of putting a corpse in your cupboard that's wearing your skin. Hatched a hundred years before while playing gulli-danda under a blazing sun; plaits, legs, flying like skittles.

Right after the funeral Sujata wanted to do an inventory of Beatrice's things. I kept telling her there's nothing left. The following day Aditi brought in a builder fellow. I heard Sujata and her talking to him about ratios of black money and white money. I called Ashwini. *Don't move from the house,* he said.

My throat hurt, my back hurt, my eyes burned and something in my heart felt like shrapnel. My papers were a mess, there were unpaid bills, overdue bills and I got the feeling something was about to be switched off—the electricity or the phone line. Clothes were unwashed. There was no food in the fridge. The only time I seemed to move was when I coughed or blew my nose.

'Do you prefer cash or accommodation?' I remember Malini asking me.

I turned away. I tried walking out of the room but she caught hold of my arm and said, *'Enough is enough, Gudda!* You *can't* stay here alone. Not after what's happened.'

'They'll *burn* the house down next, tell her,' said Sujata.

'We're *not* withdrawing the case, tell her to know that too.' Aditi.

I do not remember what I said in return or whether I said anything at all but I remember thinking I could do what our forefathers had done, that old trick of the Dahiryas—*pick up the house and run.*

But it came to me even in that fog that it was time for that cycle to end.

So I brought it to an end. I dug in my heels and waited.

Malini, Sujata and Aditi left as they had always done and the pace at which the Indian courts move, I'll probably die waiting.

I do hate that phrase 'squatter's rights', I have to say. It makes me see myself sitting on my haunches in the middle of the courtyard, shitting, or laying eggs.

Never mind the image, I tell myself sometimes. History rests on it. What you do today becomes somebody else's history tomorrow.

You have to carry on living in the present too. Violet left in search of greener pastures; Flora stayed. A few months after Beatrice's death the Congress came back to power and with it, the missionaries returned. Darla too, one morning on her way to Kathmandu. She had forgiven me for hating George Bush because by then Americans had begun hating him too and I'd understood as well that twirled and abandoned knickers, and God, were mutually exclusive. There was an evening she said, 'Let's have a little sing-song, Gudda,' so I got hold of Flora and Lajo to join us like in the old days, they were looking so lonely, and while Darla conducted the service, Flora sat on the left of me, Lajo to my right, and we banged away with our plates and pots and spoons and sang at the top of our voices and at some point Darla looked at me with affection and said, '*Goodness me Gudda, you remind me so much of your dear departed mother*!'

Acknowledgements

For the journey within a journey in 'The Third Journey' I have drawn from James Tod and Rudyard Kipling, early travellers through the Thar.

My deepest gratitude to my editors: Renuka Chatterjee of Osian's Literary Agency, and V.K. Karthika, Nandita Aggarwal, Shantanu Ray Chaudhuri of HarperCollins.

Kavita Bhanot, Will Francis, Vaiju Naravane, Dr Satendra Nandan, Dr Kavita Nandan, for their valued comments.

Saba Naqvi and Ramesh Menon, without whom these pages would have collected dust.

Tarun Tejpal, first reader and ruthless critic.

Malini Mundle, for listening to a story I told her one evening, from which the piecing together of this book began.

Kamini Tankha and Poornima Jain, without whom nothing works.

Feroze Gujral, for showing me how to go up the down staircase.